A Candlelight Regency Special

CANDLELIGHT REGENCIES

HEATHER WILD

Phyllis Taylor Pianka

A CANDLELIGHT REGENCY SPECIAL

Published by
Dell Publishing Co., Inc.
1 Dag Hammarskjold Plaza
New York, New York 10017

Copyright © 1982 by Phyllis Taylor Pianka

Dell ® TM 681510, Dell Publishing Co., Inc.

ISBN: 0-440-13537-0

Printed in the United States of America

First printing—January 1982

HEATHER WILD

CHAPTER ONE

Lady Elizabeth Cambridge lifted her face to the sunlight streaming from the dusty, canted window above the cutting table. The rain-washed sky was crystalline-blue for a change, unsullied by smoke from the new manufactory near the waterfront. Her back and legs ached from standing. It was hard to remain still, but in fairness to the weary seamstress she stood on the narrow stool without moving.

Lucy nodded for her to turn sideways as she pinned the hem into place.

"Aye, miss. This will be a right foin traveling cloak for 'er ladyship's trousseau. What a lucky thing for 'er that you and she are the same size."

"Indeed," Elizabeth agreed without enthusiasm. This wasn't the first time she had acted as stand-in for her spoiled niece.

"'Tis odd how much you and Miss Louella look so much alike, you bein' so much older and everything." The woman apparently realized that she had spoken unwisely and had the grace to turn pink. "I didn't mean to set you down for your age, your ladyship. 'Tis hard indade to be a spinster without bein' taken to task for it. I only meant that wi' that mess o' foin gold hair you could be 'er sister instead of 'er maiden aunt."

"I suppose we do resemble each other in appearance, Lucy," she said dryly, "but the similarity stops there."

"Oh, yes, ma'am. I can see that."

9

Lucy's voice was warm with sympathy, and somehow Elizabeth found that more offensive than the remark about her age. Two and twenty was not really that old. There were a number of advantages to having reached her majority even without benefit of a husband. What did go against the grain was the common knowledge that the death of her parents had left her without funds until she was reduced to accepting the hospitality of her sister and the Marquis of Farthingsham. In their great mansion on South Audley Street she was little more than a glorified maid.

She turned again as the seamstress tugged on the hem of the purple velvet manteau. Perhaps things would be different once Louella was married . . . if indeed she went through with it this time. Louella had broken more than one promise of betrothal.

Elizabeth sighed. No, things would go on much the same as before. There had never been the least degree of affection between her and her sister, Martha, who had always been jealous of Elizabeth's trim figure and hair the color of honey and snow. Even though it had taken an enormous marriage settlement to secure her betrothal to the Marquis of Farthingsham, Martha lorded her good fortune over Elizabeth until her company was almost unbearable.

The clatter of carriage wheels grated against the cobblestone in the mews, and Elizabeth wondered if her sister and her niece had finished their business with the goldsmith. But, no, they would hardly have chosen to arrive by the rear entrance like common tradespeople. Their expensive new cabriolet would drive right up to the Bond Street entrance to the fashionable dressmaker's establishment.

The carriage stopped. She could hear the horses strain against the harness. They were restless, she thought. A blooded pair by all counts. Spirited.

10

Suddenly the rear door burst open, and two hooded men blocked the entrance to the shop. Lucy gasped in surprise as she fell backward on her heels.

"'Ere, now, wot's this? You've got no right to break in 'ere. There's ladies present."

Elizabeth pulled the cloak tightly around her to conceal her state of undress and to hide the ruby pendant she wore around her neck.

One man approached her. His voice was muffled behind the mask. "Easy there, your ladyship. We mean you no harm if you do as we say."

"Wh-what is it you want?" Elizabeth demanded. "I have no money." She motioned to her worn reticule, which lay on the red brocade footstool. "See for yourself."

"It's not money we seek, your ladyship. It's you we're after," he said as his fingers closed around her wrist.

Lucy looked petrified, but she managed a threat. "Keep your filthy mitts off 'er or I'll scream for the constable."

The ruffian laughed. "I wouldn't do that." He brandished a pistol. "Now, sit quietly and you won't get hurt. But just one noise from you and I'll not vouch for her ladyship's safety. Just stay there until the carriage leaves the mews."

He turned toward Elizabeth. "Now, if you'll just go ahead of me out the door—"

"I'll do no such thing!"

"Very well." He grabbed Elizabeth around the waist and slung her over his shoulder like a sack of meal. She tried desperately to kick him, but he managed to avoid her feet.

"Stop that or someone is going to get hurt."

His pistol was pointed at Lucy, and Elizabeth was afraid to move for fear he might discharge it. Laughter rumbled from his throat. "Now, that's better, my lady." With a final warning to Lucy he backed out of the door and turned to the waiting carriage.

Elizabeth had a quick impression of peeling paint on the shabby, high-sprung enclosed carriage. It contrasted sharply with the obviously costly double pair of black geldings. An instant later she was dumped unceremoniously onto the dirty floor of the coach as the man climbed in after her and slammed the door. She started to scream, but he muttered an oath and clamped his hand over her mouth, then shouted to the driver to make haste. At the crack of the whip the powerful horses strained in their harness, and the carriage jumped forward.

Elizabeth struggled to free herself. Finding it impossible, she tried to move to a more comfortable position. The pins that held the hem of the purple cloak bit viciously into her, and she could feel the blood trickle down her ankle. Finally the man seemed to relax a bit, and she lifted her head to look up at him.

He appeared to be a seaman. In truth, she could smell the tang of the sea on the dark-colored fustian trouser legs against which her head rested. His face was still concealed by the hood, but as if in answer to her thoughts he slowly pulled the mask away with his free hand.

Her eyes widened in surprise. This man was no cutpurse. Indeed, his skin, although unfashionably browned by the sun, was the skin of a man of position. He gazed down at her, his mouth lifting at the corners.

"Now, that is much better, my lady. Quiet now, and I vow that no harm will come to you."

She willed herself to become limp. If he thought she would cooperate, perhaps he would lower his guard, and she would be able to escape. His hand eased against her mouth.

"If I take my hand away, will you remain silent?"

She nodded.

"Very well."

Slowly he drew his hand away. When it was several inches from her mouth she let out a blood-curdling scream. He swore soundly and nearly broke her neck in his hurry to silence her.

"You little vixen. I thought I could trust you." He dragged her against him, unmindful of the odd angles her arm and legs were forced to assume as he hurriedly looked out of the rear window. "Good. We're safe for the present, no thanks to you. Just settle back, my lady. We've a long ride ahead of us."

Streams of perspiration ran down between her shoulder blades, and yet she shivered with fear. What did they want from her, her of all people? She had no money, everyone knew that. Ransom was not the motive, and yet he seemed to know that she was titled. And where were they taking her? Her eyes were unable to contain her fear as she met her captor's gaze. Behind the look of excitement in his eyes she saw a glint of humor.

"You are even more lovely than I had imagined. I really don't want to hurt you, but unless you do as I say, you leave me no choice, your ladyship."

She moaned against his hand and saw indecision flicker across his face. She moaned again, more plaintively, and went limp.

He swore soundly then looked embarrassed. "I beg your pardon, your ladyship, but keeping you seems to be a bigger problem than getting you in the first place. I'll chance it again, but this time if you cry out, I shall not find it in myself to forgive you. Will you be obedient?"

She was silent, listening to the changing rhythm of the carriage wheels. They were in the country, or at least on a dirt road. The iron-rimmed wheels no longer grated against the cobblestones and the ever-present stench of the sewers had given way to the scent of newly mown hay. She braced her slippers against the door and bent her knees.

He shook her carefully as if concerned about her condition.

13

"I asked if you would be obedient." His voice was urgent.

Elizabeth nodded, and he took his hand away from her mouth. She ran the back of her hand across her lips and drew a deep breath. "Let go of me, you bastard. You'll hang for this."

He grinned. "Not likely."

"Where are you taking me?" she demanded.

"To be married. Where did you think?"

"Married! How completely outrageous. You must be totally daft." She could tell by the expression on his face that he was not jesting. "And who, if I may be so bold, is to be my bridegroom, you?"

He threw his head back and laughed. "Hardly. I've yet to see the filly who could lead me to the trough and make me drink." He stroked his chin. "And yet seeing you does give a man cause to wonder."

He leaned back against the seat, and she sat in comparative freedom on the floor of the carriage. As it slowed to round a curve Elizabeth kicked forward with her feet, forcing the door to fly open. Bending forward, she attempted to roll out of the carriage, but he grabbed the cloak and yanked her back inside. He was on the floor with her now, where there was barely room for one. His corded muscles held her tightly against his chest as he pulled the door shut.

"God's truth, he never said you had spirit! How he could have waited so long to claim you is beyond me. I'd have bedded you on sight."

Elizabeth felt a moment of pure panic as she saw the fire kindle in his eyes. It wasn't money after all that drove this man to abduct her. Indeed, if she had been frightened before, it was as nothing compared to the fear that overtook her now. She struggled against him, but he held her fast in one arm as he reached into a pocket on the side of the coach.

14

"I'm sorry to do this to you, my lady, but you leave me no choice."

Before she could move her head, he had clapped a pad of lint over her mouth and nose and she felt herself sinking into a world of cotton wool clouds. The last thing she remembered was the look of desire in his eyes as he bent over her.

She awoke to darkness save for a feeble glimmer of moonlight filtering in through a narrow window. The slant of the roof and the faint etching of daub-and-wattle-plastered walls led her to believe that she was being held in an upstairs room of a coaching inn. She willed her heart to stop beating lest it waken the man lying on the bed beside her.

He breathed deeply with the merest hint of a snore. She waited for him to exhale, but he held his breath for an unconscionably long time. Elizabeth found she was holding her own breath and was relieved when he breathed out through slightly parted lips.

She moved with guarded care, but the straw-filled mattress made scratching noises. Her captor stirred and rose on one elbow. She could feel him looking down at her, and she feigned sleep. It seemed like minutes later when satisfied, he again lay his head back on the goose-down pillow. She was not restrained, but there was no doubt in her mind that for the night, at least, escape was out of the question.

Elizabeth took stock of her situation. Except for a tendency toward being muzzy-headed, she seemed to be physically well. Instinct told her that he had not harmed her in any way save for the bruise that darkened her wrist and the puncture wound on her ankle. The thought gave her courage. In truth, he seemed more than eager to avoid bringing harm to her.

But what of the other . . . the man to whom she was to

15

be delivered? What kind of man was he who had to resort to abduction to win a bride? She shuddered as she tried to banish the demons she had conjured. She would die before submitting to that kind of man. He must be . . . No! She willed her brain to stillness lest she frighten herself beyond control.

It was dawn when she awakened to find her captor leaning over her. His blouse, open to the waist, gave her a fleeting glimpse of a snow-white bandage that covered one side of his chest and extended over his shoulder. Rolling away from her, he hastily buttoned his shirt.

"Good. I was afraid I'd have to waken you. We have only a short time to freshen ourselves, and we must be on our way."

As he got up, Elizabeth's gaze slid beyond him to a chair by the wall where the purple manteau was draped alongside his seaman's coat. Alarmed, she lifted the covers to find she was wearing only a chemise atop her small-clothes. She remembered then that to avoid mussing her gown from the heat at the dressmaker's establishment, she had carefully removed it and left it on a chair.

The fact that her well-rounded bosom spilled over the top of her laces was apparently not lost on her captor. He grinned his approval.

"Ah, now, don't be ashamed of your lovely shape, my lady. I'll see that you're properly gowned before we reach the castle. In the meantime I fear that your cloak will have to serve to hide your treasures."

He left her alone for a time while she made her morning ablutions, but from the soft rustling outside the low door it was obvious he was not far away. When he returned, after knocking first to prepare her for his entry, he was carrying a tray filled with steaming cups of chocolate, cheeses, and crusty buns hot from the innkeeper's oven.

16

Elizabeth was determined not to eat, but when he threatened to hand feed her if she didn't, she capitulated.

The currant buns were drenched with butter, and the chocolate left a faint, not unpleasant tang in her throat. She sighed. It was wise to have eaten. She needed her strength. Besides, the food had left her with an extremely pleasant glow. More than anything she would love to have crawled back into bed for another hour or two, but he was urging her into her cloak. She was just dimly aware of his encircling arm around her waist as they walked down the narrow stairway to the rear door of the posting inn. A plump, matronly woman murmured something about Lady Clendennon and dropped a curtsy as they boarded the carriage.

Elizabeth had lost track of time. Somewhere along the way she had acquired a mustard-yellow bonnet and a yellow checked dress of a cheap organdy material. Its considerable wear vouched for the fact that it had been purchased from some innkeeper's daughter. She had doubtless been a hefty soul, because the dress hung on Elizabeth like a gypsy tent after a heavy rainstorm.

They were in the carriage, moving along at a leisurely pace no doubt to spare the team of horses. She was acutely aware that her head was resting in the crook of her captor's arm as it lay against the back of the seat. She dared not move lest he know she had awakened.

Her mouth tasted like wet wool, and she longed to rinse it with clear, cool water. The chocolate! She should have realized before now that it had been drugged. The bastard! For all his courtly ways he was more a blackguard than the worst scoundrel she had ever known.

As she willed herself to be calm and plan her next move, the carriage turned sharply and entered what sounded like a smithy or stabler's yard. Her captor gently removed his

17

arm and laid her to rest against the corner of the carriage.

Her pulse quickened. Was he so intent on their next stop that he was unaware she had awakened? She felt the carriage lurch slightly as he jumped to the ground. Rising slowly, Elizabeth peered out the window. A blacksmith shop. She was right. One of the horses must have lost a shoe. They might be here for hours. This could be her only chance to escape. She quickly studied the surrounding area: a tiny village ahead to the left, smithy's forge in front, woods to the right. The woods were the only safe course. She slid down to the floor and carefully eased the door open. It grated unmercifully, then opened enough for her to slip to the ground. She dared not take time to look around and made a beeline for the underbrush that fronted the woods.

Her heart beat wildly as she sank to the ground beneath a huge hemlock tree. She listened . . . but there was no pounding of footsteps in pursuit. She was free! She caught her lower lip between her teeth and forced herself to get up. It was just a question of time until they knew she was missing. And they would come after her, there was no doubting that.

Ahead of her lay a small clearing in the woods. She skirted it and came upon a pathway that led upward toward an outcropping of rocks. Lifting her skirts with unladylike determination, Elizabeth charged forward as if her life depended upon it.

She could smell the sea. Somehow it meant sanctuary, and she forced herself to ignore the grinding pain in her side. Just as she reached the top of the hill, her captor stepped out from behind a boulder and towered over her.

"Are you taking the air, my lady?" He wagged his finger at her. "Tut-tut. Not when we are nearly there."

His infernal nonchalance irritated her more than anything. Elizabeth gave a strangled cry and made for the beach. He loped after her and caught her easily, then flung her to the sand and held her there with his knee. His eyes glittering with mischief, her captor lowered himself down beside her.

CHAPTER TWO

Elizabeth sucked in her breath as he placed himself over her. She was too frightened to plead, except with her eyes. Then too she felt a stirring of pure animal feelings inside her. He wasn't uncouth. Indeed, there was a subtle attraction about the man that must have turned the head of many a maiden.

His breath came with a quickness that had nothing to do with his easy romp down the hill. He held her there in the sand with the weight of his body as he considered his options.

"God help me, you're too much the woman for him. I should take you now and be done with it for all the trouble you've given me."

Tears formed at the back of her eyes, and she shook her head mutely. He reached up a hand to draw a curl from beneath her bonnet, then rubbed it between his fingers.

"Like spun silk. I'd give my arm to see it spilling down over your bare shoulders."

She blinked quickly and wet her lips. "Please. Let me stand. You're crushing me."

He sighed and rolled away. "Fool that I am. It's fortunate for you, my lady, that we are but an hour's ride from the castle. Were it longer, I doubt that my good behavior would tolerate your teasing."

"Teasing!" Her voice cut through the faint sea breeze.

"How can you even think such a thing? Never in my life have I so much as flirted with a man."

He raised an eyebrow. "That's not the way I heard it told. Even if it were true, your body alone could drive a man to his cups without the added spice of flirtatious glances. But be warned. His Grace will not tolerate perfidy. Once you are under his roof, you had best toe the mark. He has put up with enough nonsense from your family."

Elizabeth's head was clear enough to catch the title. "His Grace? Am I being taken to a duke?"

He threw his head back and laughed. "Aren't you the sly one, pretending you don't know? But not this time, your ladyship. Come. The carriage should be repaired. Your beloved is waiting."

Her attempt to protest gained her nothing. He grabbed her hands and swung her to her feet. The puncture wound on her leg burned as it rubbed against the sand, but she refused to cry out. Knowing what little she did about the man, Elizabeth realized he wouldn't be above lifting her skirts to have a look.

He kept a close eye on her for the remainder of the journey. Less than an hour later the crenellated turrets of the castle sprang into view through a break in the trees. He pointed to the remains of a stone sentry tower at the side of the road.

"This marks the outermost boundary of Heatherwood. From here our land goes all the way to the sea, then stretches far in the opposite direction until one meets another similar marker. Yonder lies the village of Heatherford, which is also a part of the duchy." He spoke with obvious pride.

Elizabeth was puzzled. "We must have come a long way from London. Just where are we?"

"Why, Devon, of course." He grinned. "As if you didn't know."

21

She leaned forward, conscious of his hand just inches away, ready to grab her if she so much as moved toward the door. But he needn't have worried. She was too tired to make the attempt, and even if she did succeed in escaping, where would she go? This was his territory, or at least the land belonging to the duke. No one would dare lift a hand to help her. She would have to wait until she was better prepared. She shuddered. But just how long would that be? And how could she protect herself from the duke until that time? The first thing she would do was find a weapon. If he tried to force himself upon her, he would pay dearly. At the moment it was the only thought she could cling to.

Despite her anxiety Elizabeth could not help but marvel at the wild beauty of the Devon countryside. Once they emerged from the darkness of the pine forest, the ground rose abruptly to a large clearing at the center of which the castle was set like a great white jewel. Beyond the clearing the sea provided a panoramic backdrop of cobalt-blue against a periwinkle sky. In the foreground enormous boulders made a natural barrier against invasion as if they had been placed there by some gigantic hand.

The carriage slowed to a stop to permit a flock of sheep to cross the road, and Elizabeth leaned out of the window to get a better view. On closer look the castle appeared to be constructed of stone of varying colors, leading her to believe that it had been added to over a period of time. The colors ranged from gray to pale yellow limestone to the crystalline-white of the original structure. The lower battlements were covered with ropes of ivy that contrasted darkly against the stone. The walls, stretching for some three hundred feet in length, were buttressed at several points by square towers.

They entered through the arched gatehouse, the massive wooden doors of which stood open as if they had not moved on their great hinges for more than a hundred years. Ahead of them a grassy courtyard extended as far as the middle bailey. Trees and flowers graced the area beyond the carriage turnaround, softening the otherwise harsh lines of the stone walls.

Elizabeth felt her captor's excitement begin to rise. For all his roguishness he reminded her of a little boy about to reveal a well-kept secret. It did little to ease her anxiety. She looked at him beseechingly and placed her hand on his arm.

"Please. It is still not too late to make good our departure. The duke, whomever he is, might still be unaware that we have arrived. I beg of you, don't turn me over to this despicable man."

Her captor's laughter underlined his excitement. "The despicable man to whom you refer, your ladyship, happens to be my brother. I'm delivering you to him as a gift."

Elizabeth was appalled. "Have you no sense of decency? You're no better than a barbarian."

He studied her closely. "Think now, my lady. Would a barbarian have seen fit to deliver you unscathed? It was no little sacrifice on my part to play the eunuch."

The carriage drew to a halt near the entrance to the middle bailey, from which arose the turrets of the great hall. As the driver climbed down and affixed the steps, her captor reached for the handle and opened the door.

"Now, then, shall we go in? I'll see you to your quarters and give you a chance to freshen up before the duke returns from the village."

"I'll not get out. You'll have to drag me."

"That should present no problem. If need be I can always use the pad of lint over your nose."

Elizabeth blinked back the tears. There was no doubt in her mind that he meant it. She might as well pretend to go along with his demands. She accepted the hand he held out to her and descended from the carriage.

There was a particular sweetness to the air that belied

23

the cruel circumstances of her abduction. Given a different situation, Elizabeth admitted she would have been entranced by the rugged beauty of the castle, which was perched on a rise overlooking the sea. Instead, she had to draw upon her last ounce of courage to keep from stumbling as her abductor led her toward the entrance to the Great Hall.

As they approached the massive doors a gong sounded from somewhere within, and she was not surprised to see a half dozen blue-and-gold-liveried footmen standing at attention as the butler opened the door to welcome them inside.

He bowed low. "Welcome home, Sir Arthur." He accepted the rough-looking seaman's coat and cap as if they were made of costly furs.

"Thank you, Thomas." He handed over Elizabeth's cape. "Will you send Mrs. Patchen to the Emerald Suite? Her ladyship is fatigued and would like to freshen herself. I want to be advised the moment the duke arrives home."

"Indeed, sir. Immediately."

As her captor took her arm to direct her toward a great mahogany staircase, Elizabeth tried to shake him off. "I might have known you were nobility. You haven't enough character to fit the seaman's guise you wear so easily."

He grinned. "Harsh words, my lady. You had best mind your tongue. The duke burns with a short fuse these days."

At the top of the imposing staircase they turned down a long corridor then stopped at a closed door. He opened it, motioning her inside, then followed after her.

"These will be your chambers until after the wedding ceremony."

"And when, pray tell, is that supposed to be?"

"It will be up to His Grace to set the date. In the meantime I hope the rooms will prove comfortable."

Elizabeth had only a quick impression of quiet elegance

before a tap sounded on the door and a trim woman of indeterminate age entered the room and dropped a curtsy toward Sir Arthur.

"His Grace is in the library, sir, and he's in a fine mettle over your prolonged absence. He wishes to talk to you."

Elizabeth was surprised to see her captor stiffen. "So soon? God's truth, I thought to have a little time to prepare." He stroked his chin. "Forgive me, your ladyship. I must leave you to Mrs. Patchen for a time." He took the woman's arm and walked to the door. "See that her ladyship is bathed and dressed in something more appropriate." A trace of his former humor returned. "I fear we left in something of a hurry. As soon as she is presentable send her downstairs to the library. And be as quick as possible, please."

After the door closed behind him, the woman, her face an expressionless mask, led Elizabeth to the dressing room, which was equipped with a hip tub and a built-in chamber pot. Mrs. Patchen looked apologetic.

"I regret, your ladyship, that we have not time to heat the water. Had we anticipated your arrival we would have made certain everything was in order. For the present I fear you will have to make do, but I shall start the fires going so that you may have a hot bath before you retire."

Elizabeth put her hand on the woman's arm. "Please, you must help me. That man has abducted me from a dressmaker's shop in London. I must leave here at once."

The woman drew back in surprise, and a cautious expression veiled her eyes. "You look tired, my lady. Why don't you lave your face and arms while I see if I can find a gown that will fit you."

Elizabeth knew she had wasted her breath. Obviously the housekeeper owed her loyalty to the duke and would never chance his displeasure by siding with a stranger. She sank down on a stool and resigned herself to waiting for the proper moment to make her escape.

Haste made short work of the simple toilette. Elizabeth found herself longing for the promised soak in the elegant hip bath, but she had hardly time to dry her face on the soft linen towel before the woman had reappeared with a red satin gown. Elizabeth hated red, and the gown, though of the finest material and cut, was more than ample for her slender frame. She pulled a white shawl over her shoulders to hide the generous folds. A short time later she was led downstairs, where Sir Arthur stood at the open door of a room Elizabeth assumed to be the library.

His face was tight with suppressed excitement. "At last. I had begun to think Mrs. Patchen had spirited you away. Come, your ladyship. I've kept the secret as long as I dared."

He stepped aside and motioned for her to enter the room. "Your Grace, I promised to bring you a surprise next time I returned home. And here she is . . . your dearly betrothed."

Elizabeth's eyes took a moment to become accustomed to the light in the room. He was seated at a desk, his back to the window, which silhouetted him against the sunlight streaming into the room. He rose, slowly, deliberately, and she was uncertain whether it was due perhaps to surprise or advanced age. One thing she did know, he was a tall, craggily built man, lean, yet strong as the walls of the castle keep.

"What manner of jest is this, Arthur?" When he spoke, his voice vibrated with power.

Arthur laughed boyishly. "I knew you'd never humble yourself to go after her, Marcus, so I brought her to you."

The duke moved out agilely from behind the desk and came toward them. Elizabeth drew in her breath. Here was no aging man. Standing before her was the most ruggedly masculine man she had ever seen. Black hair swept back from his face with just a hint of gray at the temples. A dark widow's peak gave him the appearance of masterfulness, and she felt her pulse quicken.

He crossed his arms in front of him and spread his legs as he confronted them. For a moment she thought she saw a glimmer of recognition, but it passed. His voice gave clue to the extent of his irritation.

"And just who is she, Arthur, if I may be so bold?"

Elizabeth saw Arthur's face blanch, and his laughter sounded forced. "I beg of you, Marcus. Do not jest at a time like this. You don't know what I've gone through to bring her to you."

"Is it your opinion, Arthur, that I'm in such desperate straits to wed that I would marry anyone whom you chose to bring home?"

Arthur was beginning to sweat. He ran his fingers around the collar of the seaman's blouse and laughed shakily. "I know it has been more than a year, Your Grace, but surely you recognize the lady Louella?"

"Louella!" Both Elizabeth and the duke echoed the name in surprise. Elizabeth was the first to recover. She was closer to tears now than she had been during her abduction, and to save herself she couldn't understand why.

"So that's it. I should have known. My name is Elizabeth, not Louella. I am Lady Elizabeth Brooks Cambridge. The lady Louella Billingsworth to whom you refer is my niece." She looked up at the duke. "But you are not Lord Aldred? . . ." Her voice was puzzled.

The duke bowed. "Indeed, your ladyship, I am not. Allow me to introduce myself. I am Marcus James Clendennon, Duke of Heatherford." He studied her face for a moment. "May I ask why you are surprised my name is not Aldred?"

Elizabeth shook her head in dismay. "This is all too confusing. The lady Louella is betrothed to Lord Aldred of Pentland, an earl, not a duke."

The duke motioned her to a chair. "Sit down, please. It seems we have a great deal to sort out."

Elizabeth seated herself gingerly on the edge of a Queen Anne chair. She wasn't surprised that Sir Arthur had chosen to remain in the background. His little surprise had proven more of a shock than he could possibly have imagined.

The duke studied her face. "I seem to see a resemblance between you and your niece, although I confess to having seen her but once and for a short period of time."

Elizabeth drew back under his scrutiny lest she see disappointment written on his face. Strangely she wanted to please him. Would he guess that she was seven years Louella's senior? Would he be thinking that she was too long in the tooth to ever be mistaken for Louella? It was impossible to read the expression on his face. He turned to Sir Arthur, who waited uneasily near the door.

"Join us, Arthur. The least you can do is see this through to the end." He turned to Elizabeth, his voice accusing. "And what of you, your ladyship? Have you presented false colors that led my brother to believe you were your niece?"

"Indeed not!" Elizabeth felt her face turn red. "In truth, I resent your suggesting such a thing. Two days ago your brother abducted me from a dressmaker's establishment where I was being fitted for a cloak. I have been held captive until this very moment."

The duke's face mirrored his surprise. "Indeed? And how was it that you were unable to escape during that time? It is a goodly ride between here and London."

Elizabeth was furious at having to defend herself. "Suffice it to say, Your Grace, that I would have drowned myself in the sea before becoming *your* bride."

The duke had the decency to turn red at her thrust. Sir Arthur stepped forward. Once again he seemed to be his old self.

"God's blood! What an unlikely thing to have happened. I had it on good word that the purple cloak was on special order for the lady Louella. I can't see how I could have been mistaken."

Elizabeth's temper continued to simmer. She was tired, her leg hurt from the puncture wound, and once again she had taken second place to her niece, Louella. She folded her arms around her and stood to face them.

"Had you but taken the trouble to ask, I would have told you that I often stand in for my niece. She has no great love for such tiresome chores as fittings at the dressmaker."

Arthur threw his head back and laughed. "Indeed, my lady. When one is in the process of abduction, one is hardly in a position to request a by-your-leave." He slapped his hand on his knee. "Fool that I am! Had I but known you were not my brother's betrothed, the nights we bedded together at the inn would have had a different outcome."

Elizabeth's face flamed as she saw the duke look from one to the other.

His voice was cold and hard. "Am I to understand that you shared the same bed?"

Elizabeth was struck dumb, but Arthur managed a dry laugh. "How else was I to keep her from escaping? Indeed, the one time she tried I had to overpower her on the beach not an hour's drive from here." He stroked his chin as if savoring the memory. "She fights like a hellcat, this one. You'd be well advised to keep her, Your Grace, and to the devil with the lady Louella."

The duke's face froze. "Mind your words, Arthur. I still consider myself betrothed to the lady Louella until I have it from her lips that the engagement is broken."

Elizabeth felt a moment of triumph. She drew herself to full height and gave a self-satisfied smile. "And I suppose when she and her husband take the air in Saint James's

Park with their fourteen children, you will still consider yourself her betrothed. She chose to marry another, Your Grace. And considering the treatment I have received from your family, it may have been the most intelligent action she has ever taken."

The two men shifted uncomfortably, and the duke rose. "It appears we both owe you an apology, your ladyship; my brother for his high-handed attempt to correct a breach of tradition, and myself for my own lack of hospitality. We will do our best to make amends and see that you are returned to your family forthwith." He bowed deeply.

Elizabeth was left with nothing to say. She felt her pride vindicated with her small triumph, but the prospect of returning to her "family" was far less than appealing. After a longer pause than etiquette permitted, she rose and responded to his bow with a token curtsy just seconds before he turned to leave the room.

Sir Arthur came toward her and took her hands in his. "I do most heartily apologize for the nuisance I've wrought, your ladyship. But in one thing I was right. You have too much spirit for my brother. It would take a better man than he to master you."

Elizabeth nodded. "Meaning you, no doubt."

He grinned and said something in response, but Elizabeth wasn't listening. Instead, her ears were attuned to the rustling outside the library door. Someone was listening. Was it the duke? Instinctively she pulled away from Arthur's grasp just as the duke came into the room. Seeing them so close together, his face darkened.

"Walkers wants to see you down at the stable. Something to do with the lead gelding, I think."

Sir Arthur nodded. "I noticed he was limping a bit during the last few miles." He glanced sheepishly toward Elizabeth. "Will you excuse me, your ladyship? I'm sure the duke will see to it that you have refreshments."

30

It was obvious from the start that they both were uncomfortable on being left alone. He *had* heard the brief exchange between her and Arthur. Elizabeth was convinced of it. Good. Then perhaps he would know his place. Admittedly she was afraid of him. For all his risqué remarks Elizabeth sensed that there was little to fear from Arthur, but Marcus was another story. His brooding, dark face and obvious strength would be something to reckon with.

She pulled her shawl closer about her. "If you will excuse me, I would like to go to my room."

He put out his hand. "Just one moment, Lady Elizabeth. I would like to question you."

"About Louella's betrothal?"

"That among other things."

She tilted her head then resumed her chair. "Very well, but if you choose to believe I have been less than truthful in telling you of her impending marriage, then there is nothing left to say."

He shook his head. "As yet I have no reason to doubt the veracity of what you say. What I wish to know is whether or not the lady Louella has willingly entered into this liaison. It is a question of honor, you see. The alliance between our families was contracted years ago between our fathers. I feel myself duty bound to follow through unless the Lady herself chooses to terminate the understanding."

He looked wretched and uncomfortable. Despite herself Elizabeth felt compassion warm her voice. She wanted to reach out to touch his arm, but she folded her hands in her lap.

"I regret if the news distresses you, Your Grace, but I assure you that Lady Louella was more than eager to terminate the betrothal. In truth, she has in the past made many alliances only to forfeit them when a better offer came along. This latest conquest is rather well known for

31

his financial holdings. That in itself would account for her change of heart."

"I perceive, then, that there is no love lost between you and your niece."

Elizabeth shrugged. "You are correct, but that does not affect the circumstances."

"Indeed? I can see how it could."

Elizabeth felt her temper rising. "Very well, Your Grace. Would you prefer to believe this?" She stood and spread her hands in a dramatic gesture as if she were relating a story to a child in a nursery.

"It happened like this. The wicked marquis, father to the lovely young maiden, was gambling one night at Watier's club. As darkness enfolded the room the wicked roué threw his cards on the table and demanded his winnings. Unable to pay, the marquis promised his virgin daughter in lieu of gold. Alas, the Lovely Louella was brokenhearted to lose the handsome duke, but there was no other way. She—"

In one swift move the duke was upon her and grabbed her shoulders. "Silence, woman. You mock me!"

Her eyes widened as she looked up at him, her pulse quickening. Despite herself, she continued to goad him. "Does that version better soothe your wounded vanity, Your Grace?" Her eyes narrowed. "Indeed, your pride has suffered much this day, hasn't it? You heard what your brother said when he thought we were alone, didn't you?"

For a moment Elizabeth thought he was going to attack her physically. The fire that burned deep in his eyes threatened to consume the two of them, but he gave a strangled groan and thrust her away.

"Go to your room at once and remain there until supper. If you choose to speak like an undisciplined child, I shall treat you as one. Suffice it to say that on the morrow I shall arrange for your immediate return to London."

Elizabeth was loath to let it end like that. It had been months since her emotions had been so alive, and she gloried in the new sensation. She folded her arms across her chest as she returned to face him.

"And what of reparations, Your Grace? Surely the penalty for abduction is transportation, if not the gallows."

Sweat broke out on his upper lip, and as she saw the rage darken his eyes, she drew a quick tongue across her lips to moisten them.

CHAPTER THREE

The duke was nearly livid with anger. "Be warned, woman. I do not take kindly to threats."

Elizabeth felt her knees go weak, but she had started this game, now there was nothing to do but see it through. She tossed her head in a semblance of disdain. "Threats, indeed. And how do you think the marquis will respond to having his sister-in-law stolen from under his care?"

"I shall take great pains to explain the circumstances. Being a man of honor, he will certainly understand. Believe this, your ladyship. It would require more than the testimony of a—" He stammered, trying to find the right word.

"Of what, Your Grace?" she taunted.

Hard put to affix a name to her kind of woman, he swore in frustration. "It will take a more influential woman than you to ruin the name of a naval hero such as my brother— a man who has distinguished himself in battle and has been knighted by the King. You would be well-advised to hold your tongue."

"I wouldn't put too much hope in that, Your Grace," she said as she turned and swept through the open door. Away from his gaze, it was all she could do not to scurry like a rabbit for the safety of her chambers. Fortunately he chose not to follow after her.

It took only one turn down a wrong corridor to convince Elizabeth that she had best keep her wits about her.

Although the mansion on South Audley Street, which belonged to her sister's husband, was of considerable size, it was nothing compared to the maze of rooms and corridors that comprised Heatherwood Castle. Finally she made her way back to the main hall, then proceeded up the great staircase to her suite.

With time to herself she was able to critically appraise her surroundings. It was appropriately named the Emerald Suite, Elizabeth thought. The gradations of colors ranged from a pale mist green of the draperies at the windows and over the bed to the deeply vibrant shades of blue-green in the border of the carpeting, so dark that it was almost black. Rich touches of gold and iridescent yellow were brought out in the velvet love seat and chairs in the sitting room. Gold-and-white lacquered furniture added a touch of French elegance to the rooms. It occurred to Elizabeth that nothing she had seen at the South Audley Street mansion could begin to compare with this fine quality.

The dressing room was most impressive of all. It was the custom in London to use a chamber pot complete with a padded lid silencer in the performance of one's most intimate needs. Here the utility was built into the wall. Closer inspection revealed a lever, which when depressed, released a quantity of water from an overhead tank, forcing it into a pipe that sluiced the chamber clean after each use. No doubt the trough emptied somewhere outside, perhaps into a stream. She had heard of such conveniences but had never seen one.

A tapping on the door called her back to the sitting room. She held her breath. "Who is it?"

"'Tis Mrs. Patchen, your ladyship. May I come in?"

Elizabeth opened the door to the trim housekeeper, who smiled and dropped a curtsy.

"Would you care to soak in a warm tub before you rest, milady? I've brought you some fresh underpinnings and a gown that should fit a mite better than the red satin." She spread it out on the bed. "His Grace said you were to have anything you wanted to make you comfortable."

Elizabeth looked at the gown. It was a delicate shade of heliotrope muslin, embroidered with darker pink flowers and piped with narrow black cording at the bodice and sleeves. The skirt flared modestly from the tiny waist. She loved it and longed to try it on, but she held back.

"To whom does the dress belong?"

"It belonged to the lady Emily."

"The duke's wife?" Elizabeth asked, holding her breath. It had never occurred to her before that he might have once been married.

"No, miss. The duke's sister. She is married now and lives on a neighboring estate."

"Will she mind, do you think? I would so like to change into something that fits."

"I'm sure she would be pleased. If you wish, I will launder your yellow check dress and see that it is pressed."

"Oh, that's not my dress either," Elizabeth volunteered before she had a chance to think. The woman gave her a quizzical look but was too well trained to ask questions. She pulled the bell rope and sent a maid and footman running to bring buckets of hot water for the hip bath.

Once alone, Elizabeth yielded herself to the pure pleasure of the warm bath. She soaked for an unconscionably long time, then dressed in fresh underclothes and lay down upon the goosedown mattress to rest. The puncture wound on her leg was softened by the bath water even though it had begun to ooze unpleasantly, but the fact that it was less painful except when it was touched relieved most of her concern.

An hour or so later, Greta, the abigail whom the housekeeper had appointed to look after Elizabeth, came in with a pot of tea and thin slices of buttered bread.

She was a singularly attractive girl who carried herself

with the confidence that her body alone could obtain for her what circumstances of birth had denied. She cooly appraised Elizabeth's unruly hair.

"Would your ladyship wish to have something done with 'er 'air?"

"Yes, Greta, but I fear I have no comb or brush."

"Indeed?" Her eyes sparkled with fun. "Then 'tis true wot they say backstairs. Sir Arthur took you from London without so much as a by-your-leave?"

Elizabeth sighed. There was no keeping secrets from the servant class. "As it happens, I left unexpectedly and had no time to pack my belongings. I suppose we shall have to see if Mrs. Patchen can provide me with simple toilette articles."

"And just 'ow long might you be stayin', your ladyship?"

Elizabeth detected a guarded note in the girl's voice, and she wondered why it should matter to a servant girl. "I rather imagine I shall be leaving on the morrow."

"That soon? Well, I've no doubt we can find somethin' to dress your 'air with." Her voice took on a decidedly friendlier note. She hurried from the room to return moments later with a collection of combs and brushes to put a hairdresser to shame.

"I fear I 'ave no great skill wi' the curling tongs, your ladyship, save wi' me own 'air, that is, but I'm willing to try. We don't often 'ave lady visitors here, other than Lady Emily, and she brings 'er own abigail."

Elizabeth could not miss the pointed hint, but she chose not to explain why she arrived unattended. "I am quite capable of doing my own hair." She pulled the combs that held its considerable bulk atop her head, and it spilled over her shoulders like a silken cloud.

"Lord a'mighty," the girl said as she watched wide-eyed. "I've never seen such pale-gold 'air in all my days." She leaned her own dark head close. "Wi' 'air like this you

37

could name your price and no buck or dandy would think twice before 'e was at your feet just pantin' to be trod on."

Elizabeth laughed. "I'm not sure that would appeal to me very much."

The girl looked shocked. "Indade, and why not? Make 'em pay, I says, and the more the better. Better than lettin' them take it free."

Elizabeth could tell by the look on her face that she meant it. "Surely you are speaking in theory only?"

"If you mean did I try it yet, no, miss, not yet, but it weren't easy fightin' off some o' those fast-handed gentlemen who come beggin' for it. I'm saving myself for the richest man I can find."

"But isn't that like selling yourself?"

The girl shrugged. "I doubt's that 'tis any 'arder to love a rich man than a poor one."

Elizabeth smiled at the simplicity of it. Unfortunately real life was considerably different. She had seen too many arranged marriages where the contract was a matter of expediency. No sooner had the marriage been consummated, than the man sought the comfort of a demirep. Many of them even went so far as to establish a pied-à-terre in the quieter sections of London, where they might visit their courtesans in private. As for the women, they kept themselves busy with their homes and children, or sometimes, out of boredom, found comfort in the arms of another man.

With her hair once again wound into a French twist at the top of her head, Elizabeth put on the dressing gown Mrs. Patchen had provided and spent the afternoon resting on a chaise longue in the oriel, a bay window extending out from one of the circular towers, supported from below by great stone corbels. Leaded glass French doors opened to a minute balcony that was itself a part of the oriel.

The secluded aerie provided a magnificent view of a garden hidden under the protection of giant yew hedges.

Beyond that lay the sea. At the foot of the steep escarpment on which the castle was built she could see the rocky abutments of a small cove where several boats lay at anchor. It looked peaceful and inviting. The plaintive cry of the gulls beckoned to her as they dipped, wheeled, and soared in a graceful, winged ballet.

It was inevitable that she compare this place with London. The thought of returning to the dirty, teeming city sickened her. What was there to go back to? More of what she had struggled through during the past year. She was not treated like family at her sister's house. Indeed, she was treated with less dignity than the servants. Servants were at least paid for their labors. What little she received was doled out grudgingly until she felt like a live-in beggar.

Her thoughts were interrupted when Greta came to help her dress for dinner.

It was with considerable trepidation that Elizabeth donned a shawl and a mobcap and went downstairs to the library, where she was told a glass of wine would be served before they dined. The perfect fit of the pale pink gown gave her the measure of confidence she needed to bolster her courage, but she was not quite certain what to expect when she once again faced the two brothers.

They rose and bowed when the footman announced her. Elizabeth dropped a curtsy and surveyed the room. On her previous visit to the library she had noticed little but the master of the house.

It was comfortably appointed with book-lined walls and deep, sturdy chairs unlike the fragile, feminine furnishings in her bedchamber. The colors were varying shades of blue, tempered by an accent of burnished gold in soft cushions that were tucked into the chairs. A sheaf of dried sea grass as high as a man's waist was arranged in an enormous aqua-blue glass bottle that stood on the floor in a corner. It was an unusal touch, Elizabeth thought, but delightful and decorative.

Sir Arthur motioned her to a chair as the footman offered a glass of sherry. Arthur lifted his glass in a toast of sorts. "I daresay, Lady Elizabeth, the rest has done wonders for you. You look ravishing in the pink gown."

Elizabeth thanked him. "It is truly lovely. I hope you will extend my gratitude to your sister."

The duke turned toward them. "Emily will not miss the gown. She has more gowns than she will ever wear. I trust that you have been suitably looked after by my staff?"

"Indeed, Your Grace. They have been most considerate." Elizabeth was once more impressed by the strength and magnetism he exuded simply by standing there. He was a man of kingly bearing, and yet he had the grace of an athlete. His skin was less dark than that of his brother, but there was a rugged vitality about it that vouched for his obvious good health.

Although he was courteous, there was no warmth in his voice as he spoke. "I have arranged for the coach to be ready to take you back to London shortly after daybreak tomorrow. With an early start we can limit the trip to two days."

"We? Am I to understand that you plan to accompany me?"

"Not out of choice, I assure you. I had not planned to return to London for several weeks."

Sir Arthur spoke, his voice edged with irritation. "I see no reason why I should not accompany her. It is not as if she would be traveling under duress."

The duke slammed his drink down on the table. "We have discussed the reasons for your remaining here, Arthur, and the matter is settled. I have said that I will accompany her ladyship, and I wish to hear no more about it."

Elizabeth felt her face turn pink. "There is no need for

40

anyone to accompany me. If truth be told, I would as leave travel on a public conveyance rather than be treated as a nuisance. I'm sure the mail coaches make daily runs from here to London."

"Enough!" The duke left no doubt as to his feelings. "The subject is closed. I have said I will accompany you, and I will not have my authority questioned."

Elizabeth stood up. "You have no authority over me, Your Grace. I have reached my majority and need answer to no man. What I do is my concern alone."

Before either of the men could stop her, she walked out of the library and climbed the stairs to her bedchamber. Her leg had begun to ache unmercifully. Once inside her bedroom, she pulled the rope to summon Greta. It was several minutes before the girl arrived.

"Was there something you wanted, your ladyship? I was having me supper."

"I'm sorry, Greta. I'd like you to ask Mrs. Patchen for some salve and a length of bandage. I'm planning to leave tonight, and I have a wound on my leg."

"Tonight? Indeed, your ladyship, I'd 'eard you weren't to leave till the morrow."

"I've changed my mind. How far is the nearest village? Is it close enough that I could walk there?"

"Oh, indeed it is. I walks 'ere every day from my cottage, and it's on the other side 'o the village."

"And is there a coaching inn located there?"

"Right next to the smithy."

"Good. Run along now and ask the housekeeper for the dressings."

Before an hour was up Elizabeth was ready to leave. The bandage on her leg was less than perfect, but it would have to do. The pain had eased some, but she prayed that the walk to the village would be a short one.

Darkness was settling over the countryside as she left.

A faint breeze from the sea stirred wisps of hair that escaped from her bonnet, and they blew across her eyes. She brushed them away impatiently. How different the road had looked from the safety of the carriage. Greta's instructions had seemed clear enough, but in the semi-darkness Elizabeth was uncertain which way to turn.

She had been walking for nearly fifteen minutes without having seen a sign of life. Occasionally a night bird screeched above her, and the sound was less than reassuring. She should have seen the tall steeple of the church by now. Greta had told her it was the nearest landmark. Her leg had begun a steady throbbing that sent pain reaching far above her knee. Elizabeth came at last to a line of huge boulders, and she knew without doubt that she was lost. Beyond was the sea, and one false step promised instant death on the rocks below. She sat down on a rock and buried her head in her arms.

It was hours later when he found her. The moon had risen full and silvery in a cloudless sky. The duke pulled his horse to an abrupt halt and slid from the saddle.

"Are you ready to return to the castle, or would you prefer to spend the night here?"

"I—I would like to return."

"Then you shall have to ride in front of me."

She nodded, not caring that he couldn't see her gesture. All that mattered now was that she be able to rest. He swung her in front of the saddle as easily as if she were a child, then mounted the horse and reached around her for the reins. Elizabeth settled against him as if it were the most natural thing in the world. He was warm, and he smelled faintly of musk and bay leaves. Never in her life had she felt so safe and protected. Despite the pain in her leg Elizabeth wished the night would never end.

Once back at the castle, the duke turned the horse over

to the groom and helped Elizabeth into a side door to the Great Hall.

"You're limping," he declared. "Is there a stone in your slipper?"

"No. It's—it's nothing. Only a slight wound on my leg from when I was put into the carriage."

"But that was days ago. It should have healed by now. Come into the kitchen. I'll have a look at it."

She drew away. "No. I can manage quite well."

"Like before? Do as I say and stop acting like a child." He put his arm around her waist and half carried her down a short flight of stairs to the main kitchen.

It was a large room with an enormous fireplace, row after row of cupboards, and sturdy worktables over which hung all manner of pots for cooking. Embers glowed darkly against the great log that banked the fire over which water simmered in a heavy kettle hanging from a crane.

He motioned for her to sit on a wooden chair while he touched a taper to the coals and lit a lamp.

"Take off your stocking."

She gasped. "I'll do no such thing. The wound is bandaged. There is nothing more to be done."

"Very well. I'll do it myself."

Elizabeth pressed her lips together in a grim line and began to roll down her stocking. He had the decency to turn away, but she knew the worst was yet to come. The bandage had slipped, but the pad of lint adhered to the wound. Gritting her teeth, she pulled it off but could not control the gasp of pain.

He turned and came over to stoop down beside her as he placed a basin of warm water on the floor. "The wound appears to be slight, but I fear that it is infected. It was stupid not to have thoroughly cleaned it before applying the ointment."

She fought to control her temper. "As it happens, my limb bends in only one direction. I have yet to learn how to turn it around to face front so that I might see what I'm doing."

"You could have asked Mrs. Patchen to cleanse it for you."

"Indeed, and so could you."

He had the decency to turn red. "Mrs. Patchen has retired for the night. If you are worried about my skill with herbs, fear not. I have had a great deal of experience treating horses."

"And are you saying that I compare to a horse?"

"Indeed, no, my lady. A horse is infinitely more obedient and a good deal less trouble."

"If you recall, Your Grace, the trouble is no fault of mine. It began when I was dragged back here against my will."

"I'm beginning to regret that I didn't leave you to spend the night on the headlands."

"I might have been better off."

"You would have had a good case of congestion to add to your infected leg, but doubtless your ill nature would have survived any disease."

Elizabeth gritted her teeth. Surprisingly his hands were gentle and efficient as he sponged away the old medication. She tried not to think about how unconventional it was for this stranger to be touching her in such an intimate way, but the very thought sent the blood singing in her veins.

His hair was dark and curly crisp from the night dew that had begun to settle. She longed to towel it down until it was dry and soft. Her gaze wandered down to the place where his open shirt revealed a triangle of hair on his chest. She caught her breath, and he must have thought he had hurt her, because he looked up quickly.

"I'm sorry. I didn't mean to cause you pain. Just a moment more and I'll have a fresh dressing in place."

A short time later he laid the scissors on the table and

reached for her hands. "Do you think you can stand?"

"Of course. There is nothing seriously wrong with me."

As he pulled her up she swayed against him and suddenly found herself in his arms.

CHAPTER FOUR

His fingers tightened on her shoulders as she leaned against him, and she could hear the steady thump of his heartbeat through the thin fabric of his shirt. Elizabeth was appalled by the feeling of wantonness that washed over her. What he must think of her!

She quickly pulled away and adjusted her skirt. "I—I must go to my room. It is very late, and I must rest before we begin the trip to London."

"There will be no trip to London until your leg is sufficiently healed to make it safe for you to travel. It would be foolish to risk poisoning of the blood when you can as easily remain here for a few days."

"I couldn't possibly. It's simply out of the question."

"I forbid you to return until you are completely well."

She felt her temper rise. "You have no right to forbid me to leave."

He swung her around to face him. "Fool woman. Do you value your independence so much that you would risk your life to prove a point?"

"I—I—it's just that my family will be worried." She turned away so that her face would not betray the lie. Indeed, Martha and the marquis would be curious, but it was not likely they would be worried enough to start an investigation into her disappearance. It was simply that as much as she wanted to remain here, she knew in her heart that it would be courting disaster. There was something about this strong-willed man that heated her blood.

He let her go and turned to pace the room. "Yes. We shall have to let the marquis know that you are safe. I shall send a messenger out at first light. In the meantime I will take you to your room. You must not walk on your foot for at least two days."

"But—"

"Enough." He held up his hand. "Come, I will carry you upstairs."

She knew better than to protest. In truth, she was glad of the excuse to settle against his chest, with her hand curved around his neck for support. His chin rested against her hair where her bonnet had been pushed back, and she felt the warmth of his breath as he climbed the stairs to her room. Putting her down on the bed, he rang for the maid.

"I'll be in to see you in the morning. Is there a message you wish to send to your sister?"

"What do you plan to tell them?"

"As little as possible. I have no wish to see my brother imprisoned or worse for his undisputed lack of judgment. It will be up to you whether or not you wish to impose charges against him."

Elizabeth shook her head. "I bear no ill feeling toward your brother. He could easily have mistreated me, but there was no permanent harm done. As for the marquis" —she shrugged—"I doubt that he will be concerned with my whereabouts once he learns I am unharmed. I was a rather convenient appendage to his household, nothing more. If you provide me with paper and a pen, I will write a message confirming what we have discussed."

The duke's dark gaze met hers and exchanged warmth. "That is most kind of you, Lady Elizabeth. You are more considerate than my brother deserves."

47

He moved a small writing desk over to the bed, and she composed the note and handed it to him for his approval.

"Excellent. I shall have the messenger deliver it post-haste."

A disgruntled Greta tapped on the door and walked in. When she saw the duke bent over the bed, she covered her ill temper with a bright smile. "Is there somethin' 'er ladyship wishes?"

The duke folded the letter and tucked it into an envelope. "See that her ladyship is helped into bed. She will be staying on with us for a few days." With a brief nod he turned and strode from the room.

The frown on Greta's face returned as soon as the duke made his exit. "I thought you was to go home tomorrow."

"I'm afraid my plans have been changed. The duke does not take no for an answer."

"Indade? It doesn't seem fittin' to me for an unmarried lady to stay in the same 'ouse without benefit of chaperon."

"There seems to be little choice for the present. My injury is great enough that he feels I must rest before making the journey to London. Besides, I have reached my majority and am answerable to no one save my conscience."

Greta sniffed. "Just the same, hit don't seem fittin' to me."

It occurred to Elizabeth that Greta was jealous of her attention from the duke. Perhaps when the girl spoke of choosing a wealthy man to pursue to the altar, she had already set her sights on the master of Heatherwood.

To Elizabeth's surprise a litter of sorts had been put together to enable the footmen to easily carry her downstairs for breakfast. She had expected to be a veritable prisoner in her chambers until such time as the duke saw fit to permit her to walk on her own. The two men rose as she was carried into the charming room adjoining the conservatory where breakfast was to be served.

Sir Arthur, his face pink and shining as if it had been freshly scrubbed, bowed his greeting. "Lady Elizabeth, may I extend my sympathy for your present incapacity?" He grinned. "But on the other side of the fence, may I say how pleased I am that you will be staying on for a time?"

"Thank you, on both counts. I daresay I am being pampered far beyond the merits of my injury. I am quite able to walk."

"I wouldn't advise it, your ladyship. At least not in the duke's presence. He left strict orders to that effect."

The duke bowed, and she inclined her head in response. She was uncertain how to react after last night's interlude, but he chose evidently to pretend it had never happened. In truth, what had really happened? Their close physical contact had left an unforgettable impression where Elizabeth was concerned, but for all she knew, to the duke the entire incident might have just been an unavoidable inconvenience.

He nodded for the footman to fill Elizabeth's plate from the sideboard, then sat down as he addressed her. "I hope that you slept well despite your injury, your ladyship."

"Quite well indeed, thank you." She looked around the room, which was painted a sunshine-yellow and was decorated with ferneries and luxuriant vines growing from baskets suspended from the high ceiling. "What an unusual and attractive room. It was my impression that castles were always cold, gloomy places in which to live."

The duke nodded. "Indeed, that is often true, but my mother was determined to make our ancestral hall into a home. She loved bright colors and growing things. The salt air discouraged propagation of flowers near the sea, so she had the conservatory added to this wing of the Great Hall."

Sir Arthur groaned. "And there you made your first

49

mistake, your ladyship. You should never have mentioned the castle unless you are willing to sit through an accounting of the history of every bit of mortar and stone it took to build this place."

Elizabeth smiled. "I would hardly consider that distasteful. Although I have visited many country homes in the past, I have never been fortunate enough to see inside a castle."

Sir Arthur grinned. "Then it pleases me to take credit for that accomplishment."

The duke frowned. "Don't pretend that your irresponsible behavior merits praise in any way, Arthur. My having to make the journey to London in a few days comes as a decided inconvenience."

Arthur brightened. "Then as I see it, we have two choices. Either I be permitted to escort her ladyship home, or we keep her here."

The duke nearly choked on his tea. "Indeed, Arthur. You become less mature with each passing day. It is difficult for one to believe that you will soon celebrate your twenty-first birthday." He mopped at the spot of tea on the tablecloth. "Consider the circumstances. For one, you were sent home from His Majesty's Service for rest and recovery, not to be seen frisking about the countryside in the company of each and every beautiful woman you find. For another, I am sure that her ladyship must be eager to return to the bosom of her family. For all we know she might have left behind a betrothed."

Elizabeth was surprised at the tightness in his voice and responded without thinking. "Your concern for my well-being is appreciated, Your Grace, but without need. I am little more than a servant in my sister's house, and as for a betrothed, there are few suitors who would pursue a penniless noblewoman, particularly one who has reached her majority."

There was an uncomfortable silence. Elizabeth realized

50

that she had said more than she should and laughed to cover it up. "I apologize if I sounded self-serving. In truth, I have no real complaint compared to the common people of Britain."

Sir Arthur's voice was gentle. "With a face and figure like yours, my lady, I doubt that your financial position will suffer for long." He turned toward the duke. "I see no reason why she can't remain here. I think we should keep her."

The duke's voice was dry. "I can think of several reasons why her ladyship would choose to leave. Besides, she is not a kitten to be kept or put out of the house. I think it best that she return to London as soon as she is able to travel. Do you not agree, Lady Elizabeth?"

She could not in good conscience answer yes. She didn't *want* to leave. The knowledge appalled her, and she was concerned lest they find out.

The duke laid down his fork and looked at her. "I asked you, your ladyship, if you agree."

She nodded. "I want whatever you think best, Your Grace."

"Indeed?" His tone was dry. "One might consider that a first knowing your unwillingness to follow instructions."

She felt the color rise in her face, but she remained quiet. The subject had put considerable strain on the conversation, and they spoke only in generalities for the rest of the meal.

As soon as he could leave decently, the duke rose and bowed to Elizabeth. "If you will excuse me, your ladyship, I fear I have duties to attend. May I ask if you have any special needs?"

"None, thank you. Since you insist that I remain immobile, I shall spend the day watching the sea from my small balcony."

Arthur jumped up. "I have a better idea. I'll have the servants carry you down to the cove, where you can watch the birds and the ships as they leave harbor. Would you like that?"

Elizabeth demurred. "I would hate to be an added burden, but the prospect is most inviting."

"I say . . . it will be no trouble at all. I shall in fact accompany you."

The duke sighed. "That comes as no great surprise. Take care that her foot is elevated, Arthur. We wouldn't want to impede her recovery."

His repeated remarks about her physical condition led Elizabeth to wonder if perhaps the duke was overly eager to see her depart. Was she really such an inconvenience to him? The thought hurt more than she cared to admit. She tried to put it out of her mind. In a few days she would be back in London, and all this would be but a vague memory. Better not to begin to like this country life too much. It would only pain the more when she had to leave it all behind.

In order to save the heliotrope dress from ruin, Elizabeth asked Greta to help her change into the old yellow check, which had been washed, pressed, and hung in the armoire. Greta's mood had not lightened until Elizabeth remarked that she was going to spend the day at the cove with Sir Arthur. When the girl went so far as to offer to brush Elizabeth's hair, it soon became evident that Greta wanted the time to question her about precisely where they were going. Just over an hour later she returned with word that the footmen were waiting with the litter to carry her down to the cove.

Sir Arthur was as enthusiastic as a little boy as he walked on ahead of them. "Right this way, follow me. I know the perfect place to sit right at the base of the rocks."

Even the footmen were amused by his exuberance as they grinned, then sobered when they saw that Elizabeth had noticed. They arranged her comfortably so that her back rested against a boulder, while a smaller boulder offered a place to elevate her leg. As soon as they finished, the footmen left, leaving her alone with Arthur. He spread another blanket a few feet away on the sand, then sank down facing the sea.

"It's incredible, isn't it? The sea, I mean. She has moods as strong as any human, and she's a demanding mistress."

"The duke said you were on leave from the Royal Navy?"

"Yes. I managed to pick up a slight shoulder wound. It was nothing, really, but they insisted on sending me home for a while."

"You were injured in battle?"

"The war with the Americans." He dug his heel into the sand. "Shabby business, that. We should have won, especially considering they had nought but a ragtag army."

"Britain is tired of war. Her armies have been spread too far and wide. They needed to come home to replenish themselves."

"It was a senseless war to begin. Had we been able to get the word to the Americans in time, there never would have been a war in the first place."

"It must be good to be home."

He shrugged. "Of course, but only for a time. Soon I will begin to miss the creak of the rigging and the snap of the wind in the sails." He gathered a handful of sand and let it sift between his fingers. "Marcus says I'm like the spindrift that blows across the sand. Nothing permanent about me . . . just air and foam . . . ready to drift again at the slightest breeze."

"He doesn't give you enough credit. When you find your direction, you'll settle down. You're still very young."

"Just a year younger than you."

She laughed. "But men are much younger than women at a given age."

53

"You're different from other women," he said, his eyes studying her closely.

"I'm almost afraid to ask."

He grinned. "I meant it as a compliment. Another woman would have been livid if I had put her through an experience like yours."

"Being abducted? Well I suppose you have to consider what my circumstances were at the time. I was leading a most unsatisfactory life. Any change would have been welcome as long as I was reasonably sure of my safety."

"You were a fool to trust me, your ladyship. It was pure luck that saved you from me . . . and the mistaken idea that you were betrothed to Marcus." She saw a mischievous light enter his eyes, and he reached for her hand.

"Now that I know Marcus has no claim to you, your safety is again in question. Were I you, I would be on my guard."

She returned the pressure of his hand. "Truly, Arthur. You don't mean that. I know you could never willingly bring harm to me."

"But men are known to lose control."

"Not you. You like to pretend, but I think you are very much in control of yourself. It is just that your brother is so strong, he makes everyone else feel weak."

"Marcus is strong both in mind and body. I'll grant you that, Elizabeth."

She looked up in surprise, and he turned red.

"Forgive my presumptuousness." He grinned. "Since we have shared the same bed, I thought it would harm nothing if I called you by your given name."

"It is rather outrageous of you. My family would be appalled."

"I say! From what little you've told me of your family, it would give me pleasure to shake them a bit."

"You like upsetting people, don't you?"

"Only when they don't know that I enjoy it."

Elizabeth laughed and withdrew her hand. "I shall remember that, Sir Arthur." She shaded her eyes against the sun. "That girl walking in the surf. Isn't that Greta, my abigail?"

"Without a doubt. None other of the servant girls would have the temerity to walk barefoot in the sand with their skirts lifted to their knees."

He continued to watch her for several minutes, and Elizabeth saw that he was restless. She settled back against the rock.

"Why don't you go talk to her. I know that's what you've had in mind for the past five minutes."

He gave her a look. "Truly, I had no such thought!"

"Arthur . . ."

He laughed. "All right. The score is in your favor. Are you certain you don't mind being left alone for a while?"

"I like being alone."

He stood. "I won't be long. She is probably waiting for someone."

Elizabeth nodded vigorously. "Yes, I rather think she is. The girl questioned me extensively about our excursion to the beach."

Arthur threw his head back and laughed. "Thank you for the warning."

Elizabeth smiled as she watched him sprint across the sand. Greta must have known he was coming, but she played the game to the hilt and refused to turn until he touched her shoulder. They remained in sight for a few minutes, then disappeared around a formation of rocks.

In the distance a three-masted sailing ship tacked in the wind and headed toward port at Exmouth. The fact that it was heavily laden with cargo was evidenced by the fact that it rode low in the water. She wondered where it had come from, but the distance was too great for her to read the markings on its flag.

Nearly an hour passed as she watched the ships and the

sea gulls as they came close to see what she had to offer. She found a nearby piece of aged lumber and a scrap of charcoal left over from a picnic on the beach. Propping the board on her knees, Elizabeth began to sketch the birds in flight. She had been working for some time when fog began to drift in, blotting out the warmth of the sun. Even the wool shawl did little to stop the chill. She pushed herself up straight and tried to peer down the beach, but there was no sign of Arthur. If he did not return soon, she would be forced to climb the precarious path on her own.

The fog worsened. Elizabeth was becoming alarmed. She had gathered her things together and was about to leave when she heard footsteps and turned.

"Your Grace—"

"God's truth! I knew I'd find you down here. Where the devil is Arthur?"

"I—he walked down the beach. I expect him back any moment now."

"Indeed. And was it your intention to wait for him?"

"I—I had not decided."

"Then you must have considered trying to climb the cliff."

She didn't answer.

"Can you stand?"

"Of course I can," she said as she quickly got up.

He stared at her thoughtfully, and she would have given a gold piece to have been able to read his thoughts. Finally he swore softly and, bending down, lifted her in his arms.

Her arm went automatically around his neck as she settled against his shoulder. "I really would prefer to walk."

"Oh, would you now? I don't recall asking your preference."

His face was close to hers this time, and if she turned slightly, her lips would graze his cheek. She yielded to the temptation, trying at the same time to make it seem accidental. The duke chose that moment to turn to ask her something, and as he did their lips brushed against each other. It was the merest whisper of a touch, but it sent flames of heat surging through her body.

CHAPTER FIVE

The duke was obviously taken aback. He stood so still that for a moment it seemed as if he had forgotten to breathe. He looked down at Elizabeth, their gazes locking. Then with apparent great effort he looked away and began to breathe in deep, ragged breaths. Without a word he attacked the steep path as if he were racing against a storm. And indeed he was, Elizabeth thought. The man was human. Her own turbulent emotions must surely have run parallel to his.

They reached the top of the cliff in record time, and he hastened to carry her to the house. Once inside, he placed her on a chair, then left orders for a footman to return for the litter and see that she was taken to her chambers. Without allowing her time to thank him, Marcus strode from the room.

There was no response to the bellpull when Elizabeth tried to summon her abigail. She hadn't expected there would be. No doubt Greta had taken full advantage of the opportunity to make Arthur notice her. She couldn't help but wonder just how far Greta would go in her pursuit of wealth. It gave one pause to wonder if Sir Arthur had money in his own right or whether he relied on the generosity of the duke to provide for him. It crossed her mind that Arthur was too good for the determined Greta, but under the same circumstances Elizabeth was hard put to know how she might feel.

Left alone, Elizabeth managed to freshen herself and brush away the sand that clung to her dress. It was damp, so she changed into the heliotrope gown. A short time later Greta returned and Elizabeth sent her to fetch the footmen to carry her downstairs to the library. Fortunately it was empty. She found an illustrated book on medieval history and prepared to settle herself for a pleasant rest when a soft, musical voice interrupted her reading.

"Hello, there. You must be Lady Elizabeth Cambridge. I hope I'm not disturbing you."

Elizabeth smiled at the attractive woman whose ample figure gave evidence to the fact that she was in the family way. "Hello. Yes, I am Elizabeth. And you must be the lady Emily about whom I have heard so much. Please forgive me for not rising."

"Please call me Emily. One need not stand on formality when one lives in the country." The woman reached for Elizabeth's two hands and spread them wide. "The heliotrope looks far better on you than it ever did on me, but I'd give up Banbury tarts for a year to be able to fit into it again."

Elizabeth blushed. "I do beg your forgiveness for having borrowed the gown without your permission. It is quite lovely."

Emily brushed it aside. "I'll wager you could find a dozen or more in the attic armoire that would fit you as well. Consider them my gift. I shall instruct Mrs. Patchen to have them brought down."

"But I couldn't—"

"You could and you must. I insist"—her face clouded —"that is unless you would consider it condescending of me. I assure you, I don't mean it that way."

Elizabeth reached for her hand and gave it a squeeze. "I'm sure you don't. I would be pleased to accept the dresses, but I did not wish to appear greedy."

The woman eased herself down into a chair. "I'm glad

that's settled. I can't wait to see you in the Persian ivory brocade. There is something about the gown that bodes good fortune. At least it always brought me good luck." She shifted her considerable bulk to a more comfortable position. "Now, then . . . just what have you done to my brother?"

Elizabeth blanched. "Sir Arthur? But I left him on the beach not two hours ago. Surely he is all right?"

Emily grinned. "Not Arthur, you goose. Marcus."

Elizabeth felt her pulse quicken. "I—I don't understand."

"No . . . I don't suppose you do. You don't know him as well as I do. Suffice it to say that he is more irritable and moody than I have seen him since my father passed on."

Elizabeth averted her face. "I am dreadfully sorry. It is true, I have been an unfortunate burden to the duke since my arrival, and I sincerely regret any trouble I have caused."

"Dear girl, you must not be so apologetic. While I do see a correlation between his temper and your presence in the house, I do not fault you for it." She patted Elizabeth's arm. "Dismiss it from your mind. Indeed, it was foolish of me to mention it."

Emily leaned back against the chair and propped her foot on a stool. "Tell me, what are the ladies of the *ton* wearing in Polite Society these days? It has been nearly a year since I've made the trip to London to visit the shops on Bond Street, and sometimes I think I will perish for a chance to browse through them again."

Elizabeth made a great effort to give an interesting, colorful description of the latest fashions, punctuated by snippets of gossip that Martha had relayed to her from afternoons spent at Almack's club for Society ladies.

"Nothing ever really changes, does it? The gentlemen still spend their evenings playing whist or gambling at the clubs. Harriette Wilson is still entertaining her various noblemen, and I mean that in the widest sense of the word. I heard tell that she's keeping a diary, and when the time comes when she no longer chooses to consort with them, she will publish her memoirs."

"It serves them right." Emily grinned. "With her wit and skill at badinage her autobiography should outsell Jane Austen. Is it true that Harriette sometimes wears knickers?"

Elizabeth shrugged. "I have never met her in person, but a few of the more adventurous young ladies began wearing knickers about the time that men gave over breeches for trousers. Some say it's a sign of moral decadence brought on by the reign of the Prince Regent. Lord Byron even went so far as to write that the waltz encouraged wantonness."

"Ha. He was always inclined to be a shade evangelical. But in truth, I doubt that the waltz will ever replace the minuet."

They were enjoying a cup of tea when Arthur came in. His gaze immediately went to Elizabeth, and she interpreted it to be a plea that she not mention his disappearance on the beach. She nodded almost imperceptibly, then tried not to smile at the look of profound relief on his face.

He strode over to Emily and gave her a brotherly hug. "I see you've met our guest. I'm glad you could come over, Emily."

She smiled with obvious affection for her younger brother. "Now that you're here I'll ask you what I lacked the courage to ask her ladyship." Emily smiled mischievously. "Did you really abduct her right out of the marquis's mansion?"

He ran a finger around the inside of his neckcloth. "I say, Emily. You know how the gossips blow things all out of proportion. Ask her yourself. Lady Elizabeth has always wanted to see a castle. Isn't that true?"

Elizabeth laughed despite herself. "Indeed it is. But I never expected to see one so grand. I am terribly impressed."

Emily groaned. "Be advised not to let Marcus know. He'll drag you by the hand over every square foot of the land before he will permit you to leave."

Marcus spoke from the doorway, and they all turned in surprise. "I am beginning to perceive that pride in one's heritage is nothing less than criminal." He walked over and kissed his sister's uplifted cheek.

She laughed and hugged his neck. "You must admit, Marcus, that you have an inordinate love for Heatherwood. Considering how much love and affection you have lavished on her, one wonders if she is perhaps a substitute wife."

His voice was dry. "Expectant motherhood has not improved your sense of propriety, Emily. But with that I will agree. Heatherwood requires more time than one could afford to give to a wife . . . but she in turn is always faithful and ever waiting to do my bidding."

Emily pointed a finger at Marcus. "Hold to that truth, Your Grace, and you will find yourself without an heir to succeed you. Remember, Heatherwood is faithful only to the one who pays her debts."

"Enough, Emily! You seem to forget we have a guest."

"Indeed I have not. Elizabeth and I have become friends." She turned to face her. "I do hope you will call on me. Come for tea tomorrow."

"Thank you, I'd like to, but . . ." She looked helplessly at the duke.

He nodded. "Certainly. I'll see that the footmen have instructions to accompany you in the carriage in order to carry your litter."

Emily's voice was kitten-soft. "Why don't you come along, too, Marcus?"

"I—I have a great deal to do, but I will consider it."

"And Arthur?" Emily asked.

"The offer is tempting, Emily, but I have an appointment to take Miss Chester for a ride in the new phaeton."

"You're certain it's Miss Chester and not Mrs. Walpole?"

"I daresay, Emily. You do have a way of cutting to the quick without batting a lash." He grinned as he said it, and Elizabeth suspected that there was some truth in Emily's pointed query.

A short time later Emily took her leave with a reminder that she would be receiving for tea on the morrow. Apparently she had stopped for a word with Mrs. Patchen, because Elizabeth had no more than retired to her quarters when a knock sounded on the door and Mrs. Patchen, along with two young upstairs maids, arrived with their arms full of clothing.

"If we might lay these on the bed, your ladyship, you might sort through and see how many of them you can use. Lady Emily expressed a hope that you would keep whatever you like, the rest to be disposed of."

She managed to hobble over to the bed with the aid of Mrs. Patchen. Gown after gown in lovely pale shades of green, apricot, blue, lavender, raspberry, and brown were spread out for her approval. Added to that were matching shawls, gloves, and a box of lacy underclothing.

Elizabeth turned to Mrs. Patchen. "Surely she couldn't have meant to give away all of these things!"

"Indeed, your ladyship, she was most specific. You've no count to worry. Lady Emily won't likely be small enough again to wear any of these things, and if she were, she would most likely choose to buy new ones. She has a fine passion for gowns, that one."

Elizabeth spent the afternoon going through the collection of dresses to see which were most suitable. Her attention was caught by the Persian ivory brocade Emily had mentioned, a costly gown cut to make a woman desirable beyond belief. It combined innocence with sophistication, simplicity with seductiveness. Elizabeth held the gown to her face. So soft . . . she would have loved to have kept it, but it was too fancy for tea, and she would have no other chance to wear it before she returned to London. And then it was only right that she leave the gowns behind. The thought of returning to London hurt, and she sought hurriedly to think of something else.

A few things needed repair, and when Elizabeth offered to do it, Mrs. Patchen was horrified.

"Indeed, your ladyship, that's not fitting work for you. I'll see that Greta tends to it."

It was no use protesting. When it came to what she considered her duty, Mrs. Patchen was adamant. She was a strange person: soft-spoken and quite intelligent for a woman in her position. Elizabeth vowed to get to know the woman better before she returned to London.

Oddly Greta seemed to welcome the chance to sit and chat while she stitched the broken seams. She gave Elizabeth a sideways look, then pretended to be absorbed in her needlework.

"I 'opes it wasn't too upsettin', your ladyship, when I took Sir Arthur away from you this mornin'."

Elizabeth was faintly amused. "Don't flatter yourself, Greta. It was I who suggested he join you."

Greta tossed her head. "Be that as it may, miss, 'e would 'ave done it anyway."

"Is he the one for whom your cap is set?"

"'E . . . or one other."

Elizabeth nearly laughed. "Ah, then it must be the duke who's caught your fancy. Tell me, Greta. Would you be comfortable wearing a duchess's coronet?"

She tossed her dark hair in defiance. "'Twould be a sight easier to get used to than beggar's rags. I'll wager I can do anything I 'ave to, to get what I wants."

Elizabeth couldn't resist teasing the determined girl.

"You were gone a long time while I waited on the beach. Are you certain you did not forsake your goal of keeping yourself pure until the right man paid the price?"

Greta giggled. "I may 'ave given him a few crumbs, your ladyship, but I'm savin' the cake until the party's over. It near drove 'im crazy, it did."

"Be warned, Greta. You can only drive a man so far. One of these days it will be you who will suffer the pain of being refused."

The girl looked at her with sudden interest. "Is that what 'appened to you, your ladyship? Is that why you are an old maid?"

Elizabeth winced at the word. "No. I was once in love with a young naval officer. He was killed in a battle three years ago."

The abigail shook her head. "I've heard tell that there are those who fall in love but once, and hit don't matter if the man is old or blind or light in the pocket." She shook her head. "'Tis too much for me."

They both were silenced by their own thoughts. It occurred to Elizabeth that she could no longer remember James's face, and yet her life had revolved around him for nearly a year. When she tried to recapture his likeness, the image of the duke kept getting in the way.

Later that day when Elizabeth was again carried downstairs, she looked in vain for the duke. It was Arthur who joined her in the salon for a glass of sherry before dinner.

"Good luck! I shall have you to myself this evening. The duke is visiting at a neighboring estate."

Despite her disappointment Elizabeth forced a smile. "Good luck? I would think you might be in a more jovial mood if you were spending the evening with Mrs. Walpole."

"I daresay, your ladyship. Mrs. Walpole would come out a poor second in a contest with you. Indeed, if your cousin is anything like you, I can see why my brother agreed to the betrothal."

"We are alike only in appearance. Our natures are foreign to one another."

"Then she is to be pitied."

Elizabeth smiled. "Sir Arthur, I do believe you are trying to butter me up. You had best save your compliments for those who would thank you for them."

"Thanks are truly in order but not on that score, your ladyship." He leaned toward her and touched his glass to hers. "I am most grateful that you saw fit not to disclose the reason for my absence from the beach earlier today. The duke would not take kindly to my consorting with your abigail." He paused as he thought about what he had said, and his face reddened. "Of course, by consorting I mean engaging her in conversation."

Elizabeth raised an eyebrow. "Indeed? I find that hard to believe, considering the length of your absence. You would be wise to watch your step where Greta is concerned. She is determined to raise herself above her present station."

"I'll keep that in mind." He moved closer and studied Elizabeth's face carefully. "Now that my brother has no claim to your affections, may I have the honor of taking you for a drive along the headlands tomorrow?"

"I thought you were seeing Mrs. Walpole."

"Confound it, you are right. Could we make it the day after? I'll warrant the ride won't compare to St. James's or Green Park, with their parade of *haute ton,* but the view is splendid."

"Thank you. If I am still here, I would like that very much. But surely the duke will send me packing before then, don't you think?"

"One can never tell about Marcus. Since he insists upon accompanying you himself, it will be a question of when he can get free from his duties on the estate . . . not to mention your own ability to travel."

"In that instance he is being overly protective. I assure you I am quite able to walk."

He laughed. "I'd advise you not to insist upon it until he is ready for you to make the attempt. Marcus, as you may have discovered, has a way of keeping things under his control."

"That may apply to you and the other members of his duchy, but he has no say over my welfare. I answer to no man."

He threw his head back and laughed. "Well said, your ladyship. But you have yet to know my brother. In a contest of wills you would find yourself sadly lacking."

It occurred to Elizabeth that *Sir Arthur* had yet to know her . . . but she didn't force the point.

The next day, just a half hour before the appointed time for tea at Emily's house, Elizabeth rang for the footmen to carry her downstairs. She wore an apricot linen dress that was gathered below the bodice to allow enough fullness for comfort. A black lace fichu emphasized the soft pink of her cheeks, and the idea was repeated at the wrist in tiny black lace cuffs. Even Greta had gone so far as to compliment her on her appearance.

An open gig had been brought around to the front, and when she was carried out to it, Elizabeth was surprised to see that the duke was in the driver's seat. Evidently her amazement was reflected in her face.

The duke made a great show of moving over to give her room on the seat next to him. "Since this is your first time in a carriage since you were injured, I thought it my responsibility to accompany you."

Elizabeth felt a stab of disappointment and was hard put to keep the acid from her voice. "I regret having to tear you away from your duties, Your Grace. I'm sure it must have been a sacrifice on your part."

"On the contrary."

Elizabeth looked quickly up at him, and he turned away in confusion. "That is to say that I see far too little of my sister, particularly now that she is in such a delicate condition and since she is alone while her husband is away on business."

"Of course, I should have realized." She had hoped for one brief instant that—Elizabeth shut it out of her mind as she focused her attention on what the duke was saying.

He pointed to several small cottages set back from the road, which was lined on each side by tall hedgerows. "Those are some of the homes of our tenant farmers. Most of them have worked our lands for several generations and are as much a part of it as I am."

Elizabeth was impressed by the fat livestock and sun-browned, healthy children who frolicked in the meadows. Several farmers paused to wave as the carriage passed by. It was apparent that they were on good terms with the duke. She was curious about the many fences that divided one section of property into smaller portions. He explained that each of the tenant families was given an amount of land on which they could raise food and livestock to feed their own household.

"Most of the women still work at some craft to provide extra income for their families. If you like, we could visit some of them so that you can see the fine handiwork that comes from our cottage industries."

"But aren't cottage industries rather outdated since the invention of the knitting looms and other machinery that can more speedily produce such items?"

"For the most part, that is true, but my people have chosen to remain on the farm. To work in the manufactories, they would have to move to the cities. One has to use very little imagination to know how hard that kind of

68

life could be for one bred in the country. Perhaps in a few days we shall spend a morning visiting some of our families."

"In a few days? I had thought I would be returning to London before then, Your Grace."

He turned to look at her, a veiled expression in his eyes. "Yes, of course, if that is your wish." He gave a snap to the whip, and the horses leaped forward.

Elizabeth had to hold on to the seat for balance. "I only meant that I have already been too much of a burden on your hospitality."

He appeared to relax. "I would say that that is the least we could do to make up for the inconvenience we have caused by your untimely . . . visit. However, we would not want to bore you unduly with our country style of living. Life in Devon is a far cry from the parties and routs of London Society."

"As to that, I hadn't noticed, Your Grace. Since the death of my parents I have not been among those favored as party guests. I do not say this with anger but simply as a statement of fact. For myself, I prefer a walk in the woods or a picnic in the park to a crowded gala at Almack's club or Vauxhall Gardens."

"Indeed?"

He appeared to take awhile to digest that information, because they continued on for a distance without further conversation. When they finally arrived at Fernwood Hall, the large country home owned by Emily's husband, the duke brought the carriage to a halt at the front walk. A hostler grabbed hold of the horse's head while a footman adjusted the step. It was clear the duke intended to carry her, and she felt her face redden.

"I am fully capable of walking, Your Grace. My wound is healing quite rapidly since you treated it."

"Then it would be foolish of us to further irritate it, don't you think?"

She sighed. This was no time to make a scene, but she would have to put an end to this nonsense. It was ghastly having to be treated like an invalid for no reason at all. She permitted him to take her in his arms. Indeed, there was something to be said for this business of being helpless. Her head seemed to settle naturally against his chest as she felt his chin graze the top of her head.

Just as they approached the front entrance Emily opened the door to greet them.

"Dear me, I had forgotten about your injury, Elizabeth. For a moment I thought my brother was about to carry you up to the bridal suite." She smiled impishly, but apparently her humor was lost on Marcus. When Elizabeth looked up at him, his forehead was beaded with perspiration and a red flush had begun to spread upward from the region at the top of his neckcloth.

CHAPTER SIX

Emily saw his discomfort and chose to emphasize it. "Indeed, Marcus. Come to think of it I've never seen you with a woman in your arms. A baby lamb, perhaps, or a suckling calf, but never a woman. I'd say that your lot in life is improving."

"For God's sake, Emily, hold your tongue. You are too old to thrash, so stop behaving like an infant."

His irritation had no apparent effect on her as she held the door wide open and dropped a curtsy. In her condition it was no easy feat, and she had to hold on to the door to support herself, finally dissolving into a fit of laughter.

Elizabeth was hard put to keep a serious face, but one look at the duke's stormy countenance gave her fair warning. When he deposited her on a love seat in the salon, Elizabeth had a chance to view her surroundings. There was none of the opulence of the castle, but the house seemed to vibrate with a tangible warmth, due largely to the influence of its mistress, Elizabeth guessed. Its large, open rooms with heavily beamed ceilings were decorated in rich colors of the earth and its harvest.

Emily settled herself in a large chair, then faced Elizabeth. "I trust that your injury is healing quite well?"

"Indeed it is. I plan to forgo the role of an invalid and begin walking tomorrow morning."

The duke swore softly. "I vow, the two of you will be

the death of me. You will walk when I tell you to, Lady Elizabeth, and not one minute before."

"And how do you plan to enforce such an order, Marcus?" Emily teased. "Is it your intention to stand guard over her during the night?"

His mouth went white around the edges. "Indeed not! I shall rely on her gentle upbringing to bow to my better judgment."

Emily arched her eyebrows. "Why is it, Your Grace, that I have the feeling you are none too eager for her ladyship to recover? Is it perhaps that you will then have to send her back to London?"

He shifted uncomfortably. "You must admit that it is a difficult time for me to leave the duchy. Of course, I cannot in good conscience permit my own problems to prevail against her safe return to her family."

"That wasn't what I meant, Marcus, as you know full well." He started to interrupt, but she waived it aside. "Don't fret. I won't force the issue." She turned to Elizabeth. "And how do you feel about returning to your family, Elizabeth? Are you perishing for want of their company?"

Elizabeth shook her head. "I confess to a regrettable lack of loyalty where my sister's family is concerned. We have not been close, and I perceive that the situation is not likely to change." She hastily added, "However, I did not intend to make it sound as though I was asking to stay on—"

"I say, now . . . would that be so bad?" said Emily, interrupting. "Speaking for myself, I'd be overjoyed to have you extend your impromptu visit, and I'm sure that Marcus would be more than pleased."

His face reddened. "That would of course be for her ladyship to decide. Our house has always been open to guests."

Elizabeth was more flustered than she had been in

years. In her heart she knew she would give anything to remain on at the castle for a few more days—a week—she didn't dare think beyond that point . . . but what did they expect her to say?

She folded her hands and looked down at her lap. "The offer is most generous. Needless to say, I would love to stay on . . . for a time . . . but I would not care to take unfair advantage of your hospitality."

Marcus cleared his throat and straightened. "There is no question of your taking advantage. As you surely must know, we have ample room."

Elizabeth was waiting for him to say that he wanted her to stay, but he didn't have a chance. Emily clapped her hands in glee.

"Good. It's settled, then. There'll be no more talk about your going back, at least for the present, and Marcus can stop this ridiculous charade of keeping you a cripple."

The duke turned beet-red. "Enough, Emily. You push me too far."

She apparently believed him, because the rest of the visit passed without incident until the duke announced that they were ready to leave. Emily gave Elizabeth an affectionate hug and promised to call within a day or two. When the duke bent to pick up Elizabeth to carry her to the waiting carriage, Emily again dissolved into laughter, and she was still laughing as she waved them out of sight.

The duke was furious. "I do hope you'll forgive my sister. Would that I could blame her behavior on her delicate condition, but alas, I fear she has always been an unconscionable tease."

"I like her," Elizabeth said with no little conviction.

He looked at her in surprise. "Indeed? Indeed!" She could tell by the sound of his voice that he was more than a little pleased by her response.

Elizabeth reached out her gloved hand and laid it on his sleeve. She could feel the muscles of his arm tighten, but

73

she kept her hand there as she spoke. "Please, Your Grace. I hope you do not for one moment think I will hold you to your invitation for me to remain on as your guest. I know that the invitation was not of your volition."

"On the contrary, your ladyship. Had I wished you to return to London, you would have departed ere this." There was a strange timbre to his voice that warmed Elizabeth to the soles of her feet. It was with considerable reluctance that she removed her hand from his arm. She curled her fingers around her palm in an effort to retain the heat that had generated between them. For a while they rode in companionable silence. Finally the duke broke the spell.

He cleared his throat and hesitated before he spoke. "When we return to the castle, I shall have a look at your injury. Perhaps, as you say, there is no longer a need to favor it."

"That won't be necessary. Mrs. Patchen can dress it for me."

He swore as his hands tightened on the reins. "Must you always seek to override my judgment? You'll do as I say, and there will be no discussion whatsoever."

Ordinarily Elizabeth would have had a quick retort, but the knowledge that she could remain at Heatherwood for yet another few days had left her in a state of euphoria. She nodded, saying simply, "Yes, Your Grace." The duke looked at her in surprise, then a smile tilted the corners of his eyes, and they settled back against the seat and rode the rest of the way in silence.

When he carried her into the house, Elizabeth savored it to the fullest. Being an invalid had some practical benefits. She would miss having those strong arms around her, miss them more than she cared to admit.

As it turned out, the duke sent Mrs. Patchen to see to Elizabeth's dressings. The woman pronounced her perfectly able to walk without causing herself harm. Indeed, according to her, she had rather expected to find a much more serious injury.

Elizabeth felt a sense of suppressed excitement as she walked downstairs to dinner that night. She was wearing a rust velvet gown that brought out the red-gold highlights in her hair. It was cut snug in the bodice to accentuate a woman's charms without seeming the least bit brazen. At the last minute she had elected to forgo the customary mobcap. She hated having to cover her hair in the summertime, and it was no longer considered a breach of etiquette.

Sir Arthur was jubilant when he saw her. "I say . . . you are looking fit! Had I known you were up and about on your own, I would have foresworn my visit to Mrs. Walpole." He took her hands and whirled her about the room.

The duke rose slowly and put his glass down on the table. "Get hold of yourself, Arthur. You're acting like a drunken sailor."

"Oh, come off it, Marcus. Don't be a spoilsport. Her ladyship will be leaving soon. Let's enjoy her company while we can."

"It was decided this afternoon that her visit is to be somewhat prolonged."

"I say, this is confounded good news. And it couldn't have come at a better time. I still have another month before I am required to report back to my command. We shall have a splendid summer."

Elizabeth curtsied to Marcus and then walked over to the window and stood beside the heavy draperies. "I shall agree to remain here for a while on one condition—that I can in some way repay your hospitality by making myself useful."

"One so decorative need not be useful," Arthur said as he lifted his glass to her.

"You're most kind, but it goes against my nature to spend too much time in idleness."

The duke nodded. "An admirable quality. I'm sure we can find something to fill your days."

Arthur grinned. "I'll make it my duty to see that you are occupied every night."

The duke frowned. "I should think, Arthur, that you would find you have enough to do overseeing the care and breeding of our horses while you are at home."

Arthur's voice was dry. "Horses need little encouragement to breed, Your Grace. Once they get the idea, they do quite well on their own . . . much the same as people. Of course, this is a little out of your line, but—"

The duke was livid. "Mind your tongue, Arthur. I perceive that it is difficult for you to remember that you are in a drawing room, not the deck of a ship, but I hope I don't have to admonish you again." He took a deep breath in an apparent effort to control his temper. "As to her ladyship, I'm sure she can find something to pass the time. I have already promised to take her to meet some of our villagers."

"Indeed? I hope it is not your intention to go tomorrow," Arthur said with a touch of smugness in his voice. "We have already planned a drive along the headlands."

The duke's face turned an unhealthy gray, and he would have said something but the footman chose that moment to announce dinner. It occurred to Elizabeth that it couldn't have come at a better time.

Throughout dinner the duke was overly quiet, but Arthur made up for it by keeping up a steady flow of conversation. He was full of tales of exploits of the British Navy, but when Elizabeth questioned him about the recent war with the Americans, he was evasive. Elizabeth assumed that the losses at the Battle of New Orleans were still a sore spot where he was concerned. As soon as dinner was over, the duke excused himself and made a hasty exit. He had seemed withdrawn and somewhat aloof after Sir Arthur told him about their planned outing along the headlands. In a different man Elizabeth might have thought it showed a jealous streak, but the duke would hardly be jealous. More than likely it was another indication that he was losing control over her life that made him appear so grim. He was a man who liked things done his way.

After dinner Sir Arthur and Elizabeth retired to the salon, where he showed her a part of his collection of souvenirs of his various military adventures.

He led her over to a glass-fronted cabinet containing a sumptuous sixteenth-century French presentation case of polished rock crystal, ebony, and gilt bronze. "This was given to me by Lord Nelson a few weeks before he was killed at Trafalgar in 1805."

She looked at him in surprise. "Am I wrong, or is that the Star of the Order of Bath that I see inside the case?"

He grinned. "You are correct. The Regent presented it to me after one of my skirmishes."

"But the Knighthood of Bath is a very ancient order."

"Indeed, but the Order as we know it was created by George the First in 1725 and was only this year reorganized."

"And so you were knighted. How proud your family must be."

He shrugged. "I suppose." Then as if trying to change the subject, he said, "These are negus tankards I brought back from an excursion to the Tuileries."

"Negus tankards?"

"Negus is a steaming brew of hot water, port, lemon juice, sugar, and spices. It has a powerful ability to warm the bones when one is forced to stand watch on the deck at night." He draped his arm casually across her shoulders. She tensed and started to move away, but his grip tightened.

"Lovely Elizabeth. Sometimes I think your hair is the

77

color of ripened wheat in the afternoon sun, but tonight it looks like honey, fresh from the comb." He pulled her around to face him. "I've always been a lucky man, but I seem to have surpassed all odds when fate brought you instead of the lady Louella to us."

Elizabeth forced a laugh as she tactfully disengaged his arm and moved away. "Indeed, Sir Arthur, your luck lies in the fact that no one would see fit to prosecute you for my abduction. Had it been Louella, you might this very moment be languishing in Newgate prison."

"They would have to catch me first." He moved toward her again and took a lock of her hair in his hand. "Why do you move away, Elizabeth? Are you trying to avoid me?"

"Should I be?"

He flushed. "You ask the most confounded questions. How is a man to answer that?"

"Truthfully, I hope."

He looked her straight in the eye in an attempt at sincerity, but the mischief showed through. "Have you ever known me to lie, your ladyship?"

She backed away, her hand brushing his as she reached for the curl he held loosely in his fingers. "I doubt that the games you play, sir, have anything to do with truth. Suffice it to say that I believe you are basically a good man, but your innate desire for conquest is certainly not limited to the battlefield."

"Gossip, my lady, idle gossip. Until now I have met no one worthy of doing battle to conquer, but for you I would be willing to risk my life."

"Is this the same tack you use with Mrs. Walpole . . . and Greta?"

He threw his head back and laughed. "Hardly. Each sortee requires a different approach. But in truth, I would forgo the other victories for the right to claim you as a prize."

She fluttered her fan in front of her face and smiled. "Alas, how sad, for you are doomed to defeat."

"Don't count your score yet, my lady. The battle has hardly begun. Given time, the victory will be mine . . . and mark this—it will be a victory that you will cheer as well as I."

She raised her eyebrows. "Indeed? If your own self-pride would merit success, you would be the winner without the battle. As for me, I shall have to struggle along without ever having known . . . what might have been."

He started toward her, but she ducked into the hallway and turned briefly to drop a curtsy.

"I bid you good night, Sir Arthur. Until tomorrow?"

He bowed with a flourish. "Tomorrow indeed, but be warned. The war has hardly begun. In another battle you are not likely to be the victor."

She smiled and waved her fan in his direction, then turned and went upstairs to her bedchamber. Sir Arthur was as appealing as a baby puppy. Had her brother, Timothy, lived, he would have been almost the same age, but he had died of the brain fever when he was only ten. She still missed him. Perhaps that was why she was so taken with Arthur. There was still much of the little boy in him.

She pulled out the pins that held her hair in its neat coil and let it cascade in rich waves over her shoulders. By all rights she should call Greta to brush it, but she was used to doing for herself, and Greta was sure to be ill-natured . . . particularly when she learned that Elizabeth was staying on for a while. For some reason Greta saw her as a threat to her campaign to marry into wealth.

She ran the brush through her hair until it crackled and bounced with a life of its own. Just as Elizabeth was about to pull the bell cord to summon Greta to help her undress, Elizabeth remembered that she had left her shawl in the salon. She toyed with the idea of letting it stay there until morning, but the thought that Mrs. Patchen might consider her untidy was unbearable. Going to the dresser, she picked up a small taper and lighted it from the oil lamp, then made her way downstairs.

It was quiet in the house, the servants either working belowstairs or retired to their own chambers on one of the upper floors. The hallways seemed to echo with footsteps of nobility long passed on to their just reward. Elizabeth felt like an intruder as she walked slowly down the staircase then entered a corridor to search for the door to the salon. Things looked so different when one was alone.

When the footmen had carried her on the litter, she had paid no attention to which door they had entered. Then later a footman had accompanied her to the salon and had announced her presence. But now she was completely alone. She approached the wide double doors with reasonable assurance, but when she turned the knob and opened it, the room was not the same. She was lost . . . but to add to her confusion the room was occupied.

Instinct told her to close the door at once lest she be discovered and put in an embarrassing position, but a glance into the room made her hesitate.

There was no light save the glow from a single candle that had been placed on the pianoforte. The duke—there was no mistaking that muscular form—was seated on the bench, his fingers drifting idly over the keys. In the dim light of the candle his eyes appeared deep-set and dark, making him seem even more formidible and unapproachable than normal. Her own lighted candle was sure to give her away should he glance up, but despite the fear of being seen Elizabeth could not tear herself away. And then the inevitable happened.

He spoke without looking up. "There is no need for you to remain standing in the doorway like a lost urchin. Come in and close the door behind you."

She hesitated a moment, then did as she was told. "W-what is this room? It seems enormous, but it's so dark I

80

cannot see anything beyond the circle of light where you are sitting."

"The room has been closed for a number of years. The draperies are drawn. That is why it is so dark." He rose. "What are you doing here? This is a strange time of night to go exploring."

"I—I do beg your forgiveness, Your Grace. It was not my intention to disturb you. I came in search of the salon where I left my shawl, but I seem to have become disoriented."

"This is the Petite Ballroom. You took the wrong corridor."

She wandered over to the pianoforte, where he stood waiting. "What a lovely instrument. Do you play?"

"No. Only a few simple pieces." He smiled. "And please don't ask me to play them. Even my music instructor refused to listen." He motioned for her to sit down.

The bench was still warm from the heat of his body as she slid across the seat, wondering if he would join her. There was room for two, but just barely. She looked at him questioningly, but he turned away and linked his hands behind his back.

"Do you play?" he asked.

"I—a little, but it has been a long time."

He nodded toward the keys. For a minute she gripped her hands in her lap, trying to recall the music that had once meant so much to her. But her fingers were stiff. Added to this was the overpowering feeling that the two of them were alone in this vast cocoon of darkness. Never before had she known a man to dominate her so completely just by the mere fact of his presence. She lifted her hands and poised them above the keys, grateful for the darkness that hid their trembling. Then Elizabeth drifted slowly into a simple melody of an old English folk tune, "Maids in the Heather and Lads on the Hill." That finished, she began to play "Starlight over the Moors."

"Lovely," he said. "No one has played as well since my mother entertained us. I can almost see the starlight this very moment."

She laughed a bit giddily. "Not through those thick draperies you can't."

"Then I shall have to open them." He strode to the window and gave them a hard snap until they spread wide to reveal tall, narrow, arched windows with many panes. He slipped the catch and opened one of them to let the fresh air flow in. "Wouldn't you say that that's an improvement?"

"Most certainly. This room must be very lovely when it's properly lighted."

"It is. I'll show it to you tomorrow, that is if you can tear yourself away from my brother long enough to see it."

"That shouldn't be too difficult, Your Grace. Sir Arthur and I plan a short drive along the headlands, nothing more. Where did you think we were going?"

The glow of her candle placed next to his was reflected like twin mirrors in his eyes as she turned to look up at him. He looked decidedly uncomfortable as he reached inside his waistcoat for a handkerchief.

"Considering the distance the two of you have come together, nothing would surprise me."

He said something else, but Elizabeth didn't hear. Her gaze was fixed on the fringe of her shawl, which protruded from his waistcoat.

She stood to face him. "I see you have found my shawl." Even in the dim light she could see his face turn red. "I—ah, yes—it was on the chair in the refectory. I had every intention of returning it to you."

He pulled it out and held it in his hand, pleating the soft material between his fingers. "You must believe that."

"Of course I do, Your Grace. Why should I not?" She reached for it, and her fingers grazed his.

With a soft sound from deep in his throat he moved

toward her and grasped her wrists, pulling her arms around him. She gasped in surprise but there was no time for words, because his mouth found hers, putting an end to idle conversation.

CHAPTER SEVEN

He had placed her arms around his waist, and when he moved his own hands to cup her head, Elizabeth somehow neglected to pull away. She thought about it, but to save herself she was powerless to move. His mouth was hungry, demanding as it invaded hers. She yearned to respond, but sheer strength of will held her back. This man was practically a stranger. To permit such liberties was unheard of in Polite Society, but she longed to answer passion with passion.

Instead, she pulled away. "Stop it. You have no right to do that. It is most unseemly."

His voice was harsh. "You speak of rights when you shared a bed with my brother? Stop acting the tender maiden. Your age and independent nature give lie to your pretense."

Elizabeth was furious. "It was through no choice of mine that I spent those nights at the inn with your brother. And though you choose not to believe it, your brother was a gentleman, which is more than I can say for you."

"I cannot begin to convince myself that Arthur laid no hand on you. My brother's fame for his conquests in the petticoat game spans three continents."

"Perhaps you see only what you wish to see. Sir Arthur has many fine qualities." She smoothed her dress carefully. "Or perhaps you are jealous of your brother's appeal to the ladies."

"Jealous! Of Arthur? You are truly daft. I've had my share of women, so don't begin to imagine I am less a man than he simply because I choose not to devote my life to womanizing."

"I suggested no such thing, Your Grace. I daresay that no one in his rightful mind would question your manliness. Indeed, there are few women who would refuse you, but I'm sure you realize that." She bit her lip the moment the words were out of her mouth. Now, why did she say such a stupid thing? It sounded as if she were trying to flatter him.

Her words had evidently caught him off guard. He dropped his hands to his sides, moved back, and stared at her.

"But you, obviously, are not one of those women."

It was not phrased as a question, and she made no attempt to answer. "I think perhaps I should go to my room." She had been knotting the shawl between her fingers, and in her nervousness it fell to the floor. He came toward her lazily, bent to pick it up, then floated it over her shoulders. At that moment an errant breeze blew out the candles, and they were left in total darkness save for a sliver of pale light that filtered through the window.

Elizabeth gasped as the room seemed to close around her. If his nearness had presented a temptation before, now, hidden from those challenging eyes, she felt herself sway toward him. With an oath he grasped both ends of the shawl and pulled her against him until she could feel the thunderous pounding of his heart. His left hand caught in her hair and once again he plundered her mouth.

When he finally stopped for breath, she turned her head. "Please. Please don't do this to me, Your Grace."

His voice was hard as the stone walls of his castle. She sensed that he bowed as he stepped away, her shawl still caught in one hand. "I do beg your forgiveness, my lady. It was not my intention to force myself upon you. In the

85

future I shall make certain to avoid physical contact, since my touch is so abhorrent to you."

"I didn't mean to—"

"Say no more, Lady Elizabeth. I understand perfectly. Now if you will just wait here, I will go into the corridor and fetch a light."

Elizabeth had mixed emotions. With a need that denied all logic she wanted those strong arms around her. The warmth of his body against hers had created feelings she was unaware she possessed, but it was unwise to let him know. Indeed, if her willingness had been apparent to him, there might have been no stopping him. Her legs trembled at the thought, and she was grateful for this moment to pull herself together.

When he returned, his face was tight and withdrawn in the glow of the candle that he protected with his left hand. "Just a moment while I close the window. Then I'll light another candle for you and see you to your room to avoid your getting lost a second time."

"I'm sure I can find my way."

"If you are concerned that I won't stop at the bedchamber door, worry no more. Once burned, the lesson is learned."

Elizabeth remained silent. Whatever she said would only serve to increase their misunderstanding. He bowed and motioned her to precede him. She nodded her head, then wrapped her arms around herself and led the way down the hall. It wasn't cold, but the dull ache in her heart sent a chill through her entire body.

He was as good as his word. At the door of her suite she paused with her hand on the knob. He clicked his heels and bowed, then handed her the candle and, turning, strode away. It was only later that she realized she had returned without her shawl.

The dainty Dresden clock on the bedside table had ticked away another two hours before Elizabeth went to bed. She undressed herself, too drained emotionally to even consider a verbal skirmish with Greta.

At breakfast the next morning Arthur was in an expansive mood, a decided contrast to the duke's tightly controlled visage.

"Ah, Lady Elizabeth," Arthur said. "How ravishing you look this morning. You must have slept well."

Elizabeth stole a glance at the duke, who seemed to be waiting for her answer. She tossed her head and smiled. "Thank you, Arthur. I slept very well indeed."

The duke's face darkened. "How fortunate. As for myself I slept very little. I seemed to hear people wandering about the corridors half the night. Hardly conducive to sleep, I'm afraid, but apparently you didn't hear it."

She gazed at him with studied calm. "If I had, it wouldn't have bothered me, Your Grace. It takes a great deal to upset me."

"Indeed? I would have thought differently."

Her face colored. "Then you have a great deal to learn about me."

Arthur forked a kipper onto his plate, then reached for another scone. "I say, must the two of you be so irritable? Either I've missed something, or I'd say you were talking in riddles."

Elizabeth leaned over and patted his hand. "How could one possibly be irritable on such a lovely day? In truth, I feel full of energy and ready to explore this delightful countryside."

Arthur preened and smiled broadly. "Splendid! Perhaps we could take a picnic with us when we go for our outing along the headlands. I know a secluded grove of trees that would be the perfect location."

"What a marvelous idea. It's been years since I went on a picnic. Shall I see Mrs. Patchen about having a hamper prepared?"

"Only if you want to. After all, you are a guest in the house and shouldn't have to do such things."

"It would be my pleasure. As I said before, I am not used to idleness and find it repressive." She feigned an innocent look as she glanced at the duke. "Shall I ask Cook to prepare for two, or will the duke be joining us?"

Arthur became suddenly flustered. "Oh, there is no need to plan for three. Marcus takes no pleasure in such childish things as picnics. He would rather work at his musty books or rattle around on his boat. Am I not right, Marcus?"

The duke gave him a look but refused to answer. Elizabeth was disappointed. She had hoped the duke would accompany them. She longed to have him accept her for what she was, not what he might think she was. He seemed to have a preconceived idea that because she was from London and had reached her majority without benefit of a husband, she was of loose morals. Perhaps he even thought her a courtesan. She hastily dusted her lips with her fingers in an effort to hide a smile. Alas, whatever he might think, she was a maiden still, and from the look of it her condition was not about to change in the near future. At least not unless she decided to play Arthur's game. The thought brought a spasm of laughter that she could not conceal.

The duke looked up suddenly. "Does the thought of my working on my boat give you cause for merriment? Sailing, although you may have not heard, is considered quite a respectable pursuit of pleasure."

Elizabeth sobered. "Forgive me, Your Grace. I was laughing at something else. And, indeed, although I have never had the opportunity to sail, I think it would be most exciting."

Arthur set his cup of tea down with a clatter. "I say, what a smashing idea. Why don't we take Lady Elizabeth for a sail in your boat tomorrow afternoon?"

The duke colored. "Don't press, Arthur. Her ladyship was simply being polite when she said she would find it exciting."

Elizabeth felt her hackles begin to rise. If he didn't want to take them, he didn't have to lay the blame on her. She forced a bright smile. "On the contrary. I would consider it a delightful experience, but I would hate to cause Your Grace undue hardship."

He sighed in resignation. "It could hardly be considered a hardship, Lady Elizabeth. I sail the *Dragonfly* as often as weather permits."

"Good. It's settled, then," Arthur said. "We'll plan an outing for tomorrow afternoon."

"I think not," the duke countered. "There is a storm building. I can feel it. We will have to wait for another day."

Elizabeth was unable to tell from the tone of his voice whether the duke was pleased or disappointed that a storm would intervene. Besides, how could he tell what the weather would be a day in advance? Did he also pretend to rule the elements from his lofty castle?

They finished the meal with a minimum of conversation. It occurred to Elizabeth that Arthur was the only one who seemed perfectly at ease. But then he was not fully aware of the undercurrents that pervaded the room.

After breakfast she spent the morning with Greta in the garden, where they had taken their sewing. Greta was mending some rents in a butter-yellow lace Elizabeth hoped to wear for dinner one evening. Elizabeth was repairing a rope of tiny silk flowers that adorned a bonnet. As usual Greta managed to bring the conversation around to the duke and his brother.

"Cook tells me you an' Sir Arthur are taking an outing this afternoon."

"Umm. News gets around quickly. Are you going to make it a point to be there, too, as you did at the beach?"

The girl smiled mischievously. "'Tis a thought. Indeed, you might ask me along as a chaperon."

Elizabeth laughed aloud. "How clever of you. But I fear that it is I who would needs become the chaperon. No, my girl, you will have to wait your turn."

Greta raised an eyebrow. "Never you worry. I can bide my time. In truth, I expects to be here a good bit longer than you, your ladyship."

"Are you prepared, then, to wait until you can persuade either the duke or his brother to offer for your hand?"

Greta pulled a curl from the wealth of dark-brown hair that cascaded down below her mobcap and stroked it against her cheek. "Aye, that I will, unless someone comes along with a fatter purse."

"Would you marry an old man?"

"The older the better, your ladyship. That way 'e'd already 'ave a foot in the grave, and I'd be on me way to bein' a rich widow."

Even Greta had to laugh at her own boldness. They were still laughing when the butler stepped into the garden and paused at the door of the gazebo.

"Your ladyship, the Reverend Mr. Fleetwood begs your permission to call and welcome you to the community."

Elizabeth laid aside her handiwork and stood. "Very well, Thomas. Ask him to join us in the garden, if you will."

He bowed and returned to the house. Greta watched his retreating back. "Fleetwood indeed. They say 'e's come to upset the town with 'is new ways. I've 'eard 'e's a real terror, this one."

"I assume you've never met him. Don't you attend services?"

"No, I don't. When I gets time to meself, I won't be spendin' it with no vicar."

"You can meet some awfully nice young men in church."

"And everyone o' them so light in the pocket they can't afford to treat a girl to a glass of ale at the Bear and Bottle." She gave Elizabeth a critical look. "And just how many eligible bachelors did you meet in church? None, I'll wager, who would appeal to a lady of quality, let alone to a poor servant girl such as the likes o' me."

"As a matter of fact I met the only man I've ever loved at the Sunday evening services that my parents and I attended regularly."

"'Im bein' the one what got killed?"

"Yes."

"Well, that's one, but I daresay the rest are just out of their cribs or too long in the tooth to even think about lookin' for a wife." She rose. "If you'll excuse me, your ladyship, I've no wish to suffer through an 'our with such as the vicar . . . whoever 'e is."

Elizabeth nodded. "Very well. You may finish your mending elsewhere if you wish." She sat down and patted her hair into place, wishing she'd had time to freshen up before her interview with the vicar.

Less than two minutes later Greta returned, her hand resting ladylike on the arm of the vicar. Elizabeth did a double-take. This was no gray-haired, rheumy-eyed, feeble old man. The new vicar of Heatherford was a strapping young Adonis with clear skin, a deep thatch of sun-streaked blond hair, and the most compelling brown eyes she had ever seen.

Greta, acting like a dowager duchess, made the introductions. "Lady Elizabeth Cambridge, may I present the Reverend Chesley Fleetwood." She stepped back to allow the vicar to come forward. Elizabeth nearly strangled as she saw Greta's sly wink.

"Reverend Fleetwood, I'm pleased to meet you. Won't

you sit down, or would you be more comfortable in the parlor?"

He lingered over her hand for just the proper length of time, then smiled. "This is perfect, your ladyship." He held her chair, then took one opposite.

Greta was making signs behind his back, and Elizabeth was afraid he would notice. She cleared her throat.

"I trust you have met my abigail, Miss Greta Brewer?"

"Indeed I have. I hope you will forgive my unannounced intrusion into your privacy, your ladyship. I had heard of your recent arrival at the castle and felt it my duty to call in person."

"You are not intruding, Reverend Fleetwood. Greta tells me that you also are new to Devon."

"There are those who have been here for ten years who are still considered newcomers. But it is true. I have yet to mark a year at this calling." He turned to Greta. "And it occurs to me that I have not seen you at services once in all that time."

Greta's face turned pink. "I'll wager that I was there a time or two."

"I think not, for I surely would have remembered."

Greta curtsied. "Would your ladyship like me to bring tea?"

Elizabeth was astounded. It was most unusual to serve tea to callers who arrived unexpectedly. The girl must have some plot stirring in the back of her head.

Elizabeth nodded. "Very well. You may tell Cook that you will serve it in the garden."

Greta sighed, then turned and nearly ran down the path. When she was out of earshot the vicar leaned forward.

"You will forgive me, Lady Elizabeth, but I must take this time to speak confidentially with you."

"Indeed? Just what is it, Reverend Fleetwood?"

"Granted the fact that rumors are often completely

without substance, I find I cannot in good conscience leave without making certain you are unharmed."

"Unharmed? I'm afraid I don't follow you."

He appeared boyishly flustered, an endearing attitude, Elizabeth thought as he continued.

"You see, my lady, the talk around the village is that you are being held prisoner here at the castle. That you were . . . kidnapped from Carlton House right from under the nose of the Prince Regent himself."

Elizabeth was beside herself. The next time she heard the story, they would be saying she was the Prince Regent's mistress. She leaned forward and patted the young man on the hand.

"Suffice it to say that I am indeed from London, and I did make the journey here somewhat without preparation, but as for being kidnapped . . . why, I have never even set foot in Carlton House, and I have only met the regent a time or two when he was just the Prince of Wales."

He took both her hands in his. "I am greatly relieved to hear it. Needless to say, the duke is an important man, and it would not be an easy thing to face him with such an accusation. Please forgive my impertinence, your ladyship."

She returned the gentle pressure of his hands. "There is no need to apologize. Indeed, it was kind of you to be concerned over my welfare, but I trust you will be able to put an end to these ridiculous rumors?"

He smiled. "The truth would be more believable if the duke would attend services once in awhile. He is in a position to set custom for the village. It is a rare place that is not made better by regular attendance at church."

"I'm sure you are right. My influence over the duke is very limited, but I shall be happy to pass the message on to him and his brother."

"Yes, his brother would surely benefit from one of my less merciful sermons." He smiled, knowing that Elizabeth understood his meaning. Apparently everyone knew about Arthur's escapades with the various women of the area.

Greta returned carrying a Sheffield tray laden with a tea service and a plate of apricot tarts. There was a slight frown on her face as she put the tray on a low table and moved it into place. "Would you like me to pour, your ladyship?"

Elizabeth was amazed at the girl's impertinence but at the same time amused. "No, thank you, Greta. I see there is an extra cup. Would you care to join us? I'm sure the reverend will not object."

He rose and got a chair for her. "Indeed not. Perhaps I can take the time to persuade her to join our small congregation at Sunday services."

Elizabeth poured tea for each of them, then offered the plate of tarts. "I fear Greta is not inclined toward church-going."

Greta batted her eyelashes at the vicar, then demurely folded her hands in her lap. "Beggin' your pardon, my lady. It is not a question of being disinclined. 'Tis so busy I am on the Sabbath that I can scarce find time to go. And when I do, the thought of going unaccompanied is enough to make me weak from fear."

The vicar was immediately sympathetic. "My dear child, you must never feel alone. When you are of the faith, you are able to rise above such feelings of shyness and inadequacy. I beg of you, don't let another Sabbath pass without giving yourself over to Divine protection."

"Thank you, Reverend. I'll do me best, but I'm afraid to try it alone."

"Have no fear. I shall guide you every step of the way. Perhaps I could visit you before then and begin to instill in you some of the faith that will make you strong."

Greta bowed her head in humility, then looked up at him, as appealing as a newborn calf. "You are most kind, sir, but it would not be right to ask you to spend time away from your wife and family."

"Aha! Then it is settled. You see, I have no wife, so let us hear no more excuses. If you are free this evening, you may come by the vicarage, and we will begin your instructions."

Greta glanced at Elizabeth, and she nodded. That poor vicar. If only he could begin to guess what he was letting himself in for. Greta, shy? Even Sarah Siddons had never given a greater performance at Covent Garden.

A short time later the vicar took his leave. Elizabeth walked him out of the gazebo, and when she returned to confront Greta, the girl had disappeared.

Later, when Elizabeth rang for Greta to assist her to dress for the picnic, Greta was apparently walking on another plane. She appeared distracted when Elizabeth tried to pin her down as to her odd behavior, and Elizabeth finally gave up and allowed her to continue to work in silence.

Arthur was pleased by Elizabeth's appearance in a sprigged muslin of a soft pink with a matching lace sunshade. A touch of pink on the ruffles of her bonnet and gloves made the outfit complete. Granted, the skirt was a little too full to be in fashion, but it suited Elizabeth, giving her a youthful, innocent look.

They stowed the picnic hamper in the boot next to the coachman's seat, and Arthur got into the carriage beside her. They were hardly out of the drive when she felt his arm go around the back of the seat, just grazing the top of her shoulders. His hand rested there for a moment, then he turned slightly toward her until his knee brushed hers.

"Elizabeth. How I've wanted to get you alone like this. I curse myself for the time I've wasted." His hand came down over her shoulder, and he pulled her against him.

CHAPTER EIGHT

To say that Elizabeth was angry would have been incorrect. Rather, she decided, she was amused. Admittedly his strength caused a slight stirring of sensation in her body, but she knew herself well enough to realize that it was a purely physical response to a man and not Arthur in particular. His face was so close to hers that he would have kissed her, given the least bit of encouragement, but she placed her hands on his chest and gently pushed him away.

He released her, and it occurred to her that had the duke been in his place, he would not have been so easily put off. The thought quickened in her, and Arthur took courage to try again, but Elizabeth was not one to use one man while pretending he was another.

"Please, Arthur. You mustn't behave so outrageously. I thought we were going to be friends."

"Why can't we be *good* friends, Elizabeth?"

"Is it your idea that we become lovers, Arthur?"

He grinned. "A jolly good suggestion. At least you managed to finally do away with the title. I mark that a step in the right direction."

She opened her fan and drifted it in front of her face. "Before you avail yourself of any more ideas, Arthur, suffice it to say that I will not go beyond the bounds of friendship. I enjoy your company too much to become one of your little interludes for which, I might add, you are quite famous."

"It doesn't have to be just an interlude, Elizabeth. You must know how taken I am with you."

"And with Mrs. Walpole and at least a half dozen other women in the village."

"*They* were interludes. With you it could be different."

She smiled, knowing he was only half serious. "Are you asking for my hand, Arthur?"

He turned red and ran his finger around the inside edge of his high, starched neckcloth. "I would say it is a little premature for such a step, but I confess to having given it some consideration."

Elizabeth laughed and tucked her hand in the crook of his arm. "Forgive me, Arthur. I shouldn't tease you so unmercifully. We both know I am too old for you. I think of you as my younger brother. Does that upset you?"

"At the moment I can think of nothing more deadly. Perhaps I can change your mind now that you are staying on permanently."

"Permanently! Whatever gave you such a notion?"

"Well, why not? You've no special need to return to London, and we have plenty of room here. I think it's a splendid idea."

"I fear your brother would hardly share your enthusiasm. I suspect it is all he can do to tolerate me on a temporary basis, let alone permanently."

"I can't understand why the two of you are at such odds with one another. Granted, Marcus is not always the most outgoing man I know, but he is fair to a fault. Have you and he had words? I felt as if the air was charged with lightning at breakfast this morning."

"I fear he considers me an inconvenience. Either that, or he is afraid I will ruin your reputation."

"Ridiculous on both counts. It must be the fact that you

are a very lovely woman. Marcus was never at ease with women."

"But he told me he had taken his share of women." The moment she said it, Elizabeth regretted it.

Arthur looked at her in surprise. "He said that to you? I wouldn't have thought Marcus capable of going beyond the bounds of good taste to brag of his conquests."

Elizabeth lifted an eyebrow. "But you do."

He laughed. "Touché. But I am me, and he is Marcus."

"You say that with a great deal of respect and perhaps a touch of envy in your voice," Elizabeth mused aloud.

"Very astute. Yes, I admire Marcus more than I can ever say, and would ever dream of letting him know," he added with a grin. "Although Emily and I delight in teasing him for his passion to bring honor to the House of Clendennon, Marcus is the best man I have ever known. I used to think I wanted to be like Marcus, but we are so different that I find it hard to believe we are even brothers."

"I told you before, Arthur, that you give yourself too little credit. You've proven yourself in your duty to the King. Your circumstances are different than Marcus's. Were you the firstborn, you would doubtless have found your satisfaction in preserving the duchy. As it is, when you are not serving the King, you find yourself at a loss to know what to do. Chasing women seems an easy and entertaining pastime, and you appear to have settled for that."

He grinned. "Perhaps you are right, Elizabeth, and I shall not give up until I have pursued you to the wall and you are ready to admit defeat."

She laughed. "You are absolutely hopeless. The vicar was right. You need the benefit of his Sunday sermons . . . along with the rest of us, I daresay."

"The vicar? When did you see him?"

"He called today to make certain that I was not staying at the castle under duress."

"My God. And what did you tell him?"

"That you had kidnapped me from Buckingham Palace, where I was acting as mistress to the King."

Arthur sucked in his breath, and his jaw dropped until he apparently realized she was playing him the fool. Then he grabbed her by the shoulders and playfully shook her. "Had you not just praised me for my sense of honor, I would this minute cover your body with kisses as revenge for your jest. Indeed, I am sorely tempted to do so anyway."

"I wouldn't, Arthur. Given enough provocation, I have been known for my ability to scratch like an angry kitten."

"I'll remember that."

She gave him a sideways look. "The vicar seems to think that your attendance at church would go a long way toward putting down the untidy rumors that have been circulating since my arrival at the castle. I told him I would do my best to convince you and your brother to attend on the next Sabbath."

"Don't waste your breath on Marcus. He has no love for the church since the death of our mother."

Elizabeth would have questioned him further, but they were distracted by the breathtaking panorama of the sea breaking upon the rocks far below. Arthur bade the driver stop, and they alighted for a better view.

The wind from the sea had freshened since they left the castle, and Elizabeth was chilled through the thin fabric of her shawl. Arthur put his arm around her, and she accepted his gesture for what it was—a brotherly concern for her comfort. He breathed an oath, but she saw that he was smiling.

"Marcus is right again. We will have a storm on the morrow. The sky is filled with the signs of it, and so is the sea."

Elizabeth studied his face. It bore the look of a sailor too long absent from the deck of a ship. She had seen the same look on James's face before he left on the voyage that was to be his last. For the first time she realized that her life with the man whom she thought she had loved would never have been the dreamworld she had conjured. A sailor was a sailor forever. The sea was in his blood.

As she watched the waves curl and foam against the small spit of sandy beach, she felt her own life wash clean of the debris that had cluttered it for so long. How odd that here, standing on this rocky headland with a man who was still a stranger to her, she had finally laid to rest the ghost of her first love.

Their picnic proved to be pleasant if uneventful. Arthur talked a little about the sea and his life aboard ship, although he was still unwilling or unable to talk about his wound or the Battle of New Orleans. Elizabeth suspected it was a matter of injured pride that decreed his silence on the subject.

When they arrived back at the castle, Mrs. Patchen approached Elizabeth with a message from Emily.

"I hope I have not exceeded my authority, your ladyship, but Lady Emily was here to call while you and Sir Arthur were out. She expressed a desire to return for dinner, and I told her that I was certain you would not mind."

Elizabeth was taken aback. "Speaking for myself, I couldn't be more pleased, Mrs. Patchen, but I have no right to either approve or disapprove her visit. Surely that decision should be left to His Grace, or in his absence, Sir Arthur."

"Yes, your ladyship. However, His Grace informed me that I should consult you about your preferences for dinner. I merely assumed—"

"I see. I did tell the duke that I would make myself available for such duties as were needed. I think perhaps we need to clarify what he has in mind. As for dinner tonight, I'm sure the duke and Sir Arthur will be pleased that their sister will be present."

The housekeeper tucked her hands into the long sleeves of her uniform, and once again Elizabeth was impressed with the woman's look of quality. "Does your ladyship have a menu in mind for the evening meal?"

"I'm sure you know what the family prefers much better than I do, Mrs. Patchen. I'll leave the decision up to you."

The woman nodded her head in satisfaction, and with a curtsy returned to her duties.

With the abundance of flowers available in the conservatory, it seemed strange to Elizabeth that there were rarely cut flowers in the house. Upon questioning the gardener she learned that it was simply because Mrs. Patchen had no time for such frivolous things, and no one else bothered. Elizabeth decided it was a duty she could perform quite capably and took it upon herself to arrange flowers for the dinner table that evening. She chose pink primroses to match the long tapered candles Mrs. Patchen said would grace the table along with the pink-and-gold embossed china. When she was satisfied, Elizabeth arranged a huge basket of daisies and purple delphiniums to stand atop a bare pedestal in the salon. Pleased with the effect, she went upstairs to dress for the evening meal.

Greta was far from her usual cocky self when she came in to help Elizabeth dress. Elizabeth was puzzled until the girl finally spoke up.

"It's seein' the vicar I'm worried about. I don't know what to wear."

Elizabeth nodded. Apparently this visit meant more to the girl than she cared to admit. In truth, the vicar was a handsome man, clean-cut, mannerly, and yet appealing in a purely masculine way. Could the girl have become smitten so quickly? She longed to chide her, but prudence warned her to keep silent lest she wound the girl's pride.

"I doubt that any woman knew at once what to wear on any given occasion, Greta. If it were me, I would wear something simple and a trifle demure."

"Aye. A trifle demure."

"By that I mean something that doesn't show too much of what one has to offer."

"Huh! 'Tis no wonder you stayed an old maid."

"That wasn't the reason. It isn't marriage that men are looking for when they feast their eyes on a woman's half-bare bosom."

"Aye, but a body has to get their attention somehow."

"You can find a better way. Besides, you must remember that the vicar is a man of the cloth."

"And a more beautiful man I haint never set me gaze on. I could stare into those brown eyes for the rest o' me life."

Elizabeth laughed. "And what happened to your great plan for marrying into wealth?"

"Who's talking marriage? Blimey! Can you see me a vicar's wife?"

The image set them both laughing, but Elizabeth sobered first. "Then what did you have in mind, Greta? I can't perceive of you trying to seduce the vicar." She smiled. "Not just out of respect for his office, but I thought you wanted to save yourself for the man who could pay the highest price."

"Indade, your ladyship. I still hold to that plan, but I'm mighty partial to men wi' gold hair. What 'arm can come from just talkin' to 'im? As for beddin' wi' 'im . . . I'll make up me mind when the time comes."

"He seems a nice sort, Greta. I'd hate to see him hurt."

"Aye, and so would I, but when the likes o' me takes a man to bed, hit won't hurt 'im none, I'll stake me life on that."

102

"What I meant was that it could damage his profession. A man of God is supposed to be above such desires."

"I wager we'll find out soon enough. Hit won't be me who spreads the gossip should 'e decide to lift me skirts."

Elizabeth felt a twinge of sympathy for the unfortunate vicar. If Greta made up her mind to seduce him, he would lose the game before he realized it had even begun.

There were times when Elizabeth rather envied the casual approach some younger people took toward flirtations. Most of her friends had shared stolen kisses with any number of bucks and dandies in the Dark Walk between the hedges at Vauxhall Gardens. Indeed, at the time of her coming out she had experienced brief caresses with one or two special young men behind the draperies at routs and parties. And then there was James. He had been a sweet young boy, more prone to drag her off to watch the ships come in to the Pool than to a lovers' trysting place. But he had loved her, and Elizabeth had thought she was in love with him. Now she was beginning to wonder if her emotions had been genuine.

Despite the fact that her lovemaking with James had gone a small bit beyond the propriety of kisses, she had never experienced the mind shattering feelings that resulted from the merest touch of the duke's hand on her arm. She was hard put to know why he affected her that way. Although he was an attractive man, he was in no way as handsome as the vicar. And yet the vicar had left no lasting impression; had created not the least whisper of carnal desire in her blood as he had apparently done to Greta. The same was true with Arthur. If anything, she was tempted to mother him.

She sighed. It was a waste of strength to attempt to sort out her feelings. What did it matter in the long run? She would soon be returning to London. The duke was generous, but she doubted that he intended to let her stay on indefinitely as Arthur had said. Indeed, she could not in good conscience accept such hospitality for very long.

Greta brought the violet organdy dress to slip over her head, putting an end to Elizabeth's musing. A short time later she was ready to go downstairs to the salon.

Surprisingly Emily was already there, enjoying a small glass of wine. She hauled herself out of the chair and put her hands out to greet Elizabeth.

"How truly lovely you look, Elizabeth. I hope you don't mind my early arrival. The house seems terribly empty with Gerald away on business."

Elizabeth smiled her pleasure. "Indeed, had I known you were here, I would have come downstairs much sooner. It's a delight to see you. Are you feeling well?"

"Indeed. I couldn't feel better. My son has just begun to kick a wee bit, to let me know he is thinking of me."

Elizabeth smiled. "Are you so sure it is a son?"

"In truth, it matters to me not a whit. Like all men, my husband would like a son, and I would like to please him. Were we concerned about succession I would indeed pray for a boy, but I am more comfortable with little girls. Alas, my husband is away so often that he would see little of a son if he had one." She raised an eyebrow and slanted a look at Elizabeth. "Of course, the duke is in a different position. He, to say the least, is badly in need of a son."

Elizabeth's voice was dry. "Considering his age, if he is not aware how to go about getting one, then I would perceive there is little hope for him."

Emily giggled. "Silly. You know what I mean. It is not easy to bring about a proper liaison to assure noble bloodlines while at the same time providing a suitable wife who would bring honor to the family line." She fluttered her fan in front of her face. "Oh, listen to me. I sound like a snob and a busybody. Marcus will wed whom he pleases and when he pleases . . . but I do wish he would accomplish it soon."

Marcus spoke from the doorway. "In the meantime, Emily dear, I don't think you need concern yourself with the state of my bachelorhood. It is hardly a topic for parlor conversation."

Emily laughed, completely undaunted by his severe tone. "How little you know about parlor conversation, Marcus. The state of your unweddedness was the most-talked-about topic in the county . . . until Arthur's return with Elizabeth in tow."

The duke swore competently. "I was inclined to think there were no disadvantages to living in the country, but I must reassess my opinion. Nothing can equal a country village for its abundance of idle gossip."

Arthur arrived a moment later, and they all toasted each other with a glass of sherry before they went into the refectory. Elizabeth was pleased at the appearance of the table, and both Emily and Arthur commented on the lovely flowers she had arranged. Marcus made no comment, and Elizabeth felt the omission as much as she would have suffered from a rebuke. It somehow spoiled the rest of the meal despite the fact that the food was excellent and the conversation between Emily and Arthur was witty and entertaining.

When it was finished and they were about to leave the table, Marcus gave Emily his arm, which she accepted with a great show of affection.

"Darlings . . . I have a marvelous thought. Why don't we show Elizabeth the Petite Ballroom, or have you already had a tour of the castle?" she asked, turning to Elizabeth.

"Well, I—"

Marcus interrupted before she could say she had already seen the ballroom. "Her ladyship has been too occupied with tea parties and picnics to tour the castle, but I think we might instead repair to the drawing room, which is considerably less musty."

"Nonsense," Emily argued. "The ballroom has been aired once a month if Mrs. Patchen has had anything to say about it."

"Oh, come on, Marcus," Arthur said. "Elizabeth might enjoy seeing the barrel organ." He turned with a bow and offered his arm to Elizabeth. "It was made by George Astor and Company back in 1780. There's a hand crank that turns a cylinder to play the most delightful tune."

Elizabeth shot a glance at Marcus. His face was grim, but it appeared he had no choice but to go along with them. Why had he given the impression that she had not seen the ballroom? Was he afraid she would say something about their having been there together? She compressed her lips. If anyone told about that night when their emotions had run away with them, it wouldn't be her.

Her apprehension mounted as they entered the darkened room, but Emily's lighthearted laughter covered up whatever moodiness might be affecting Marcus. She and Arthur dashed about flinging draperies aside and opening the windows to liven the dead air. Once that was accomplished, Arthur dragged Elizabeth over to a niche between the windows where a large parlor organ stood against the wall.

"Here it is." He waved a flourish. "What good times we used to have dancing to its merry tune!"

It was a tall instrument with a large, exposed horizontal cylinder that was covered with hundreds of tiny pinpricks of metal. The instrument was brass-mounted in a polished-wood cabinet with gold-embossed trim.

As Arthur slowly began to turn the handle Elizabeth covered her mouth in surprise. "Why . . . it's like a music box."

"Indeed." Emily laughed. "And we have spent many a happy hour dancing to it. Remember, Marcus, how you used to pretend you were the King and I was one of your servant girls whom you chose to be your dancing partner?"

"Yes. And you always managed to stumble over your feet . . . just like some untrained country girl."

Emily held out her hands. "I don't stumble anymore, Marcus. Come dance with me."

He swore in apparent irritation, but Elizabeth saw the affection flow between brother and sister as he took her into his arms and carefully danced her around the room. In spite of her state of expectancy Emily managed to give an impression of grace and youthful exuberance as they pivoted and turned.

Even though the music was slow Emily was breathless as they danced near. Just as they came close she whirled out of Marcus's arms and pushed Elizabeth toward him.

"Oh, do take my place. I'll make my son dizzy."

Neither Marcus nor Elizabeth had any choice in the matter. She went into his arms, but her body refused to relax, and she knew that they must have looked ridiculous together. Nor did Marcus help. He held her at arm's length as if she had a touch of leprosy and he feared contamination. After what seemed like an interminably long time, Arthur tired of turning the crank and let the music wind to a stop.

Emily had wandered over to the pianoforte, where she ran her fingers across the keys. As she was about to sit down on the bench, she bent over and picked up something and held it to her face. It was the shawl.

She stood, a conspiratorial smile on her face. "Someone has been telling stories. How does it happen that the shawl I gave to Elizabeth is here in the ballroom when she has never been here?"

Elizabeth felt her face go white. She wet her lips, then looked at Marcus, who also appeared to be in a state of distress. He studiously avoided her gaze and did nothing to fill the awkward gap in conversation.

Elizabeth felt compelled to explain. "I—I'm afraid I was less than honest. In truth, I did come to the ballroom one night, quite by accident. I made a wrong turn in the corridor when I thought I was going to the refectory."

Emily studied them both with care. "And Marcus was there."

Elizabeth stammered. "No, I—I—that is—"

"Oh, do behave yourself, Emily," Marcus ordered. "You sound like the Royal Inquisitor. Come. I think we've seen enough." He took Emily's arm and steered her toward the door.

Arthur looked completely bewildered, but he offered Elizabeth his arm, and they left without speaking. A short time later Emily said her good nights and Marcus offered to see her safely home.

Arthur and Elizabeth remained in the library after they had gone. He came over to where Elizabeth was sitting and took her hands in his.

"What happened that night? Marcus *was* there, wasn't he?"

They both looked up as they heard Marcus at the door. "That is none of your damned business, Arthur."

Arthur straightened and stood his ground. "I say that it is. I am, after all, responsible for Elizabeth's being here."

"That does not make you responsible for her welfare."

"Then I will make it my responsibility."

"Not in my house you won't!" There was no mistaking the fury in the duke's voice.

Elizabeth stood, her body shaking. "Stop it, the two of you. I will not have you fighting like a pair of dogs over a bone. No one is responsible for me but myself. I make my own decisions . . . and at this moment I have decided to retire to my room." Both men appeared to relax, and she carefully let out her breath as she walked between them.

The duke straightened his coat. "My sister has asked

the pleasure of your company in the carriage as she returns home to her farm."

Elizabeth hesitated, knowing full well that if she agreed, it would mean a return ride in the dark, alone with Marcus. "Is your sister not feeling well?"

"She professes to being somewhat tired."

"In that case I can hardly refuse to accompany her."

Marcus nodded, and she preceded him out the door. She didn't have to look back to know that Arthur was left standing there with his hands on his hips in an attitude of bewilderment.

CHAPTER NINE

Marcus was silent as he ushered Elizabeth into the waiting carriage. Elizabeth looked quickly at Emily, who managed a radiant smile in spite of her supposed fatigue.

She reached out her hand to pat Elizabeth's arm. "How sweet of you to accompany me home. I perceive there was no great need, but it is comforting to have another woman about when one is in the family way."

Marcus's voice was grim. "You would do well, Emily, to have your housekeeper accompany you when you go out. I daresay she has a bit more experience in the birthing of children than her ladyship is apt to have."

"Nonsense, Marcus. Women know these things by instinct."

He sat across from them as the carriage made the short journey down one lane and up the next to Emily's estate. When they arrived at her door, she invited them to come in, but Marcus declined without consulting Elizabeth. He got out of the carriage long enough to make certain Emily was in the safe care of the butler, then returned to the carriage and climbed in, taking his former seat across from Elizabeth.

Elizabeth let out her breath. She had wondered if he would sit next to her, and she was both relieved and yet disappointed that he chose not to. The silence was awkward. Finally he cleared his throat and looked at her.

"I must beg your forgiveness over the shawl incident.

It was foolish of me to pretend that you had not seen the Petite Ballroom. By faith, I cannot find a good reason for my having allowed the misunderstanding to come about . . . except that my sister is too inclined to see plots where none exist."

"You've no need to apologize. Let her play her game. She seems to enjoy it, and she means no harm. On the other side of the coin we have done nothing to cause us shame."

"Yes. You are right. I'm sure the less said about it the better."

"My shawl. What happened to it? I fear she must think me terribly careless of the things she has given me."

"I—I picked it up."

He pulled it from his waistcoat, and as he handed it to her their fingers touched. Immediately their eyes met, and Elizabeth knew beyond a doubt that he was thinking thoughts similar to hers. This was the way it had happened before. He had started to give her the shawl, and she had ended up in his arms.

But it wasn't to happen a second time. Although the light was dim, she saw a guarded expression cross his face, and he seemed to retreat within himself. She relaxed. No, this was not to be a repeat performance. Somehow the thought left her less than content.

They were a short distance from the castle when the carriage lurched sharply and Elizabeth was thrown against the side. The duke swore softly, asked if she were injured, then stuck his head out the window.

"What the devil happened?"

"Blimey, 'tis the axle, Your Grace. She's fair split on me, I'm thinking, and I dassn't drive on until I see to the damage."

Marcus looked at Elizabeth. "I'm afraid I'll have to send home for our own conveyance. You could wait in-

111

side, but with the seat at such an angle I fear you would be less than comfortable."

"It isn't far. I would much prefer to walk the short distance."

"But that is ridiculous. The night is dark, and the road is at best uneven. Wait here and I shall return within the half hour."

"Why should you force your driver to harness the horses when I can walk home in less time than it would take to rouse him?"

"Except for your tendency to get lost in the dark."

She groaned. "Must you be so ungentlemanly as to remind me? It happened once, only once. You make it sound as if it were a daily occurrence."

"I meant no such thing."

"But it sounded that way, Your Grace." There was no homage in the way she used his title, and her irritation was not lost on him.

"Very well. Since you insist on having your own way, begone. And don't cry out as you go over the cliffs into the sea."

Elizabeth bit back a reply and practically fell as she turned and walked quickly away. She had gone no more than a few yards when she heard him walking behind her. She smiled to herself. She was right. He would not permit her to walk the short distance home unescorted. She made a mental promise to treat him with a little more consideration and respect . . . beginning tomorrow.

In the meantime, so that he would not think she was waiting for him, she walked a little faster. His steps also quickened until he came alongside her.

"Forgive me. I should not have spoken to you with such forcefulness."

"Please don't apologize, Your Grace. I know you were simply trying to be considerate. I too regret having spoken sharply. My only excuse is that I dislike having you treat me as a child. I am quite capable of taking care of myself."

"Indeed?" He stopped walking and put his hands on her shoulders. "Then why are you going in the wrong direction?" He spun her around until she was forced to retrace her path, then gave her a swat on the bottom as if she were an intractable infant. "Run along home to bed, little girl. Just stay on the road, and you can't miss the castle. It's the large stone building surrounded by a high wall." He laughed as she fought back tears of anger.

"Damn you, Marcus. You're no gentleman at all."

His laughter continued to ring in her ears even after she had reached the safety of her own bedchamber.

"Fool! Fool!" she said aloud, not realizing that Greta was curled in a chair in the sitting room.

"Yes, your ladyship. Did you want something?"

"I—no. I merely thought aloud." She walked over to where Greta was sitting. "Is something wrong? You look faint."

"No, your ladyship. I was just sitting here thinking."

Elizabeth smiled. "About the vicar, no doubt. I trust your visit with him was successful?"

Greta shrugged. "'Is bloomin 'ousekeeper was there bendin' 'er ear over every word we said."

Elizabeth chuckled. "Good. The man is wise despite his comparative youth. What did you talk about?"

"'Twas 'im what did the talkin' . . . and readin' from the Good Book." She sat up straight and pressed her palms together. "But I hain't never 'eard nobody say the words like he does. Seems to me it was more like music than just plain talkin'. If a body could believe all them things what he said . . ." Her voice trailed off without finishing, and Elizabeth left her to her thoughts.

A short time later Greta, apparently having recovered, came into the bedroom, where Elizabeth was working at the catches on her dress. She fixed her with a speculative gaze.

"You were out when I came 'ome."

"Yes. We saw Lady Emily home after dinner."

"We? Meanin' you and 'Is Grace?"

"Yes."

"Glory! No wonder Sir Arthur was in such a lather."

"I'm sure I don't know what you mean."

She grinned impishly. "Yes, ma'am."

Elizabeth turned to her. "You would be well-advised to tend to your own affairs, Greta. I admit to having been too lenient with you, but unless you guard your tongue, I shall have to see that you are properly disciplined. Do you understand?"

"Oh, indade, your ladyship. I understands a great many things."

And from the look in her eyes Elizabeth suspected the girl was not exaggerating. She was too wise for her years, and much too impudent for a servant. Unfortunately she liked the girl too much to ever punish her.

"Will you be needin' me tomorrow night, your ladyship?"

"Why? What did you want to do?"

Greta gave a toss to her mane of dark hair and sent Elizabeth a sidelong look of triumph. "'Tis the vicar who asked me to visit. 'E hankers to read to me again from the Good Book."

Elizabeth sat down on the edge of the bed. "It is not my wish to interfere in your personal life, Greta. I know what you have in mind, but someone is bound to be hurt. I don't want it to be you, nor do I want the Reverend Fleetwood injured in any way. You're playing a dangerous game."

Greta hung Elizabeth's gown in the armoire, then stuck her head around the door and grinned slyly. "I'm very good at games, my lady. Will there be anything else before we say good night?"

"No, I think not. Good night, Greta."

Greta curtsied and smiled with what Elizabeth interpreted to be a condescending look of pity. "Good night, Lady Elizabeth."

It was a full week later before Elizabeth again saw the duke. Arthur appeared somewhat surprised by the duke's absence, but he said that it was not unheard of for Marcus to keep to himself for good portions of the day and night. During that time Arthur took it upon himself to make certain that Elizabeth was well entertained. The people of the village grew used to the sight of the two of them tooling about the countryside in one of the small buggies with Arthur at the reins.

It occurred to Elizabeth that she was doing little or nothing to justify her presence at the castle, and the thought bothered her. When she tried to discuss it with Arthur or Emily, they seemed surprised that she felt it necessary to make herself useful.

When Marcus finally put in his appearance at dinner one night, he was more quiet than Elizabeth had ever known him to be. Unfortunately Arthur was in a mood to show off, and his conversation kept returning to the excursions he and Elizabeth had made into the countryside.

Marcus finally laid down his fork and fixed Arthur with his wooden gaze. "I perceive, Arthur, that you have not lacked for female companionship during your leave from the King's Navy. Indeed, from what I deduce, you have forsaken the local fare for your own special variety of import."

Elizabeth gasped, and Arthur motioned her to silence.

"If you have a complaint about my behavior, Marcus, I think it is something we should discuss in private."

"Indeed? And why should we not discuss the matter in front of her ladyship, since she is directly concerned?"

"Really, Marcus. You are behaving most indiscreetly.

115

If this is what your recent retreat has accomplished, I would suggest you forgo the luxury, as it does nothing to improve your humor."

"At least we agree on one point. Better that I should remain in evidence lest my brother and our guest make complete fools of themselves."

Arthur leaped up from the table. "Retract that at once, sir, or I shall be forced to demand satisfaction!"

Elizabeth jumped to her feet. "Stop it. Stop it at once. There is no reason for the two of you to be at one another's throats."

Marcus grabbed her shoulder. "Enough. Go to your room and remain there until I send for you."

She saw the pain and anger etched across his face, and the sight made her heart wrench with sorrow. Bursting into tears, she ran from the room and up the stairs to her bedchamber.

It was there that Arthur found her still weeping ten minutes later. He had knocked on the door, but Elizabeth had not wished to see anyone and chose not to answer. She was lying on the bed when he entered, her face red from weeping. He stood there awkwardly, obviously not knowing whether to speak or leave her alone.

Elizabeth forced herself to get up. "Arthur, you really shouldn't be in here like this."

He was distraught. "I had to come. He shouldn't have said those things to us. I'm so dreadfully sorry, Elizabeth."

She reached out to pat his arm. "You've no need to apologize. It's not your fault, but I cannot continue to stay here if my presence is the source of trouble between you and your brother."

"Don't even think of leaving. Trust me, Elizabeth. I can set things aright." He put his hands on her shoulders and drew her close to him. "If you were to leave now . . ."

116

Before she knew what was happening Arthur had pulled her against him and crushed her mouth with his.

At that unfortunate moment Marcus strode into the room. His voice was deadly calm. "It was as I thought. Get out of this bedchamber, Arthur, before I throw you out."

"You shall have to kill me first, Marcus. I have decided to marry Elizabeth."

Elizabeth just barely managed to gather her wits in time to move between them. "Do as he says, Arthur, please," she begged.

He hesitated a moment, then turned quickly and left the room.

Marcus had not moved, nor did he show any intention of doing so. She looked up at him, her eyes filled with the pain of their misunderstanding.

"You're wrong, you know. There is nought but friendship between Arthur and me."

"Come now, Lady Elizabeth. I saw and heard with my own eyes and ears. Do you take me for a complete fool?"

She studied his face. "I didn't, Your Grace, until now."

Her icy calm served only to fan the fires of his rage. "What is it you want from me, Elizabeth? Is it money?"

She smiled. "Money, Your Grace? You *are* a fool. I doubt that you could ever give me what I want from you."

He looked confused.

She shook her head. "In truth, I think you are right. Perhaps it is time for me to return to London."

He studied her face, and for a brief moment she thought he was going to reach for her. But he shook his head as if to clear it.

"If that is your wish." He bowed. "We shall leave at first light."

"I would like first to say good-bye to Emily and the others."

"You can write them a letter. I am well aware of Emi-

117

ly's powers of persuasion. If you think I shall permit her to put them to work on me in this matter, you are misguided."

She nodded. "As you say. If you will excuse me, Your Grace, I have much to do before the dawning."

He bowed and walked toward the door, turning once as if to say something, then drawing a deep breath and departing.

Elizabeth looked around the rooms she had come to love. It was over—the happiest time of her life, too good, too precious to be more than a fleeting dream. She regretted having to leave so abruptly, but maybe it was better this way. Once she was out of their lives, the brothers could regain their sense of balance. Greta would solve her own problems . . . and Emily's husband would be home to share her dreams. Although she had intruded on their lives for a brief time, she had never really been a part of them. But despite the years of heartache she knew must lie ahead, she wouldn't have missed it for all the gold of the kingdom.

She was sitting on a chair near the window when Marcus came for her at dawn. If he had knocked at her door, she didn't hear him. She was in a state of numbness that shielded her from the pain of leaving forever the house—and the man—she had come to love.

His face was white against the dark wool of his cloak, and from the expression on his face Elizabeth wondered if he were having second thoughts.

She broke the silence. "I'm ready, Your Grace." It occurred to her that the words could not have sounded more final than if she were going to meet her executioner.

"Your bags . . . have you sent them downstairs?"

She shook her head. "I came with nothing, and that is the way I shall leave."

"Don't be ridiculous. Emily gave you a wardrobe full of gowns. I know she meant you to keep them."

Elizabeth shook her head. "Shall we go?"

He grasped her by the shoulders, and his face was so close that his breath disturbed a curl that escaped from the side of her bonnet. "Damn you for your pride and willfulness, Elizabeth."

Tears burned her eyelids as his fingers dug into her shoulders, but her pain went beyond the flesh. This was the last time he would hold her. The knowledge was almost too painful to bear, and she pulled away lest she break down and sob.

The coachman was ready and waiting atop the State carriage when Elizabeth went downstairs. Without waiting for Marcus to assist her, she climbed in and settled the purple cloak over the yellow-checked gingham Arthur had bought for her just a few short weeks ago. It seemed like years . . . so much had happened during that time.

Marcus climbed onto the seat facing her and gave the driver the signal to depart. She was going back. She blinked her eyes rapidly to stop the tears. But in truth she could never go back, because things would never be the way they used to be . . . before Marcus.

They rode silently mile after aching mile. Elizabeth was hardly aware of the passing countryside. It was only when they entered the villages that she seemed to come alive. The normally friendly farmers stared at them with looks that in some cases seemed to approach hatred. She was hard put to understand.

Just as they were leaving a fairly large village, a trio of young men shouted strings of obscenities, and one of them, a wiry, dark-haired lad, reached down and threw a clod of horse dung, hitting the window near Elizabeth's face.

Marcus yelled at the driver to give the horses their head, and the team surged forward. With the carriage moving at full speed, Marcus grabbed hold of the framework and moved over to where Elizabeth was seated.

"Are you all right?"

"Yes, just shaken. What happened? Why are the villagers so angry at us?"

"It's not us in particular. They blame the nobility for the enactment of the Corn Laws. Had I my wits about me, I would have taken another carriage instead of this, which bears the Clendennon Family crest."

She was profoundly aware of one of his knees, which had grazed hers as he moved across the aisle, and she tried to cover her feelings with conversation.

"But I thought the Corn Laws were meant to protect the poor."

"I'm sure that is what the Tory government would like us to believe. By placing a high tariff on imported wheat, the price of our own wheat has become outrageous. In addition to that, there have been several years of poor harvest. This doesn't hurt the rich landowner too much, but the poor farmer cannot raise enough to feed his family."

"I suppose that is why so many families in the North and the Midlands have gone to work in the mines and manufactories."

"Indeed. What with the long hours and low pay, their lives are little better than wretched. But in the South there are few industries, and if a man travels even a short distance from home to look for work, he stands a good chance of being arrested as a vagabond."

"But how can such a situation exist? Why do the farmers not demand reform in Parliament?"

"My dear Elizabeth . . ."

She looked up in surprise at the unexpected term of endearment, but apparently he was not aware he had used it. He continued.

". . . the smallholder and the farm laborer are the ones

120

who suffer most under the Corn Laws, but they have no great representation in Parliament. It is the men who prosper from the Corn Laws, the big landholders and the wealthy farmers with the price of wheat in their pockets, who run the Tory government." He crossed his legs as he leaned back against the seat. "Granted, a few sympathetic Whigs and some angry radicals have been pressing for reform, but the Tories see it as money stolen from their pockets. If there is ever to be reform, it is a long time hence."

"But I don't understand. Why was there no ill feeling in your village? Arthur and I were treated with great affection as we drove through the countryside." She noticed a muscle tighten in his cheek at the reference to Arthur, but he made an apparent effort to control himself.

"There are some villages where the situation is entirely different. My family has long believed that our tenant farmers should have ample land to permit them to raise crops and forage for a few sheep and pigs. Where there is food in a man's belly, there is not likely to be rioting in the streets."

Elizabeth knew he was right, and she respected him for his sense of fairness. If only he could have treated her with the same measure of understanding.

They rode on for another hour or so until they approached the outskirts of a larger, more prosperous-looking village. The number of wagons and dogcarts entering the town was unusual for so late in the day, and Elizabeth became apprehensive.

"So many people. What are they all doing here?"

He apparently noticed the tightness in her voice and put his arm across the back of the seat protectively while still making certain to avoid touching her.

"From the sound of it, I'd say it was a country fair. I doubt that we have cause for concern. The town seems prosperous enough. At any rate we have little choice but

121

to take shelter for the night. The team is in need of rest even if we could manage to push onward."

He leaned his head out of the carriage to speak to the driver, then settled back against the seat. He was closer this time, the warmth of his thigh pressing hers. Elizabeth found herself wondering if it were intentional. They would be stopping at the inn for the night. Would he find an excuse to share her room as Arthur had on her previous journey? She trembled at the thought. He apparently mistook it for an attack of the jitters, and his arm settled around her shoulders protectively.

CHAPTER TEN

There was laughter aplenty in the street as the driver picked his way around pedestrians dressed in holiday clothing and dogcarts loaded to the top with all manner of merchandise, most of it handmade. For the moment Elizabeth forgot her apprehension and leaned forward to get a better look.

There were baskets and furniture made of osier rods, which commonly grew along the water. Hours of painstaking labor had gone into the cutting, peeling, and bleaching of the willow whips to bend and weave them into the proper shapes. Directly ahead a brilliantly painted gypsy wagon boasted handmade candles and matches—not to mention all manner of potions guaranteed to enhance one's beauty or masculinity. They passed a small hand-pulled cart filled with quilts made of brightly colored squares of flowered cotton material. She turned to Marcus.

"It's pleasing to see that the cottage industries have not completely disappeared. It would be frightful if the time came when the skills of handcraftmanship were entirely forgotten."

"Indeed. It would be a pity. Fortunately the people of Heatherford have retained many of the skills learned from their ancestors." He sat back against the cushion. "I do regret that I had no opportunity to take you through my village as I promised."

Elizabeth folded her hands and returned his steady gaze. "I too am sorry to have missed it. Those few villagers whom I chanced to meet seemed most pleasant and friendly."

"Indeed. Except for a few new people like Rupert, my driver, most of the village families have lived on Clendennon land for generations. They have suffered through the hard time along with us, and as we prosper, they prosper. That is one reason we work so hard to keep the estate from losing money. A great many people are dependent upon it for their livelihood."

They were approaching the section of the village where the fair was to be held. Rows of stalls bordered the street, and up ahead Elizabeth saw additional stalls and pens filled with sheep. pigs, and goats. Alongside the street a man driving a dogcart loaded with crates of chickens was attempting to replace a wheel that had come off. The crowd good-naturedly lifted the side of the cart, and he was able to slip the wheel in place and affix a wooden pin to hold it there. They all cheered and threw their arms around each other after it was accomplished.

Elizabeth relaxed visibly when she saw the happy attitude of the fairgoers. They were so different from the people of those other villages.

The carriage with its regal crest attracted considerable attention, as might be expected, but no one moved aside to allow them to pass as would have happened in London. Everyone seemed intent on reaching their destinations before the onset of darkness. There was food and shelter to arrange for the animals and for themselves, and after that the task of setting up their booths for the fair, which doubtless would begin on the morrow.

Marcus studied the obvious excitement in her face. "You enjoy this, don't you?"

"Very much. I attended a country fair once when I was a child, but not since then."

"Would that we could linger on to view it completely, but I fear we must continue our journey to London in the morning."

"Yes, I understand."

"Perhaps we could visit those stalls that are already set up after we dine tonight . . . assuming you are not too fatigued."

"Could we? I can be ready as soon as I have refreshed myself." She studied his eyes, and the warmth she saw there kindled the fire in her blood. She turned quickly lest he see the need that haunted her eyes.

"Oh, look! The horse auction. Oh, Marcus, have you ever seen such beautiful animals?"

He leaned close to peer over her shoulder. "Indeed not. They are some of the finest blooded mares I have seen in months. I'd give a good price to own that bay with the white stockings." He gazed at her in speculation. "Would you like to stop and look at them for a moment?"

Elizabeth clasped her hands together. "Oh, do lets!"

He leaned his head out the window and told Rupert to pull over to the side. The driver found ample space near the shed and drew the carriage to a halt. Marcus opened the carriage door, then waited for Elizabeth to rise. When she started to reach for the step, he scooped her up in his arms and carried her a few feet away before he put her down. In that moment their eyes met and held, and Elizabeth would have given her life to have remained there for the rest of the day.

His voice was husky when he spoke. "You had best watch where you step. The grounds near the horse pen are not safe for ladies' slippers."

It occurred to Elizabeth that she was much safer on the ground than she had been in his arms. The current that flowed between them was threatening to become a raging torrent.

He offered her his arm, and they walked over to the rail

fence that confined the twenty or so horses in the small paddock where a goodly number of people had gathered to watch the spirited mares. The crowd here was more bawdy than those in the rest of the village had appeared to be. Perhaps the heady aroma of ale, which was even stronger than the barnyard odor, had something to do with it. At least three or four of the men were far into their cups.

"The horses are quite wild. Are they as yet unbroken?" Elizabeth asked.

"I would say so. Trained horses would not be so skittish, even with all the noise of the crowds, but to my way of thinking that makes them even more valuable. A poor trainer can break a horse's spirit if it isn't handled properly."

The horses galloped around the perimeter of the small paddock, each fighting for space near the front. One of them reared up on her hind feet and, wild-eyed, pawed the air. The crowd let out a roar. For a moment it appeared the horse might jump the fence, but it was nudged by the rest of the herd and caught up in the constantly moving tide.

The crowd moved closer, and Elizabeth was shoved against the rail. She was unhurt, but she gasped involuntarily.

Marcus glared at the man. "Attend to your manners, my good fellow. You could have injured her ladyship."

The man, obviously muzzy-headed from bending his arm at the pub, swept off his grimy cap in a theatrical bow.

"Sh-sure an if it haint the king and queen. M-move back the rest o' you scum and l-let them th-through ba-fore they fall in the m-manure pile." He grinned, showing black and broken teeth. "C-come to think on it, the manure pile hain't sech a bad idee."

Another voice took up the jest. "Jolly right. Let the

126

nobs see how it is to live like animals—the way some o' us 'as to. Them and their Corn Laws."

A cheer went up from the crowd. Marcus put his arm around Elizabeth and spoke as softly as possible. "I think we should leave. Hold onto my arm and don't let go for anything."

"All right. I understand."

"Excuse me, madam." He spoke to a portly woman who blocked the way. "We would like to come through."

She folded her arms across her bosom and laughed. "Madam, is it? Aye, 'e's a fancy one, or I miss me bet. 'Im an 'is lady, too, in 'er velvet robe fit for a princess. Come on ducs, gimme a kiss. I hain't never been kissed by no dandy before."

"E's a bloody duke, 'e is. That's 'is carriage standin' by the shed."

The mood of the crowd was growing nastier by the second. Marcus tried to push their way out of the close area, but they were forced back against the paddock rail.

Elizabeth was beginning to panic, but she fought to control it, knowing full well what a mistake it would be to show fear. She forced a smile. "You lead, Your Grace. I'll follow."

He took her hand and squeezed it, then put his arm around her waist. The fat woman grabbed hold of Elizabeth's cloak. "Look 'ere at this now. Me an my 'Enry would 'ave to dig potatoes for a year to pay for somethin' like this. I'll wager she 'as a dozen to spare."

"Right you are, Lolly. Mayhap we should take it offen 'er."

"A bloody good idee," another voice chimed in. "My Sarah could use a dress."

The duke straightened to his full height. "Enough. Have you no sense of decency? What do you hope to gain by acting like a pack of ruffians? You came to enjoy the fair. Don't spoil it before it's begun."

127

"You talk about decency, Your Grace, but decency bloody well don't fill my younguns' bellies, nor pay the rent my landlord demands."

"But rioting won't help. Only Parliament can set aside the Corn Laws. Your only hope is to work through Commons."

Laughter rippled through the crowd.

"Commons, indeed. They are the very ones who profit by keeping the law in force."

"Right you are," another agreed. "We need to take 'em out one by one and 'ang 'em from the gallows."

Marcus tried to push their way through the crowd, and the people in front dropped back a foot or two, but about that time someone on the edge of the mass threw a clod of manure and it splattered against the fence rail near Marcus's head. He was white-faced now, fully aware of their impending danger. It was less than a minute later when someone threw the first stone.

The crowd surged forward again, and Elizabeth was behind Marcus, caught against the fence. He shielded her effectively from the flying missiles. Most of them were too small to do any real harm anyway, but one rather large stone hit Marcus a glancing blow on the forehead. Elizabeth heard the dull thud, and her heart nearly stopped beating as she saw Marcus's hand go up to his temple and come away stained with blood.

She stifled a scream. "Marcus, you're hurt. We must leave at once."

He looked at her, but there was no recognition in his eyes.

Oh, Dear Lord, she thought. They're going to kill us.

A roar went up from the crowd at the sight of the blood on his head. He was still standing but seemed dazed and disoriented. For the moment at least, the barrage of stones had ceased as all eyes were fixed on Marcus's face. Elizabeth was still caught between Marcus and the paddock fence, and because of his height, was partially shielded from the crowd. She knew their time was growing short. The next stone to be thrown would signal the crowd to finish them off.

As if sensing the blood in the air, the horses were on the verge of trampling each other in their haste to get out of the cramped paddock. Elizabeth felt something gouge into her back. She knew instinctively it was the wire loop that held the gate closed. With a determination born of fear she slipped the wire over the top of the post and felt the gate begin to swing inward. Grabbing Marcus around the waist, she pulled him backward with all her strength, using the framework of the gate for added support. As it swung inward, propelled by their weight, the crowd began to surge forward with them. At that moment the lead horses spotted the opening in the rail fence and turned toward the crowd.

"Stampede, stampede!" The high-pitched screams cut throught the air as people fought to get clear of the wild horses. Agonized cries of those who were trampled added to the chaos, which looked like a scene straight out of Hell.

Elizabeth slapped Marcus, trying to bring recognition to his face, but he only staggered, glassy-eyed, against the fence. Hooking his arm over her shoulder, she managed to steer him toward the edge of the crowd. "Marcus, now is our only chance. We must go!" she shouted.

At least he was able to walk. They half ran as they dodged horses, toppled booths, broken crates, and people nursing their wounds. So great was the havoc that none seemed to notice their departure, and no one appeared to follow. One look assured her that it was no use trying to get to their carriage. Whether from the stampede or the work of the mob, the carriage lay on its side, one wheel broken, the other bent at a strange angle. Neither the team nor the driver was anywhere in sight.

They had to find shelter as soon as possible. Although

the crowd was still occupied with the wild horses, which had scattered the damage as far as Elizabeth could see, the time would come when the villagers would start looking for the two of them.

If they could reach the church, the vicar would surely give them sanctuary. But her heart sank as she remembered seeing that tall, white spire at the other end of the village. Too far. With Marcus hanging on the edge she was not sure how long he could hold out. If he worsened to the point where he could not walk, it would soon be over for them.

She chewed her lip in frustration. He was leaning more and more of his weight down on her shoulders. Shelter. They needed a place to hide until the darkness was complete. That would give her time to make plans. The tumult of the crowd was lessening. She had to hurry.

"Marcus, try to walk faster. We must find a place to hide."

"Castle. Safe."

His voice was a blur, and she knew he was only dimly aware of what was happening. It was on her shoulders whether or not they escaped. His arm tightened around her, and she felt her resolve strengthen. She'd take care of him if it was the last thing she did.

She found a small shed standing next to a dung heap, but there was a door and it was unlocked. Elizabeth half dragged the duke inside, then told him to lean against the wall while she cleared a place for him to lie down. He needed rest. His legs were getting shakier as the minutes sped by. She moved a rusty hoe and tipped over a table with a broken leg. After several tries, she managed to get him to step over the table then get down on the floor so that it offered some measure of concealment. Lying down beside him, she cradled his head on her breast. At first he was tense, but as she continued to stroke his hair and murmur soothing words, he relaxed and closed his eyes.

130

Fortunately his wound had stopped bleeding. She wished there was water to cleanse the cut, but it was the least of their needs for the present. She rested her head against the dirty wall and measured their chances. They had to return to the castle. London was much too far to attempt, and only Heaven knew what manner of trouble might confront them between here and there.

His face was dreadfully pale. Would he be able to even walk as far as the edge of the village? No. She immediately discarded the idea. But the carriage was gone . . . and to the best of her knowledge, so was the driver. From what the duke had said Elizabeth judged he was new to the staff at Heatherwood. Whether or not he could be relied on for help was purely conjecture, even if she succeeded in finding him.

The sound of approaching voices caused her heart to throb painfully. If the villagers found them now, they were finished for certain.

One of the men spoke. "There's no call to waste our time here. Can you fancy a duke hidin' behind a dung hill?"

There was laughter, and Elizabeth thought she heard them move away, but it was several seconds before she dared release her breath.

Full darkness came at last. Never in her life had Elizabeth been so weary, but she forced herself to stand. Marcus groaned. The air was cool, but his skin felt warm even though he shivered. She stripped off the purple cloak and spread it over him, leaving enough to make a pillow for his head. He sighed and appeared to sleep.

Elizabeth stepped carefully over the table and moved to the door, opening it a crack to see if there was anyone nearby. It was silent save for a few people wandering around in the general direction of the horse paddock. Perchance they were still trying to salvage something from the wreckage caused by the riot.

It was time for her to make a decision. She had to find some kind of conveyance to get the duke back to the castle. To take a public coach would be dangerous, and to buy a private carriage would be terribly expensive. Perhaps she could steal one. No, not unless she found a team already harnessed to a wagon . . . and that would be courting discovery.

Her most reasonable chance of escape lay in buying a wagon, but she had no money of her own. All she possessed was what she was wearing when she was kidnapped. That included the purple cloak, which was now soiled beyond hope, her small clothes, which had little value, and the necklace that had belonged to her mother. Her hand closed automatically around the ruby and pearl pendant that had been her sole link with the past. It was valuable, not extravagantly so, but for her the worth went far beyond monetary value. It was the one thing she had refused to give up. To lose it now was to cut all ties with her past.

The duke slept without moving. His face was so dear, but so frightfully pale. In truth, he meant more to her than anything else in the world, and she must do her best to return him to the castle.

Stepping outside, she closed the door softly behind her. To her left lay the scene of the riot from which they had so narrowly escaped; to the right was a number of small cottages. It occurred to her that perhaps she could get help from one of the villagers, but she had no idea whom to trust. She turned and followed a dirt path from the shed to another building a good distance away. As she approached she heard the sound of iron meeting iron. The blacksmith shop! Perhaps he would have a wagon for sale.

She looked down at the soiled yellow dress. It was unlikely that he would suspect she was of the nobility. Her face and arms were covered with enough grime to put an urchin to shame. But what would he think about the necklace? Would he assume she stole it? And if so, would he rouse the constable? She prayed that she could get through it without causing suspicion. If she were arrested, only Heaven knew what would happen to the duke. Although constables were supposed to enforce the law, they had to abide in the community. It might be easier for a constable to turn his back and let the crowd rule. She drew her lips into a firm line and picked her way down the path.

The smithy looked up when she entered. His hammer stopped for an instant as the iron he was pounding glowed yellow-white and then cooled to dull red. Motioning for a young boy to take over, the smithy wiped his hands on a dirty rag and came toward her.

"And what would the likes o' you be wantin' at this time o' night? If hit's money, you came to the wrong place. 'Tis the pub what caters to your kind o' woman."

"No. You misunderstand, sir. I came to purchase a wagon and team. I know that it would be easier to buy one at the stables, but my—husband is ill. He was injured in the riot this afternoon when our wagon overturned and was destroyed. Now I must find some kind of conveyance so that I can take him home."

He came close and studied her face. "Blimey. You're quality folk. And to think I mistook you for a hoor. Beggin' your pardon, ma'am, but hain't nothing going right these days. The fair comin' to town has upset the whole place, bringin' in all manner o' rabble and rioters. Hit's like the whole world's gone daft."

He stroked his chin, which was already streaked with dirt where rivulets of sweat had run down his face. "So you'll be needin' a wagon and team?" He turned and yelled at the boy who was still pounding the strip of iron. "Bend it easy there, Timmy, lest it break." Then turning again to Elizabeth, he motioned her outside. "Over there by the fence is a wagon what I took in trade for a gamey horse. It hain't much good, but then neither was the horse.

133

If you take it slow, the wheels could last a week, maybe two."

Elizabeth was appalled. "Is it the only one you have?"

"Indeed it is, miss."

She chewed the inside of her lip. "Very well. But what about a team? Do you have horses for sale?"

"Aye, ye're lucky there. I just bought a fine pair of geldings this afternoon." He took her around to the side of the barn where the pair of blacks nervously pawed the ground.

"Why, those belong to the duke!" she said before she could stop herself.

He cocked his head. "Indade. The driver who sold them to me had another pair, but he sold them to the stabler. He said the duke wanted to get shut o' them in a hurry."

"How much do you want for them?"

He named a figure.

Elizabeth gasped. "But that's entirely too much. I don't have enough money for them and the wagon, too."

He sighed. "Peers we been wastin' our time. Just 'ow much do ye have, miss?"

She slowly reached for the necklace. "All our funds were stolen when the riots started. I have this. Would you be willing to take it in trade for the horses, the wagon, and some blankets?"

He looked skeptical. "Hit's no business o' mine where you got it, but I could 'ang if it's stole and I get caught."

She sighed. "It isn't stolen. Before her demise it belonged to my mother, the Baroness of Wenndon. You were right. I am of the nobility, and I place my life in your hands by telling you this."

"Hit weren't no bloody secret, your ladyship. Your dirty dress can't hide yer foine ways. But don't fret. You've nought to fear from me." He shifted uncomfortably. "All right. The wagon and team is yours, and I'll see to hit that there's a pair o' rugs to soften the ride a mite."

134

He looked around the darkened yard. "And where be the likes o' your 'usband?"

"My—oh, my husband is resting yonder in a small shed. If you could harness the team to the wagon, I'll bring him around. We must leave tonight so that I can get him to a doctor as soon as possible." She lifted the chain from around her neck and handed the pendant to him, but he stepped back.

"Lady, if you have far to go, you'd best learn how to do business. Never give a man his due until 'e 'ands over the merchandise. 'Tis many a nob what's been cheated out of 'is share." He started toward the shed adjoining the smith. "I'll be harnessin' the team. You'd best go get your man an' bring him round back."

She nodded. "Thank you. Thank you most kindly."

Elizabeth was shivering uncontrollably by the time she found her way back to the narrow path that led to the shed where Marcus lay sleeping. The tall weeds along the path were covered with sticktights, which pierced through the fabric of her dress and petticoats until they rasped against her skin. The soft material of her slippers was caked with mud and filth, which she cared not to think about. Even so, she was grateful that she had been successful in finding a conveyance. Once they were on their way she would soon forget about the small discomforts.

She opened the door to the shed, and for a moment the intense darkness nearly overwhelmed her. "Marcus." She called again. "Marcus." But there was no answer. He must be sleeping more soundly than she had expected. Inching her way across the littered floor, she found the leg of the upturned table and bent down to shake him. But her hand encountered bare floor. Marcus was gone.

CHAPTER ELEVEN

Marcus gone? That couldn't be. Elizabeth searched franti-
cally, but there was no other place for him to hide in the
close confines of the small shed. Had someone discovered
him and spirited him away? The purple cloak lay in a heap
where Marcus had left it. She picked it up and fastened it
around her shoulders, but despite its welcome warmth,
she felt cold sweat trickle down at the back of her knees.
Dared she risk calling his name, or would that serve only
to bring the curious who might prove unfriendly?

Elizabeth ran out of the shed and cursed the fact that
she had no lantern to light up the darkness. "Marcus.
Marcus," she called softly. There was no answer.

Slowly retracing her pathway from the village, Elizabeth felt her heart contract with fear. There was no doubt
in her mind as to what the mood of the villagers would be,
considering the afternoon's events. The amount of damage
to their stalls, not to mention the severe injuries some of
the people had sustained, was enough to raise the ire of
even a friendly community.

She was about to start searching in another direction
when she saw the shadow of a tree move slightly. The hair
stood up at the back of her neck. Had someone been
following her . . . or was it Marcus? She whispered his
name, and the figure separated itself from the shadow.

"Where were you?" Marcus asked. "I woke up, and I
was all alone."

His voice sounded strange, but she didn't stop to question it. "Marcus. Thank God you're safe. Come." She tucked her hand under his arm. "I've found a wagon for us."

He laughed shakily. "I know this is a dream. A wagon, indeed."

"It's not a dream, Marcus, but we must hurry. In order to be safe we must put miles between us and this village before dawn."

"Nonsense. I don't choose to go. I am far too tired to attempt a journey before teatime."

She tried to see his face. He sounded far from normal, but she had to pierce that veil of fog that clouded his brain. "You will do as I say, Marcus. Now, come. There is no time to waste."

"Yes, Mother. Since you insist."

Elizabeth was taken aback, but time was slipping by too quickly for her to set him straight. He came toward her, his legs moving unsteadily, but with her shoulder to lean on he managed to walk quite evenly. As they approached the smithy she had second thoughts.

The blacksmith had been unexpectedly decent. Was it some kind of ploy to woo her into a state of complacency so that he could summon the constable? Her mouth felt dry. Dear God, did she dare take the chance of exposing Marcus to the danger? Yes. She had to. For now, at least, there was no other choice.

She heard voices as they approached. Marcus started to say something, but she put her hand over his mouth as she pulled him into the more intense darkness of the building. Two men stood beside the blacksmith as they engaged him in conversation, but it was impossible to determine what they were saying. How long they stood there she didn't know, but Marcus was growing restless. There was no sign that the team had been hitched to the wagon. The feeling

137

of dread had become a solid lump in the pit of her stomach.

Elizabeth feared that Marcus had about reached the limit of his endurance and that she would no longer be able to control him, when the two men finally took their leave. As soon as they were out of sight the blacksmith hastened around the corner of the smithy in the direction of the paddock. For an instant Elizabeth dared hope that all was going according to plan.

She looked at Marcus. He would have to go with her. She could not risk his straying away at a time like this.

"Listen to me, Marcus. You must be very quiet and not say a word until I tell you to. Do you understand?"

"I'm dizzy. It is as if the world is spinning around."

"Will you be silent?" she asked softly.

"If that is what you wish."

"Good. Then come with me while I talk to the blacksmith."

She hurried them past the open shed where the boy was pumping a pair of bellows over an open fire. He was so busy that he appeared not to notice them as they continued on around the corner.

They were in the barnyard area where the horses were kept while waiting to be shod. Beyond was the fence where the team should have been, but there was no sign of them. Suddenly she felt a hand on her shoulder and nearly screamed until she realized it was the blacksmith.

"Aye, there ye are, miss. I was afeared you'd been frightened off."

"Those men. Were they—"

"Lookin' for you? I can't rightly say, seein' as how I never took time to inquire yer name. They asked had I seen a man and woman, and I swore to as how I'd not."

She could sense his grin, and she allowed herself to smile. "You've been a good friend to me tonight. We shan't forget you. I give you my word on that."

138

"The team has been fed a ration of oats and is fair set to travel. I bid you and yer man a safe journey, my lady."

She lifted the necklace from around her neck and placed it in the cup of his hand. "Thank you. Perhaps we shall meet again one day."

"Hit ain't likely, your ladyship, seein's how we come from different sides o' the heap, but I wish you and your mister a safe journey. I put a bucket for water and a bag o' oats for the horses in the back o' the rig. You'll find a loaf o' bread and a slab of cheese under the seat. 'Tis a mite far to the next village."

He helped them into the wagon and told Elizabeth which way to go to get back on the right road. He was true to his word in that there was a pile of rugs on the floor of the wagon. On his suggestion Elizabeth made a bed for Marcus out of her purple cape and wrapped herself in one of the rugs to ward off the cold. She couldn't begin to guess what she looked like, but she knew that both from smell and appearance it would take someone a very close look indeed to realize that she was anything but a poor farm woman.

Finally they were on their way. For the most part the village was asleep. It had been a long and trying day for those who had arrived from the country for tomorrow's opening day of the fair. Fortunately for Elizabeth they were more concerned with bedding down for the night than they were with the passing of yet another wagon. Even so she breathed a grateful sigh once they had left the village behind.

Driving a team was new to her. She was quite an accomplished horsewoman and had, as a girl, frequently driven a dogcart, but this was her first attempt at pulling a wagon. It occurred to her that it was probably a good thing the team was tired. They were a spirited pair and might have been less easy to control had they not already been exhausted from the day's journey. She would have to stop after awhile to allow the horses to rest for the night, but for now it was important to put as much distance as possible between them and any chance of pursuit.

It bothered her that she might take the wrong road at some point during their journey. Marcus delighted in making sport of her penchant for getting lost, but this was one time she must keep her wits about her. The road was fairly straight, and she could tell from the wagon ruts which was the main road and which were simply side roads. Occasionally there would be a wooden sign nailed to a fence that pointed toward the next village. Elizabeth was grateful that she had remained awake when they had ridden in the carriage. As a result, most of the way was somewhat familiar.

Marcus slept fitfully. How different it could have been if he were himself, completely in command of the situation, sharing the seat next to her. Indeed, it would have been an adventure instead of a harrowing experience. She yearned to have someone share the responsibility if just for an hour, but it was on her shoulders, and only God knew just how long it would take them to get home.

The road was monotonous. More than once she started to nod off, and had it not been for the hard seat, which rubbed against her bones, she might indeed have fallen asleep. It must have been just after midnight when she saw a grove of trees alongside a stream near the road and decided to stop for the remainder of the night. The horses needed rest, and indeed, so did she. Marcus continued to sleep, and as soon as she tended to the horses she got back into the wagon and curled down beside him. He stirred slightly, then settled back against her. Even without touching his skin Elizabeth knew that he was feverish. His body through the layers of clothing was unnaturally warm. She closed her mind against the thought. It was all she could do at the moment to rest in preparation for the journey at dawn.

But sleep was as elusive as the night fog that drifted across the meadow to settle along the streambed. Elizabeth was ever conscious of Marcus's body so close to hers that she could feel his heartbeat. The wound had robbed him of the arrogance he usually wore. Indeed, he looked as vulnerable and sweet as a little boy. There were those times when he had imposed his will upon her that she had longed to see such a gentle expression on his lips, but she had been wrong. It was that very strength of character that had caused her to fall in love with him. For love it was. At first she had deemed it merely a wild fever of the blood, a need to make of herself the complete woman she longed to be, but she knew differently now. Her feelings for Marcus went far beyond the cravings of the flesh. She squeezed her eyes shut, as if by doing so she could put an end to the pictures in her mind. Sleep finally came in bits and pieces, punctuated by the night sounds so new to her ears.

At dawn she led the horses to the stream, and when they finished drinking, managed to again connect them to the tongue of the wagon. Her nails were split and broken by the time they were ready to go, but she felt a deep sense of satisfaction. She patted Marcus on the shoulder as he drifted between sleep and a state of half wakefulness.

"Didn't I tell you I could take care of us, my dearest?" she whispered, bending over to kiss the place just between his eyebrows. He didn't hear, of course, but the words had not been meant for his ears.

Elizabeth managed to bathe his wound, then in his lucid moments helped him drink a few swallows from the clear water of the stream. He refused the bread and cheese, which to her tasted exceedingly good. It worried Elizabeth that he seemed to be no better after his long rest. Perhaps sleep was the wrong thing. The thought nagged at her like a mosquito she could hear but was unable to swat, and she tried to push it out of her mind. There was nothing she could do for him now but get him home to the castle.

The hours dragged by as they rode mile after mile in the warming sun. She stopped again in the heat of the day to rest and water the horses, then pushed on. After long consideration, Elizabeth had determined that travel at night was too great a risk. There was always the question of being waylaid by highwaymen, but even the possibility of taking a wrong turn was too much to lay to chance.

Just after dusk she spied what appeared to be a deserted barn a short distance from the road, then managed to guide the horses into the barnyard, which was overgrown with tall weeds. One side of the structure had tumbled down, but there were enough remaining walls to hide them completely from view and protect them from the night damps. Marcus was awake at times, but he was out of touch with the present situation and was apparently unaware what had happened. She managed to get him to look after his physical needs and eat a small portion of cheese, but he soon drifted off into his state of waking sleep in his impromptu bed of moldy straw. Weary to the bone, Elizabeth unhitched the team from the wagon and led the horses into the barn. The risk was too great to leave them outside. If the horses ran away during the night, she would have lost her last hope of ever getting Marcus home.

The cheese was gone, and there was no more bread. She had hoped that they would find fruit along the way, but all the trees had been picked clean. Marcus stirred restlessly on his pallet of straw. It was no wonder. The straw had the odor of rats about it. But she had to rest. How much distance remained between here and the castle, she could not begin to guess. All she knew was that they were on the right road. They had to be.

As she sat down next to Marcus she felt him move toward her. At least he was responding to touch. It was

142

a small improvement and a welcome one even though his eyes remained closed.

They slept for a considerable period of time, nested together like spoons, his arm holding her against him, or her arm around him. Oddly she was content. They had come this far, surely it could not be much farther.

The sound of the horses snuffling in the straw awakened her. Marcus lay on his back, his hands tucked under his head for a pillow. His waistcoat was pulled up an inch or two, and Elizabeth spied the string from a money pouch protruding from the the waistband of his trousers.

Of course! Why hadn't she thought of it before. He would have money for the journey to London. With it she could buy enough food to see them through until they were home. She reached down to slip it out from under his belt, but in that moment he grabbed her wrist and held it in a bone-crushing grip.

"Marcus, please. You're hurting me. Let me go."

There was no recognition in his eyes as he pulled her down on the straw and held her there with the weight of his body.

"Thief, wanton." His voice was thick and slurred. "I'll teach you what we do to ladies who steal."

Elizabeth tried to push him away, but as ill as he was, she was no match for his strength. "Marcus, stop this. I only wanted to take some money to buy food. We shall be in desperate straights if we have to go another day without eating. The horses will die."

She could feel his passion begin to build. With his free hand he pulled at the neck of her gown until one shoulder lay bare to the breast. His voice came harshly from his throat, and he lowered his mouth to her cool skin. She shuddered as the heat of his fever scourged her throat. He was burning up. Was there no way to make him understand?

His hand slid down the length of her, exploring the soft

curves through the thin, dirt-caked fabric of her gown. He groaned as he pulled her even closer against him. For a moment the wild thought entered her mind that perhaps just this once she might surrender to—but no. She couldn't bring herself to do it no matter how much she needed him, wanted him . . . and the satisfaction his body could afford.

His hands became more demanding as his mouth searched the depth of hers, waiting for a response. It took all her will to deny the inner urgings of her desire, but as she lay inert beneath him, he reached for the buttons on her dress. Indeed, unless she were stronger than him, the moment was fast approaching when there might not be a choice at all.

At that moment Elizabeth heard footsteps coming toward the barn through the tall grass.

"Marcus," she whispered. "Someone is out there. We must be quiet." Apparently he understood, for he lifted his weight and leaned away. Elizabeth took the opportunity to crawl out from under him and made a hasty effort to repair the damage to her dress while she peeked out between the boards of the door.

It appeared to be a lone man, a farmer by the look of him, although it was difficult to tell in the dim light. He had gone over to look at the wagon. A moment later he came toward the barn, slowly, like an animal judging its prey.

Elizabeth was more frightened than she dared let Marcus know. She tried to make her voice sound normal. "Stay in here while I see what he wants."

Marcus looked at her, confusion in his eyes, but he remained on the ground where he lay.

Elizabeth extracted a few coins from the bag of money she had managed to take from Marcus during their scuffle and hid the rest inside the purple cloak. Then she opened the barn door and stepped outside, closing it behind her.

"Good day to you, sir. Are you the owner of this barn?"

The man grinned. "And just who might be wantin' to know?"

Elizabeth forced a smile. "I hope you will forgive me for taking advantage of your kindness. I was in need of shelter for the night."

He took stock of her trim figure and golden hair, which now spilled down over her shoulders. "Hit must be you're a mite cold in that thin dress you're wearin'. Ye look like ye could use a bit o' warmin' up."

"Thank you, but I am quite comfortable now that the sun has started to come up. Is there is village nearby where I can buy something to eat at a small cost? I have but a few coins."

"Sure, and we'll get you plenty to eat, little lady, but first we'll go inside the barn."

"I don't believe that will be necessary."

He came so close that she could smell his fetid breath. "Hit don't matter wot you think, 'cause after I get through wi' ye, there won't be no need to think."

"Don't touch me, or you'll regret it."

"And just what will you do?"

"I don't have to do anything. My husband will do it for me."

She noticed the faintest hesitation, then the man laughed. "Aye, and just where is this husband o' yourn?"

"In the barn. He has a pistol."

"If you 'ad a man and 'e had a pistol, there hain't no way 'e would o' sent you out 'ere." He pushed his way past her and shoved the barn door open.

Elizabeth's gaze flew to the pile of straw, but Marcus was nowhere to be seen. Had he gone out a rear window? She felt relieved that he was safe, but at the same time was possessed by an inevitable sense of desolation that she was left to face the intruder alone.

As the man lunged toward her, his hand snaking

145

around her wrist, Marcus loomed out of the shadows, brandishing a long piece of timber above his head.

"Let go of her or I'll kill you." His voice was low and threatening, so like its old self that Elizabeth's heart soared.

Marcus moved toward them, his gaze fixed on the man. "Get out of here and let us alone. We shall depart as soon as I get the horses hitched to the wagon."

The man swore profoundly as he backed out of the door. "You'll bloody well pay for your threats, or my name ain't Hiram Brown. Next time I comes back, me brothers will come along. Then we'll see what kind o' tune you likes to dance to." He walked quickly toward the wagon and, putting his shoulder to it, toppled it over on its side. The ancient wood splintered as the axle gave way with a snap, and Elizabeth felt her last vestige of hope disappear as the man took off at a run.

She turned to Marcus. "He'll be back, and with reinforcements, I fear."

Marcus was leaning against the door. The piece of lumber had slipped from his hands as if he had used his last ounce of strength. "Where are we?"

"We're returning to the castle. I have no idea how far it is. We've been traveling for more than a day." She looked at him in alarm. "You'd best sit down before you fall."

"Have we no weapon? Where is the coachman?"

"Gone. We have nothing, save the horses," she said as she shook out her cloak then put it on as she handed him his money pouch. "We'll have to take them and go. Can you manage to get astride?"

He nodded but didn't move.

"Come. I'll assist you. She helped him stand, then made a step of her hands laced together, bracing them against her knee. "Put your foot in my hands, then pull yourself up."

146

He gave her a scathing look, then by sheer force of will managed to haul himself aboard without her help.

But staying there was another concern. Motionless, he might be able to handle it, but if they were to attain any semblence of haste, he would surely fall off. Elizabeth decided that the only way to keep him astride was to ride behind him and hold on to him.

As quickly as she could she gathered their few possessions and placed them in the bucket, then made a loop of the reins from the other gelding and slipped them around her wrist. Later, if she found it impossible to manage the extra horse, she would have to let it go, but until then she needed the added security should the other horse chance to go lame.

Leading the horses out to the damaged wagon, Elizabeth prayed that Marcus could stay alert at least until they were away from immediate danger. She pulled her gown up to her knees, then climbed onto the overturned wagon. After a little coaxing, the horse came near enough for her to mount behind Marcus. It was a queer feeling, riding astride, and without benefit of saddle, but she managed to grip her knees against the horse's flanks and prod him into motion. The other gelding followed along after the first tug on the reins, and Elizabeth felt a tiny seed of hope begin to swell.

There was little she could do but point the horses in the right direction. It was next to impossible to see around Marcus's big frame. He was quiet, and she assumed he had drifted off again. Once he started to lean too far to the left, and she had to shake him.

"Wake up, Marcus. You cannot lie down until we have gone a few miles. The risk that we might be pursued is too great."

He made an effort to straighten but again drifted off to sleep.

Elizabeth urged the horses into an easy trot. It was

147

harder to keep Marcus upright, but it was worth it to gain the added time. It must have been two hours later, although it seemed like four, when she finally permitted them to stop to rest.

The horses foraged on the dry grasses despite the bits in their mouths, but there was nothing to take the edge off her own hunger save the cool water from the stream. It took awhile to find a step to assist her onto the horse, but she walked until they came to a stone fence and was able to mount so that they could resume the journey.

There were few wagons on the road and even fewer carriages. At one point a maroon-and-black mail coach loaded to the limit with passengers and baggage passed them going in the opposite direction. Had they been going the other way, Elizabeth would have considered hailing them, but it would have been difficult. Few coachmen would take the chance of stopping for fear that they were highwaymen in disguise.

As they rounded a slow sweeping curve that skirted a row of run-down-looking cottages, a pair of mangy-looking dogs charged out to meet them. At first Elizabeth was merely conscious of their approach, but as they came nearer she saw the wild killer look in their eyes. Prodding the horses into a gallop, she warned Marcus to hold on.

Their sound alone was enough to frighten a man to death. With lips drawn back to reveal yellowed fangs, they snarled and snapped at the horses' feet. One of them grabbed hold of the purple cloak, and Elizabeth felt herself slipping toward the ground. She screamed, more frightened that she had been at any point during the entire journey.

CHAPTER TWELVE

Elizabeth's scream woke Marcus out of his stupor. Grabbing the free end of the reins, he lashed out at the dogs, first one and then the other. Elizabeth pulled the gelding she was leading in closer so that it could not be attacked separately, and the dogs were caught between the horses. This, added to Marcus's furious onslaught, apparently served to frighten them, and they dropped back at once, then gave up the chase. It took considerable time to quiet the horses, but when Elizabeth slowed them to a walk, it appeared that neither of them was injured. She breathed a prayer of gratitude.

"Marcus, do you have any idea where we are?" she asked.

He ran his fingers through his hair and groaned. "Can't seem to sort things out. Muzzy-headed. Did someone put a potion in my glass of wine?"

"No, Marcus. You received a blow to the temple. Does your head hurt?"

He remained silent as if considering her statement, then shook his head. "No. It doesn't pain me, but there are times when I see double images, and other times when I lose touch with the present. I'm so dreadfully weary."

"I know, but we dare not stop just yet. If we can continue on until we come to a stream where we can water the horses, then we might afford the luxury of a brief rest."

He nodded as if he understood, but Elizabeth perceived

that he was still far from normal. Not once did he mention the fact that she was riding behind him and effectively holding him so that he would not fall. Under ordinary circumstances the duke would have been appalled at such an attempt to cater to his needs.

They continued on for perhaps an hour. When they passed through a small village, Elizabeth managed to buy oats for the horses with the money she had taken from Marcus's pouch. She also bought wine and some meat pastries, which she carried with them. Rather than delay too long in the village she decided to stop along the road to eat. There would be less chance of encountering trouble. A guarded inquiry elicited the information that they were just a few hours away from Heatherwood Castle.

Marcus was becoming increasingly more difficult to hold astride the horse. She had considered leaving him at an inn along the way, but although her conscience told her that he would be perfectly safe left in the care of an inn-keeper's wife, Elizabeth wanted him beside her. She wanted to be certain of his safety and not leave it to the ministrations of a stranger. But after another hour on horseback, she was beginning to regret her decision. He continually dozed off, causing him to lean forward until it required most of her strength to keep him from falling. Finally she gave in to his needs and guided the horses to an outcropping of rocks at the edge of the forest by the sea.

The sand looked warm and inviting. Once they had dismounted she tethered the horses to a tree, allowing them enough rein to graze, then spread her purple cloak on the sand. Marcus needed no second invitation to lie down. In truth, she was as weary as he. Every bone in her back and thighs ached from the unaccustomed ride, but the mental fatigue was even more enervating. Neither of them was capable of eating. They had gone so long with limited food that they were no longer hungry. She considered opening the wine but decided to save it for later when

150

she would have to rouse him for the final leg of their journey.

Marcus was already asleep when she curled up alongside him on the velvet cloak. The horses snuffled and moved contentedly just a few feet away while a flock of sea gulls, curious at the human intrusion, dipped and circled overhead in an aerial minuet danced to the unheard music of the soft sea breeze. Elizabeth yielded to an urge and brushed a kiss across Marcus's forehead, but unaware, he slept on. As she drifted off to sleep a smile played across her lips. If only Lady Louella could see what had become of her precious purple manteau, she would be horrified. Somehow that thought bothered Elizabeth not in the least.

Something was pulling at her dress. Her eyes flew open, but the sun had darkened behind a cloud and it took a moment for her to remember where she was. She blinked her eyes to clear them and in the same instant took stock of their surroundings. Marcus slept soundly, so close that she could see the dark smudges beneath his fringed lashes. All seemed well . . . but something had wakened her. Cautiously she started to rise. In that moment a sand crab scurried across her chest and buried itself beneath her shoulder.

Elizabeth screamed, and the frightened crab clamped its claw on the soft skin at the base of her neck. She screamed again, and Marcus was immediately alert.

"Wait. Don't try to pull it off. You will only make things worse." Carefully he grasped the crab and pried its claw apart, then flung it toward the water.

Elizabeth was sobbing hysterically as he reached out to comfort her, and she went into his arms like a sailor running before a storm. Marcus bent his head to the wound on her throat and put his mouth to it, drawing the blood to rid the wound of impurities. Then he spat on the ground.

151

"It was only a small cut. Let me cleanse it, while it is still open, with a few drops of wine."

She nodded her acquiescence. The wine burned unmercifully and tears rolled down her cheek, but she forced a smile. "I much prefer your first method of cleansing the wound."

His eyes burned darkly, and she could not determine if it was merely the fever . . . or fever of the blood. Replacing the cork in the bottle, he slowly laid it down as he moved toward her. Elizabeth lay back against the cloak, willing her heart to stop pounding, but it was soon forgotten as his face came down to meet hers and his arms enfolded her in a tender embrace. His mouth brushed her eyelids, her earlobes, her lips, and she felt her fears dissolve in the languorous warmth of his touch. It was a caress born less of passion than of their joy in being together and having shared the experiences of the last two days. Searching his face, she saw in his eyes the reflection of her love.

Elizabeth freed her hand from where she had knotted it in the hair at the back of his neck. The way Marcus was looking at her and the stirring in her thighs reminded her that they were alone and she was vulnerable to her desires. She traced her finger across the rough stubble of his new beard.

"I fear it is time we leave, Marcus."

"So soon? Could we not rest here for another hour? We are but a short ride from the castle."

Elizabeth smiled. "Indeed, that is all the more reason to make haste. Come. Let us be on our way before we are tempted to delay yet another night."

They set out soon afterward, and although Marcus had protested that he be allowed to take over the management of the horses, Elizabeth refused, and he was soon dozing while she struggled to hold him upright.

It was teatime when they finally arrived at the castle

152

gate. Elizabeth guided the horses toward the great bell, which was mounted by the arch, and gave a yank to the rope. A moment later a servant appeared and nearly fainted with shock.

"Saints above us, what has happened, your ladyship?" he said as he reached for the horses' heads. "Is that His Grace you've got there?"

"Yes. We ran into an angry mob, and His Grace was injured. Please summon a footman to help you assist the duke to bed."

"At once, your ladyship. At once."

Elizabeth slid down from the gelding's back and led the two horses to the entrance of the outer bailey. Marcus was beginning to waken, and she patted his knee.

"We're home at last, Your Grace." Unaccountably, Elizabeth was struck with shyness. While they were alone she had not hesitated to call him by his given name, but things had changed once again. They were on his land, and as before, she was an intruder.

He tried to focus his eyes on her face, but the effort was too much. He had summoned his last reserve of strength to comfort her as they lay on the beach.

Before Elizabeth was willing to turn herself over to the sheer luxury of being pampered, she made certain that someone was sent to fetch Arthur, who was taking the air with a village maid. Dr. Farragut, the village physician, was also summoned, but when Elizabeth suggested they wait awhile to inform Emily of the duke's injury, Mrs. Patchen agreed.

"Indeed, your ladyship. I think it is a wise decision, what with Miss Emily in the family way. The shock might cause her undue concern. Dr. Farragut will advise us if it is important she be told at once. From my experience with wounds of this sort, I perceive that once His Grace has rested sufficiently, he will soon recover."

She turned her attention to Elizabeth's disheveled ap-

pearance. "As for you, my lady, a hot soak would doubtless be most welcome. After that the doctor will want to
see you, and then you must retire to your bed for a long-
overdue rest."

Elizabeth allowed herself to be soothed by a quick bath
and a change of clothing before the doctor arrived, but
refused to permit him to examine her. As for Marcus, the
doctor agreed with Mrs. Patchen that what Marcus
needed was good, nourishing food and twenty-four hours
of uninterrupted sleep. The wound had begun to heal
rather well with no sign of infection.

Greta brought a cold collation of meats, cheeses, and
bread, along with a tureen of hot oxtail soup and a pot of
tea. She appeared in considerable awe of Elizabeth.

"Is it the God's truth that you saved 'Is Grace from a
mob 'o rioters?"

"I wouldn't go so far as to say that, Greta, but it is true
that we were caught in the middle of a mob, and the State
carriage was destroyed."

"And you've been all this time gettin' back . . . spendin'
the nights in a barn and the like?"

"Yes. I was afraid to trust anyone in the villages."

Greta's eyebrows raised and she smiled suggestively.
"And you an 'im were all alone . . . sleepin' in the 'ay an'
everythin'?"

"Those thoughts are not worthy of you, Greta. Kindly
refrain from such crude insinuations."

"Yes, my lady. I do beg your pardon."

To Elizabeth's surprise the girl looked appropriately
contrite.

Apparently she noted the expression on Elizabeth's
face, for she explained, "The vicar tells me that I 'ave a
sharp tongue and I should try to be more 'umble."

Elizabeth smiled. "Are you still having sessions with
the vicar?"

"Indeed, your ladyship. Every night. 'E's teachin' me to

154

act like a lady." She dropped a graceful curtsy. "Now, if you will excuse me, I must tend to me duties belowstairs."

She left with the dinner tray, and Elizabeth settled back against the down pillows, luxuriating in the feel of cool satin that smelled of lavender and attar of roses.

Her gaze wandered to the French doors and the faint tracery of treetops seen through the filmy curtains. If things had gone as planned, she would be in London now, looking out over the rooftops from her crowded bedchamber. The return trip had ceased to be the nightmare it had seemed at the time. Now that they were safely home, she saw the riot as a blessing in disguise. Was it the hand of providence that had seen fit to return her to the castle . . . with the man she loved? She squeezed her eyes shut. Better not to think of it now, because in her heart she knew that it was just a question of time until she would again have to set out for London, leaving all this . . . and Marcus . . . behind.

Without knowing it Elizabeth had slept the clock around. It was teatime when she awoke the next day. Greta, who was doing some mending in the sitting room, came into the bedchamber when she heard Elizabeth stir. There was a peculiar glint in her gaze.

"Faith. 'Ave you woken for good this time? Hit 'peared to me you'd spend the rest o' your life between the covers."

Elizabeth stretched and swung her legs over the side of the bed. "I feel like I've slept forever. Has Miss Emily been told about our return?"

"Indade, she'd been 'ere most of the day but took 'er leave about an hour ago. Sir Arthur saw 'er 'ome."

"Is she all right?"

Greta gave her a look. "If you can call bein' as big as a barn all right." She hummed a line of a folk tune, something Elizabeth considered completely unlike Greta, then

155

tried to make her voice sound casual. "Will you be wantin' to get up? 'Is Grace 'as been 'angin' outside yer door for the best part o' the day."

"The duke?" Elizabeth flushed at the stupidity of her remark. "Yes, of course I'll get up. Hurry. Lay out my clothing while I make my ablutions."

Greta tried to suppress a grin. "I 'spect you'll want the peach gown wi' the white lace?"

"That would be fine, thank you." Elizabeth knew that Greta considered this a special occasion. She was partial to the peach gown.

Marcus was standing at the end of the corridor, looking down over the garden maze, when Elizabeth left her room. He turned as he heard her footsteps, and her heart swelled with gratitude when she saw how well he looked.

She dropped a curtsy, and he answered with a low bow. "Good morning, Elizabeth. Or is it afternoon? I confess to losing all track of time since we left for London."

He reached for her hands as she approached and held them wide. "Our adventure must have agreed with you. I've never seen you look so lovely."

"I—thank you, Your Grace. I trust you are feeling well again?"

"Indeed, quite well, except for an occasional throbbing in my temple. Had it not been for your quick thought and unbelievable bravery, I daresay my fate would have been quite different."

She walked to the window to avoid his gaze, which she found most disconcerting. "I can't forget, Your Grace, that had it not been for having to escort me to London, you would not have been put in such a dangerous situation in the first place. I do most heartily regret having been the true cause of your discomfort."

"If we are placing blame, Elizabeth, we would have to go back much farther. Suffice it to say that we are victims of our destinies. You, however, chose to give fate a run for

156

her money—a fact for which I am grateful, since I would hate to pass on without having left an heir to Master Heatherwood. Please accept my gratitude. If there is anything you desire, all you have to do is call it by name and it is yours."

Elizabeth was more flustered than she had imagined she could be. "Please say no more. I do not seek a reward. Indeed, that we both arrived safely is reward enough, Your Grace."

He grasped the ends of his buff-colored waistcoat as if he was uncertain what to do with his hands. "Much of our journey is still lost in the haze of my illness, but I seem to recall that you did me the honor of calling me by my given name. If you would not consider it too presumptuous of me, I would be pleased if you were to continue to do so."

She nodded. "If you wish."

He held out his arm. "May I escort you downstairs, Elizabeth? I believe Mrs. Patchen has been keeping a veritable banquet of food hot on the sideboard in readiness for your awakening."

Elizabeth accepted his arm with considerable trepidation. This was a new side to Marcus she had not seen. In one respect it made her presence in the house more difficult. She had grown used to their verbal battles and knew how to deal with them, but a polite, gentle, considerate Marcus might be more than she could handle.

The footmen, standing smartly in their blue-and-gold livery, smiled up at the duke and Elizabeth as they descended the stairway, and to save herself, Elizabeth could not rid herself of the feeling that she belonged there as surely as if she were his wife. Once seated, the duke excused the footmen and butler from the dining room. As far as Elizabeth could guess, his reason could only be that he wished to speak confidentially.

She wasn't far wrong. He had no more than tasted his jellied salmon than he laid down his fork.

"I do not know quite how to approach this delicate subject, Elizabeth. Indeed, prior to our unsuccessful journey, I found it somewhat easier to talk to you, but I find myself in an awkward position."

Elizabeth felt her heart sink. It was apparent that he intended to waste no time in planning another trip to see that she was safely returned to London. She carefully placed her cup in the saucer and folded her hands in her lap.

"You need say no more, Your Grace. I understand perfectly and feel a degree of sympathy for your position. You refer to my return to London. I have decided to take the next available mail coach bound for the city. It was just short of ridiculous to force you to travel such a great distance simply for the purpose of seeing me home. I am perfectly capable of using commercial transport, assuming, of course, that you are willing to advance me the funds for the purchase of my fare."

He reached over and covered her hands with his. "Elizabeth, Elizabeth. Did you truly think that that was what concerned me? Alas . . . I have come to realize that Heatherwood would seem bleak indeed without your lovely face."

She caught her breath. "Surely you don't mean—"

"That you are to stay? Yes. If you are willing."

She was astounded. "I—I don't know—" She saw the look on his face, then quickly continued. "What I mean to say is that I am truly honored by your invitation and confess that to stay here would exceed my wildest dreams . . . but I wonder, Marcus. Would it be . . . socially correct?"

He threw his head back and laughed. "After what we have been through recently, I find it amusing that you would be concerned over mere social whims. Do you truly believe, Elizabeth, that anyone would question your living here under my protection?"

She winced as he spoke. "The word 'protection' sometimes implies a great deal, Marcus."

His face flamed. "Indeed. It was not my intention to suggest—"

She smiled at his confusion. "I know that, but will your people think otherwise; the servants here at Heatherwood and the farmers who work your land? I do not wish to put myself or you in a position that might be suspect."

"You surprise me, Elizabeth. Since you make it a habit to flaunt your independence, I find it something of a novelty that you are so concerned over local gossip." He ran his hand through his hair. "Suffice it to say that I will see to it that the vicar lets it be known that you are a respected guest here at the duchy . . . and nothing more."

Elizabeth raised her eyebrows. "Indeed? It was my impression from having spoken with the vicar that you have had very little to do with the church in the past."

"Be that as it may, but it is I who pay the man's salary. He will say what I tell him."

"Just how well do you know the Reverend Fleetwood? He said he was new to the village of Heatherford, but it was my feeling, young though he is, that the vicar is not a man to be ordered around."

"Never underestimate the power of my position, your ladyship. The reverend may be of the anointed, but he is still mortal and answerable to earthly influence. Until we, and not Polite Society, decide otherwise, you are to be considered a guest in this house and are free to come and go as you choose. I shall instruct my staff accordingly."

Elizabeth nodded. "Thank you, Marcus. For the present I accept your hospitality and will ever be indebted to you for your generosity."

He reached over and covered her hand, where it rested on the table. "Speak not of debts, Elizabeth. You hold the markers on my life. Nothing I own would equal in value the gratitude I feel toward you this day."

Her eyes met his steady gaze, and she felt a warmth spread over her that was unlike anything she had ever experienced. She felt safe, protected . . . and above all, happy.

As he continued to hold her eyes in his compelling gaze, he turned her hand palm upward and lifted it to his lips for the briefest caress. Then he curled her fingers over the place where his mouth had been. They were silent for a moment, each caught up in the skein of their own weaving. Finally he spoke.

"To get back to my original thought, there are things that I am sadly unable to remember about our unfortunate journey. I think perhaps it would be wise if you were to enlighten me."

"There is not a great deal to tell. We were being pelted with rotten fruit and—and other things by the crowd at the fair. A few rowdies began throwing stones, and one of them chanced to hit you in the head. You became dizzy, and I released the horses that stampeded, scattering the mob. We made our escape during that time."

"Yes. I remember most of that. Do go on."

She drew a deep breath. "We concealed ourselves for a time in a small shed behind the smithy. When darkness fell, I ventured forth and bargained with the blacksmith for the purchase of a wagon and the two remaining horses that he had purchased from, I would assume, your driver. The other horses were sold to the local stable master."

He nodded. "We shall have to make an effort to regain them. They are blooded horses from the finest stock." He motioned for her to go on.

"We owe a debt of gratitude to the blacksmith. He risked no small danger to himself in helping us escape. There were injuries during the stampede, perhaps even

160

deaths. The villagers would not have hesitated to extract similar justice."

"I shall see that he is repaid. But surely he did not give you the wagon and horses out of the goodness of his heart." His voice grew wary. "Just how did you pay the man for his services?"

Elizabeth felt reluctant to talk about the loss of her mother's necklace. The thought of it was too painful. She shrugged. "I exchanged a personal possession. What does it matter? I really prefer not to talk about it." She settled back in the chair. "Do you wish me to continue?"

He nodded.

"We traveled until I felt that we were a safe distance from the village, then we stopped in a grove of trees beside a stream. At daybreak we started out again, stopping periodically to rest the horses. We spent another night in a barn where we encountered a ruffian who destroyed our wagon. You were able to frighten him off, and we made our escape astride the horse, bringing the other gelding in tow. That is about all."

He tapped the table with the fingers of his right hand. "I suspect there is a great deal you are leaving out, but I won't press you at the moment. You should be resting."

"I couldn't possibly. But I would like to see Emily."

"She will join us for breakfast tomorrow. She wanted to see you before then, but we were hoping you would sleep much longer than you did."

"And Arthur?"

"I expect he will return before dinner. He took Emily home and doubtless stayed for tea. Is there anything else you would like to eat before we leave the table?"

"No, thank you." She smiled. "I fear I have more than compensated for the meals we missed on our journey."

He rang for the butler to clear the table, then turned again to Elizabeth. "Just how did we manage without food?"

"I bought cheese, bread, and a bottle of wine, and of course oats for the horses."

"You bought them?"

"Yes." Her face turned dark red at the memory. "I took some coins from your money pouch."

He smiled. "Then that must have been how you paid for the team and wagon."

"No. It was later, in the barn, when I took the money from your pouch."

He gave her a strange look and would have pursued the subject, but the butler entered with his tray, and they left the table.

Marcus took her arm and directed her toward his study. "I must have been far gone indeed for you to have been able to take my money belt. You seem a trifle embarrassed because you took the money, but you should have taken it all. There was precious little missing."

"You were not well, Marcus. You thought I was trying to steal from you."

"Dear Lord! I can't have been very gentle with you. Exactly what happened, Elizabeth?"

"I—" She paused as she remembered how close he had been to stripping her bare. "In truth, nothing untoward happened. You were interrupted by the ruffian who came upon us where we were concealed in the barn."

His eyes burned like coals as he grasped her shoulders and brought her around to face him. "Dear God, if I harmed you in any way, I'll never forgive myself."

"No harm came to me, Marcus."

"I must know this. Was it a dream or were we at one point lying on the sand . . . on the velvet cape."

"I—yes. For a time."

"And did I hold you in my arms?"

"Y-yes."

"And kiss you?"

She nodded.

"Were you angry?"

She shook her head.

His voice was low and vibrant. "I am most fervently glad it was not a dream."

Elizabeth caught her breath as his mouth came down over hers.

CHAPTER THIRTEEN

For all his strength the duke was unbelievably gentle, and yet his embrace left no doubt as to his virility. Elizabeth swayed against him as her arms twined themselves around his neck and her lips softened against the demands of his mouth.

"Elizabeth," he whispered. "Elizabeth."

Her name sounded special when he said it, but she would much rather to have done with words. Now that she had tasted his kisses, she could not get enough of them. But propriety made her pull back.

"Marcus, you must not."

"And indeed why not? Do not pretend that I am forcing you."

"The servants. They are sure to see us and misunderstand."

"How could they misunderstand? They will think that my blood cries out for you . . . as indeed it does."

"They will also think that I am a woman of little virtue . . . which I am not."

He let her go with obvious regret. "Forgive me. I did not mean to place you in a difficult position. It is only that I am attempting to reconcile my present feelings for you with the vague memories of our adventure. I fear they will continue to haunt me until I recapture them bit by bit. To be frank, after coming to know the brave woman you are, it distresses me that I treated you so badly before we set out for London."

"Say no more. What has gone before is not worthy of comment. We can begin again . . . can we not?"

"That is my most fervent desire." They had reached the door of the study, and Marcus motioned her to precede him. "Would you care for a glass of wine? Or perhaps you would like to join me. I am going to the South Wing to look for some papers that have been stored in the old library."

"May I? I have seen very little of the castle since my arrival and must confess that I am intrigued by the many rooms that I have yet to explore."

He offered her his arm. "It would be my pleasure to show them to you. Indeed, I would have offered before this, but Emily and Arthur make such a point of my over-fondness for the castle that I am reluctant to inflict it upon visitors."

Elizabeth placed her hand on his arm. "I can't imagine anyone not wanting to see it. The generations of memories accumulated here must fire the imagination."

"How true. As you can imagine, the castle was built as a fortification against invasion. The first Duke of Heatherford was a companion to Sir Francis Drake on his voyage to circumnavigate the world in 1577. He was later killed in the unsuccessful expedition against the Spanish West Indies."

They moved down the corridor past a series of glass cases set into the wall. "The armor displayed here also dates back to the reign of Queen Elizabeth. A bit farther on down you will see gowns that some of the Heatherford duchesses wore to the royal coronations."

He took her through a dozen or more unused rooms that contained relics from all corners of the earth, collected by the Clendennon family. They were a family whose influence reached from kingdom to kingdom, and the

165

things they left behind bore silent testimony to their power.

Marcus and Elizabeth came at last to the old library, the most remarkable room in the South Wing. It was not a large room, but it was a veritable museum of old books and rare, classical pottery dating back to the eighth century B.C. The magnificent Gothic ceiling, which boasted intricate Spanish paintings on carved wood, was as compelling as the hand-woven Chinese rug that Marcus said had originally belonged in a Venetian palace.

Elizabeth ran her fingers across the heavily embossed gold lettering of a Bible that reposed on a lectern. "What a truly beautiful example of the art of calligraphy. Is it from the Carolingian Dynasty?"

He nodded. "Yes. It goes back to the time of Charlemagne, who had all service books and classical documents rewritten in letters such as these."

Turning the fragile yellowed pages with reverence, she came to the end, where the names of the Clendennon family had been recorded. She looked up quickly. " 'Alicia Marie, dead of a broken heart at age seventeen.' Your sister?"

He nodded. "I fear that my mother took a bit of poetic license when she entered the account of my sister's death. Alicia was stricken with consumption. Doubtless that had more to do with her passing than her sadness over the loss of her beloved."

"What happened? Was he killed in battle?"

"Nothing so dramatic. He was a papist. His family refused them permission to marry unless she accepted the faith. She had been reared in the Church of England, as we all were, and asked to be relieved of her vow of loyalty to the church. When permission was refused because she would not completely disavow that loyalty, the betrothal was called back. A few weeks later she died."

"How terribly sad. What happened to her beau?"

"He married a young Catholic girl and gave her a houseful of children, then promptly took to the gaming tables to get away from them. My mother suffered the most. She had been close to Alicia, who was the eldest child, and she never quite recovered from her death."

"Was that when your mother left the church?"

He gave her a curious look. "Your powers of deduction are astounding. Yes, she forbade us to go to the services, although she made a special effort to continue to support its charities."

"I must confess that I had a clue. The Reverend Fleetwood suggested that something had happened to turn your family from the church. He also tried to enlist my services in convincing you to join the congregation on Sunday."

"And are you a regular churchgoer?"

"I was until I took up residence with my sister and the marquis. They did not choose to attend services, and it would have been awkward if I had insisted on going."

"Would it please you if we joined the villagers at the chapel on Sunday next?"

Elizabeth folded her arms across her waist and tucked them in her sleeves. "Yes. It would please me very much. In the short time I spent with Reverend Fleetwood I found him most personable. Did you know that he is attempting to convert our Greta?"

"Our Greta?" His voice reflected his astonishment.

Elizabeth misunderstood his surprise and thought he was questioning the word "our." "I beg your pardon, Marcus. It was not my intention to be presumptuous."

He looked at her for a moment, then smiled. "Do not apologize. She is, after all, your abigail for as long as you wish. I was simply nonplussed that anyone could presume to bring Greta into the fold."

Elizabeth smiled. "It does seem an unlikely feat, but I'll

warrant there has been a decided change in Greta since she has taken to visiting the rector."

"Any change would of necessity be an improvement. Very well, if it is your wish, we shall all attend services come next Sabbath."

Elizabeth reached out to touch his arm. "Please, Marcus. It wouldn't seem right if you agreed only to please me."

He covered her hand with his. "Suffice it to say that we have been far too negligent regarding the spiritual needs of the community. If, as you say, the new vicar is worth his salt, we might consider regular attendance at church to be quite in order."

Elizabeth closed the Bible and waited while he replaced the velvet dust cover then turned to look at her.

"Since you have an affinity for old books, perhaps you would like to see a copy of the Koran, which was scripted in 1659. If you will excuse me a moment, I'll fetch it from the storeroom."

While he was searching the shelves of a small room that opened off the old library, Elizabeth wandered back to look at a collection of crystal paperweights displayed in another case. At that moment Arthur burst into the room.

"Elizabeth! God's blood! I thought I'd never find you." He pulled her into his arms and held her against his chest. "When Emily and I heard what had happened, it was all we could do to keep from waking you, but the doctor said you needed rest." He held her at arm's length. "I should never have let you go off alone like that with Marcus. The nerve of him, stealing you away in the middle of the night. Indeed! He might be a great man in his duchy, but it takes a man of experience and wit to deal with the rabble."

"Arthur, please. You're crushing me." She managed a laugh as she pulled away from him, painfully aware that Marcus could hear what they were saying. "I appreciate the warm welcome, but you are so wrong about the riot.

168

No one could have stood fast against that mob without being in danger of losing his life. We were outnumbered twenty to one."

"I'd venture it was a profound lack of judgment to have gotten into such a situation in the first place. You could have been killed. I would never have put you in such a position."

Elizabeth had tried to quiet Arthur, but to no avail. At that moment Marcus made his presence known and there was no mistaking the fury written on his face.

"Enough! How dare you question my judgment? It amazes me, Arthur, that you continue to stay here, since you have so little respect for my ability to be in charge."

Arthur's face flamed. "Are you asking me to leave, Your Grace?"

"I would certainly not hinder you should you choose to depart. The matter is up to you."

Arthur's face drained of color save for a red splotch on either cheek. His voice was soft and thin as he faced Marcus. "I would not care to remain in the house simply through the grace of your sufferance." He drew himself up to full height and clicked his heels in military fashion. "Suffice it to say that I will quit the house before dinner."

Elizabeth was appalled. One moment the brothers had been the best of friends, and the next they were veritable enemies. To make it worse, she was caught in the middle. She stepped between them.

"Dear Heaven . . . can I indeed trust my ears? The two of you are acting like a pair of fighting roosters. Must you bare your verbal spurs without considering the outcome?"

. Marcus reached over and removed her hand from his sleeve. "Stay out of this, Lady Elizabeth. I can fight my own battles."

Elizabeth fought back the tears. "If you let him leave, Marcus, I'll never forgive you."

Marcus contemplated her face for an instant, then

looked at Arthur. "Stay, then, and be damned." Turning abruptly, he strode from the room.

Elizabeth looked up helplessly at Arthur, who studied her face with unusual intensity.

"My God, Elizabeth. You've gone and fallen in love with him."

She was unable to answer him, but apparently the expression in her eyes said it all. He put his arms around her and held her as a father holds a heartbroken child. His lips brushed her hair.

"It's all right, Elizabeth. Let me talk to him. I know I can make him see things for what they are."

She pulled away. "No, no, you mustn't. Please, Arthur, don't say a word to him about the way I feel."

"Very well. If you insist. But I think you are making a mistake. I know I could be of help."

"No. Marcus cares for me, of that I am certain, but the question is, how much does he care? If he should choose to offer for me, it must be of his own volition, not simply out of gratitude or because he was shamed into it."

He nodded. "The man would have to be out of his mind to lose a woman like you. He will doubtless have his temper under control by dinner time. You will be able to work it out with him, of that I am convinced."

"Thank you, Arthur. You're a true friend."

Elizabeth dressed for dinner with exceptional care that night. She carefully rehearsed the words she might say to effect a reconciliation between the two brothers. Admittedly she was concerned about the way Marcus felt about her, but above all, nothing, not even her love for the duke, could be permitted to drive a wedge between the two men. If necessary, she would leave Heatherwood before she would allow that to happen.

Greta was apparently puzzled by Elizabeth's inattention. "Be ye alright, your ladyship, or are you still muzzy-headed from your fright?"

"I'm fine, Greta. My thoughts were gathering wool. Did you ask something?"

"Indade. Will you be wearin' the pink lace tonight? Your face is as pale as a tub o' milk. You'll be needin' something to put some color in your cheeks."

"The pink lace will be fine."

Greta selected the gown from the armoire and laid it on the bed. She stood there for a moment as if contemplating what to say, then finally drew in a deep breath. "Would you consider it forward of me, your ladyship, were I to offer a circlet of pink asters to wear in your 'air? I made them up meself just after tea, so they're not likely to wilt on ye."

Elizabeth was touched. "How thoughtful. Thank you, Greta. It would be a true pleasure to wear them."

Greta went into the sitting room, where she had concealed the flowers in a drawer of the secretary. When she came back she seemed unusually shy and eager for approval as she handed the flowers to Elizabeth.

" 'Tis not much, your ladyship, but it's glad I am to 'ave you 'ome safe."

Elizabeth was about to protest that Heatherwood was not her home, but in truth, she had come to think of it as home. How sweet it was that others too felt that she belonged here. She took the coronet of flowers and held them to her cheek.

"How lovely, Greta, and how dear of you to do this for me. The fern that you have woven between the flowers adds the perfect touch."

"Aye." She studied the lace dress and the way it clung to the soft curve of Elizabeth's bosoms then fell straight to the floor to end in a demitrain. "I'll wager 'Is Grace will take more than a second look. 'Tis indade a step up from

171

the yellow checked rag you came 'ome in. If you hain't got 'im 'ooked yet, ye stand a good chance tonight."

Elizabeth gave her a look. "For a moment, Greta, I had begun to think you had reformed, but I see you haven't changed so much after all."

She had the grace to turn pink. "Chesley says that a chicken doesn't grow feathers overnight."

Elizabeth raised an eyebrow. "So it's Chesley now, is it? My, my. Have I missed something?"

Greta assumed an innocent look, but there was an underlying hint of something Elizabeth found hard to define. She confronted the girl.

"Greta, you didn't—you haven't actually gone through with your plan to seduce the vicar? I thought you were speaking in jest."

For a moment the girl's face clouded over, and suddenly she burst into tears. "I tried to, your ladyship," she wailed, "but 'e wanted no part of it. 'E said hit weren't right to seek the pleasures o' the flesh out of wedlock."

"And . . . ?"

Greta spread her arms in helpless gesture. "And nothing. Wot else is there? The likes 'o 'im hain't about to offer for the likes o' me."

She looked so distraught that Elizabeth held out her arms, and the girl went into them as naturally as if Elizabeth were her mother.

"Don't cry, child. It's heartbreaking, I know, but when the right man comes along, both of you will want the comfort of marriage. Don't despair. You're bound to find him before long."

Greta pulled away and dried her eyes. "Indade, that's wot I tell meself, but it didn't happen to you, and you've reached your majority."

"But we are different people. Marriage is less important to me than it is to you." Elizabeth nearly bit her lip over the lie. Marriage had become *very* important to her

172

. . . but in truth, it wasn't just marriage she wanted, it was the man; one man.

Elizabeth straightened in an effort to put the duke out of her mind. "Believe me, Greta. I am sorry about your sadness over the vicar. I suppose his attitude has brought an end to your meetings with him?"

"Oh, indade no, miss. Beggin' your permission, I was 'opin' to see 'im tonight if you can spare me for a toime."

"Are you sure you really want to? Won't you merely be rubbing salt into an open wound?"

Greta's face reflected her torment. "I can't 'elp meself, your ladyship, no more than you can leave the castle." She drew in a deep breath. "Besides, 'tis not courtin' I'm seeing 'im about. Chesley is giving me instructions for joining up wi' the church come Sunday."

Elizabeth took the girl's hands and held them in her own. "I'm so terribly proud of you, Greta. You *have* changed . . . and it's for the better. I'm not saying that nothing bad will ever happen to you once you've professed your faith, but it gives you something to lean on."

"Would you consider it forward of me, my lady, if I asked you to be there? I confess to being right edgy about the service."

"I'll be there, you can be assured of it. And thank you for asking me. Now I think I'd better go down to dinner before Cook decides to proceed without me."

As she descended the stairs Elizabeth touched the circlet of asters, which with Greta's assistance she had arranged around the smooth chignon from which descended a cluster of honey-blond curls. Such a thoughtful thing for the abigail to do, and so completely surprising from one who had been wholly concerned with her pursuit of finding a rich husband. Greta's mental attitude was maturing, a fortunate thing, since her voluptuous figure gave lie to her actual youth. She would need her wits about her if she were to evade the unprincipled men who would try to lift her skirts for a quick romp in the hay.

Elizabeth sighed. Her own sense of modesty had ruled with iron-bound rigidity since the day she had stopped being a child. Short of being taken by force, she had not questioned her ability to remain pure . . . until now. But dear Lord, if Marcus asked, could she refuse him? She closed her mind against the thought. For a while tonight they had been so close. She had seen the desire in his eyes . . . yes . . . and more. She was almost sure that she had seen the beginning of love. Or was it simply gratitude to her for having saved his life? He had changed so abruptly when Arthur entered the room. Could it have been jealousy? But why? Arthur meant nothing to her. Surely Marcus must know that. She sighed. No doubt they would have gotten over their little tiff by now and everything would set itself right at dinner. She'd see to that.

But Marcus didn't put in an appearance at the dinner table. Arthur was there, dressed with enough care to put Beau Brummell to shame, and he rose to greet Elizabeth with open arms.

"How smashing you look, Elizabeth. Marcus is a fool to miss this." Although she sought to conceal her expression, he apparently saw and understood. "I'm dreadfully sorry, my dear, but Marcus has chosen to remain in his chambers. We will dine alone tonight."

She tried to keep up a pleasant run of conversation, but it was almost beyond her ability. Feigning weariness, which was not altogether a lie, she begged off early with the promise of joining him and Emily for an early breakfast. Elizabeth was grateful that Greta had been promised time off to visit the vicar. This was one of those nights when she wanted nothing more than to be left alone.

The following morning Elizabeth had scarcely completed her ablutions and begun to dress before there was a tapping on the door to her chambers and Emily bounced in.

"Forgive me, Elizabeth. I simply could not delay a moment longer." She flew across the room despite her considerable weight and flung her arms around Elizabeth, who laughed in delight.

"Emily. Are you all right?" She grinned. "But of course you are. You look the picture of health. I was so worried lest the news of your brother's accident cause you undue concern."

"I was worried beyond belief about both of you and will certainly take Marcus to task for spiriting you away with such unforgivable secrecy."

"No. Please don't say anything about that. It is better that we ignore it. Marcus was in something of a mood last night. He and Arthur argued. I hope that we will be able to smooth things over."

"Marcus and Arthur always argue."

"But this seemed rather more than a casual difference of opinion."

"Aha. They argued over you, then."

Elizabeth's face flamed. "Not specifically, but I perceive that had it not been for me, there would have been little to have kept them from settling their differences. Marcus seems to think that the relationship between Arthur and me goes considerably beyond friendship."

"I confess to have wondered the same. It is not like Arthur to allow such a delectable piece as you to slip away from him."

"Don't underestimate Arthur. When one treats him as a gentleman, he acts the part. We are the best of friends, Arthur and I, despite our unfortunate beginning. But for all his worldly experience he is still a young man. Too young for me," she added with an impish grin.

Emily hugged Elizabeth, then held her at arm's length. "Good. Because I decided the first time I saw you that you were going to marry Marcus and become the next Duchess of Heatherford."

CHAPTER FOURTEEN

Elizabeth knew that her mouth was standing open in a most unladylike way, but there was little she could do about it. Emily grinned at her and nodded.

"Yes, darling. You heard aright. I've decided that you are the one I want to marry Marcus."

Elizabeth felt her face go red, and she turned away to stall for time. "Emily"—she laughed as her voice shook—"you are incurably outrageous."

"And I always get what I want. Marcus will vouch for that."

"I fear this is one time you shall be disappointed."

Emily put her arm over Elizabeth's shoulder. "And if I am, how would you feel?"

"What a ridiculous question!"

"Not at all. I'll ask it the other way around. How would you feel if Marcus were to offer for your hand?"

"Any woman would be proud and flattered. Surely you must know that?"

Emily smote her forehead with the palm of her hand. "Stop being deliberately obtuse. Do you love him or don't you?"

Elizabeth felt the tears begin to gather behind her eyes. "Please. I really don't want to discuss it. Can we not go down to breakfast?"

Emily nodded. "Of course. We don't need to talk about it, my dearest. I didn't know he meant quite that much to

177

you. Forgive me for prying, but I want the best for Marcus, and I think that means you."

They were silent as they went downstairs. Save for one of the servants who was watering a great hanging basket of ferns, Arthur was alone in the breakfast room. His face lighted as he saw Elizabeth and Emily.

"I say. What a picture the two of you make; Elizabeth slim as a reed, and Emily big as a hay barn."

Emily gave him a playful punch. "Behave yourself, Arthur, or I'll tell everyone about your latest paramour."

"Pray tell, how would you know which lady I am seeing?"

"I shan't divulge my sources, but if a certain Mr. B. heard about it, he would be obliged to call you out."

Arthur's eyes widened, and then, grinning, he recovered himself. "Oh, no, you don't. You can't trick me with pure conjecture."

"Whatever you say. Where's Marcus? I thought he'd be down by now."

There was an uncomfortable silence that Arthur finally broke. "I fear we had words before dinner last night. He dined in his room, and I haven't seen him this morning. I presume he intends to breakfast alone."

Emily heaved herself out of the chair. "Well, we shall see about that. If you will excuse me, I will return in a few minutes."

When they were alone, Arthur looked sympathetic. "Leave it to Em. She'll fix it up proper. As for me, I'll do my part to get the two of you together—" His face broke into a grin. "That is if you are absolutely determined to treat me like a brother."

Elizabeth gave him a look, and he reached over to pat her hand.

Emily was as good as her word. Moments later she breezed into the room with her hand tucked under Marcus's arm. There was no doubt that Marcus had come

178

against his will. His eyes were smoky blue, shaded by his dark brows, which drew together in the middle.

Arthur rose and bowed. "Splendid that you could join us, Marcus. We've been talking about the fact that you promised to take us sailboating."

Elizabeth looked up at him in surprise, but he ignored it and continued. "I say, tomorrow would be the perfect day, unless you aren't up to it yet. You do look a little peaked."

Marcus seated Emily, then took his own place at the head of the table. "Rubbish! I feel perfectly fit."

"Bloody marvelous! Would you prefer to go in the morning?"

"Actually, Arthur, I rather think that another time—"

"Then the afternoon. In truth, it would be better. The fog will have burned off by then. Does that sound pleasing to you, Elizabeth?"

"I—I don't know. I—"

Arthur stuck out his lip as he studied her. "You had something else planned?"

"No. Of course not. I simply feel it is an imposition."

Arthur tipped his chair back until it teetered on two legs. "Imposition indeed! I can't fathom any request of yours being an imposition. Can you, Marcus?"

"On that we agree." There was no missing the dryness in his voice, but Arthur chose to ignore it.

"Good. It's settled, then." He looked apologetically at Emily. "I don't suppose you would care to join us, old girl?"

Emily laughed. "Kindly watch your language. No, I think I'll wait at least untill my son is christened before I make a sailor of him. Otherwise he might be born at sea."

They all looked at her at the same time.

"No. Don't start imagining things. I'm not about to give birth. Doctor Farragut assures me there is yet another

179

month. That means I shall have to wear a gypsy tent to your birthday party, Arthur."

"You will doubtless start a new rage." He smiled. "Perhaps we should wait until after the child is born to celebrate my birthday."

"Nonsense. Mrs. Patchen has been working on the arrangements for weeks."

Marcus heaved a sigh. "Besides. Invitations have already been prepared and many of them have been sent out. The musicians have also been hired."

"I say." Arthur grinned. "It's going to be a proper rout. Even better than I could have hoped, since Elizabeth will be here to do us honor."

Elizabeth buttered a scone. "It sounds like a festive affair. Who are the guests to be?"

"Local people, for the most part," Marcus said.

"But don't expect it to be your usual country ball," Emily added. "Our family doesn't believe in separate ballrooms for the nobility and common folk. Those who partake of our hospitality must be willing to rub shoulders with the tenant farmer as well as the nob. It's not as much an extravagant party as it is a gathering of friends."

Elizabeth nodded. "I like that. While living with the marquis I saw enough of the ways of the beau monde to last a lifetime."

They talked for a while about the arrangements for the party, which was set for two weeks hence.

"Have you invited the vicar?" Elizabeth asked.

There was a small silence, then Marcus answered. "I haven't as yet, but I suppose we must."

Emily took his hand. "Oh, Marcus, I wish you would."

Elizabeth looked at Marcus. "Perhaps we could extend the invitation when we see him at church next Sunday."

Marcus turned dark red. "I have had time to think it over, and I would prefer to reconsider my offer to attend the service."

"Please don't say that. Greta is to be taken into the church that day and is counting on all of us to be there to bolster her courage."

Arthur nearly exploded as he tried to swallow a mouthful of hot coffee. "Don't expect me to be there. I haven't seen the inside of a church in over ten years."

Emily nodded. "We could have vouched for that, Arthur, without your having told us. However, since Elizabeth has asked that we be present, I don't see how you can refuse. Why, only moments ago you said that no request of hers could possibly be considered an imposition."

Marcus laughed. "Speared on his own sword! I'll wager it will be worth the trouble just to see Arthur squirm."

Even Arthur joined in the laughter, and they all breathed a little easier once Marcus lost his stiffness. Breakfast, which Elizabeth had dreaded, turned into something of a party all its own. It was late into the morning when Arthur offered to see Emily home. Elizabeth hoped that the time alone with Marcus would provide an opportunity to give new life to their friendship that had begun to blossom last night, only to wither when Arthur appeared. Unfortunately, once they were alone, Marcus bowed and begged to be excused.

Elizabeth rose and placed her hand on his arm. "Please, Marcus, I hope you don't feel obliged to take us sailing on the morrow simply on my account."

He stared for a moment at her hand on his sleeve, then moved aside casually. "I told you once before that it was no imposition to take you sailing. Besides, I had already planned to take the boat out tomorrow. Two more passengers will hardly matter that much. Of course, if you would rather not go, I would hope that you don't feel duty bound to accept the invitation."

There was a decided chill in his voice that did little to lift her spirits. The small hope that he might care for her was beginning to wilt from lack of warmth. She dropped a curtsy, then backed toward the doorway.

"It was my impression that the invitation was forced upon you. However, since you put it so bluntly, I would be pleased to go sailing."

She hoped for a softening in his manner, but he inclined his head without saying a word. Elizabeth, taking it as a dismissal, turned and went upstairs to her room.

Marcus secluded himself in his chambers for the rest of the day, but Arthur, after his return from seeing Emily safely home, sent word to Elizabeth that he wanted to show her the stables. Elizabeth made a special effort to be cheerful even though she would far rather have spent the afternoon alone. When tea and then the dinner hour arrived and Marcus still had not put in an appearance, she was glad for Arthur's company. More out of depression than fatigue she retired early to her chambers and stayed there until the following morning.

Arthur too felt the duke's prolonged absence from the family circle and commented upon it the next morning. Elizabeth was more than a little disturbed.

"I fear that it is mainly my fault that Marcus has chosen his own company rather than joining us at the table. In truth, as each day passes I find less justification for my remaining here."

"Nonsense. I'll grant you that Marcus has been in a dark mood at times, but much of the blame must fall upon me." He grinned. "Marcus and I get on well as brothers as long as I am at sea most of the year."

"Would it not be better to postpone the sailing trip until another time?"

"Indeed not. I'll wager that by teatime, when you return, the two of you will be on much better terms."

As soon as luncheon was over, Elizabeth went to her room to change for the boating excursion. She chose a dark-gray dress of heavy cotton with a wide white collar

182

embroidered with pink and lilac flowers. Mrs. Patchen had personally seen to the cleaning of the purple cloak, which Elizabeth knew must have required hours of painstaking work. She insisted that Elizabeth wear it instead of the lilac shawl to ward off the cool sea breezes. A gray bonnet with pink and lilac embroidery to match her dress would serve to keep her hair in place. A sunshade would doubtless be of little value on such an occasion. When she went downstairs, Marcus was already there. He bowed as she entered.

"I see you have brought your cloak. Wise. The wind at times becomes rather brisk."

"It was Mrs. Patchen's suggestion. I fear I know very little about sailing. In truth, although I eagerly anticipate the experience, I am a bit uneasy."

He smiled. "I find it exceedingly difficult to believe that anything could frighten you. The past month has seen you kidnapped, wandering alone at night on the cliffs outside the castle, and caught up in a riot that would have been the death of most men. Yet you seem to come through with little more than a few bruises."

It occurred to Elizabeth that all of her wounds were not visible. She was glad that he could not see the damage done to her heart.

"Without meaning to sound self-serving . . . I have become strong out of necessity. I have been told that it makes a woman less womanly to be able to take care of herself, but when my parents died, I learned that to survive one must take control of one's life. If I seem brave to you, it is only a facade."

"Be assured that no facade will be required today. The weather is perfect for sailing."

His words were encouraging despite the fact that there was no real warmth in his voice. He strode over to the window, and Elizabeth watched as, silhouetted against the light, he gazed out at the sky. He was dressed in a pair of

183

black fustian trousers and a black wool sweater that snugged in his waist then rose to wide shoulders, which were punctuated with iron-hard muscles. His hair was swept back from his face in deep black waves. She had never seen him look so masculine.

They both turned as Arthur came into the study. Marcus frowned.

"Not dressed yet? Or do you plan to wear that velvet jacket on the boat?"

"Hardly. The truth is, I fear you will have to go without me. I have an errand that cannot be put off."

Marcus swore quietly. "Confound, Arthur. You have an irritating way about you. Just what is so important that you find it necessary to leave at this precise moment?"

"A messenger has just brought word that the other two horses that were sold when the coach was destroyed have turned up at a stable over in Milfordshire. I plan to ride over there and lay claim to them."

"Indeed! But you can't go alone. I'm sure Elizabeth will consent to postponing our sail until another day."

"But of course."

"Nonsense. There is no need for you to go. I have already made arrangements for the stableboy to accompany me." Evidently he saw the look on Marcus's face. "Don't concern yourself, Marcus. I do not intend to resort to force . . . unless it is necessary. I expect to pay a reasonable price for the return of the animals." He started toward the door. "I'm off now. Have a pleasant sail." Once his back was turned toward Marcus he winked at Elizabeth and grinned. "I trust the two of you can manage without me?"

There was dead silence after he left. Elizabeth didn't know what to say. Should she suggest they wait until another day when Arthur could join them? No. She had given Marcus an opportunity to reclaim his invitation. Now it was up to him.

Apparently he was taken with the same indecision. He looked at her for a moment, then straightened. "It seems we have been deserted. If you can abide my company for another few hours, we might as well go down to the harbor."

It was with a heightened feeling of expectancy that she followed him to the small open carriage that would convey them down to the cove where the boat was berthed. Neither of them spoke, and Elizabeth wondered if he were as breathless with anticipation as she. Indeed, the only words he said were the few instructions he gave to the man at the docks as they were helped aboard the trim craft.

The boat had been readied in anticipation of their sail. As Marcus hoisted one of the smaller sheets the dockman let loose the bow line and waved them off. Elizabeth was seated comfortably in the stern next to Marcus, who manned the tiller. As the sail slowly filled, Marcus eased the tiller to the left, and the boat moved forward, slowly at first, and then with a surge of speed that nearly took her breath away.

She stole a glance at Marcus only to discover that he was watching her. She felt herself blush, then laughed to cover her embarrassment. "It's like racing with the wind. No wonder you love it."

He gazed at her in speculation, started to say something, then apparently changed his mind. It disturbed Elizabeth that he was so quiet. In truth, she hated idle chatter, but this was not a companionable silence. There was an awkwardness about it that drove her to invent things to fill the void. He managed to answer but just barely.

After they rounded the point where the town of Brixham was visible in the distance, the wind picked up, ballooning the sail with a jerk that caused the boat to heel over abruptly. Elizabeth looked at Marcus, but his attitude of nonchalance reassured her. He valued his own life whether or not he was concerned for hers.

Was he deliberately taking chances just to prove his skill? Elizabeth suspected that he was still smarting over what he considered to be Arthur's criticism of his inability to escort Elizabeth back safely to London. There was no doubt in her mind that he was envious of Arthur's military record and perhaps chagrined by his own comparatively safe life in the duchy and in London, when he sat in The House of Lords.

She longed to reassure him, to hold him in her arms as she had during their return home. She had seen his weakness, and he had turned to her for strength. But he was strong now. Could he, in truth, could any man forgive a woman for being witness to his failure, whether or not he was accountable for it? He would have to be strong indeed. Perhaps it was too much to expect.

The wind died as abruptly as it had begun, and the boat drifted slowly in the pattern of the current. Capricious, Elizabeth thought, and she sighed, likening her own circumstances to the whims of fate.

Marcus turned to her. "Are you weary of the sea?"

"Indeed not. At this moment I wish we need not return at all."

He looked surprised. "But you sighed. I thought perhaps—"

"I fear my mind was woolgathering." She dared a further comment. "I was thinking about the riot and your illness."

His face grew even more sober. "Indeed. It is much on my mind also. I regret to having failed you so miserably. Perhaps Arthur was right. I should not seek to undertake missions beyond my own small realm."

Elizabeth was appalled by his attitude of defeat. "Indeed! How can you permit yourself to grovel in self-pity? It is difficult for me to acquaint your present attitude with your former reputation, about which I have heard so much. No one doubts your courage. What must you do to prove your manhood to yourself? Do battle unarmed with a raging dragon? Spare me your maudlin mood, Your Grace. You are not Arthur, and for that we can all be grateful. As for myself, I much preferred your company when you were out of your head."

His eyes blazed dangerously as his mouth hardened into a thin line. Without removing his gaze from her face he lashed the tiller to hold their course. "You tempt fate, Elizabeth Cambridge. Do not bait me, for I have endured all I can this past day."

Despite herself she goaded him. "Your ills are of your own making, Your Grace. You need no enemies other than yourself."

He grabbed her wrists and held them iron-fast. "If that is true, then why do you play the villain by defying me? Why do you delight in turning my resolve into porridge?" He let her go and averted his face. "I swore I would see you returned to London before the month was out, but here you are, a gnat caught in my hair."

"Is it your wish that I leave?"

"Arthur and Emily would give me no peace if I permitted you to depart."

Her voice was dry. "That was hardly an answer."

When he faced her, his eyes reflected his turmoil. "Heaven protect me from independent women."

She saw the need in his eyes, the vulnerability of his mouth, the strength of his stubborn will, and she found she was wise in womanly ways. Reaching out to him, Elizabeth placed her hands on each side of his face.

"Yes, Marcus. Heaven protect you." As she leaned forward her eyes closed of their own volition and she kissed him slowly, deliberately on the warm curve of his mouth. He remained still, but she heard the soft intake of his breath as she brushed her lips back and forth against his.

187

Pulling away slightly, she dared a look. His eyes were closed, but a single vein throbbed near the still raw-looking scar on his temple. She bent his head and touched the vein with her lips.

His arms came around her, seeking the softness beneath the purple cloak, but gently, as if he were afraid to break the spell. She felt the warmth of his hands through the fabric of her gown, and her body responded with warmth of its own. His mouth came down on hers, cautiously at first but with a growing ardor that ignited the fires of her being. His kiss was long and complete. When he lifted his head, he stared at her face as if he wanted to memorize it.

"I remember now . . . the nights we spent together in the barn and along the stream. I wanted you so desperately that I would have given my life to have taken you then and there. It was fortunate for you that I was incapacitated."

She met his gaze and slowly shook her head. "I don't consider myself fortunate, Marcus."

She felt him tense. His voice was husky when he spoke. "What are you trying to say?"

"Surely you can guess."

"I would much prefer that you tell me lest I choose the wrong meaning."

"I'm not sure that I have the courage."

"I find that hard to believe. Perhaps you don't want me to know."

"Perhaps."

"But why, Elizabeth? Surely you can afford to speak the truth after all we have been through together. Just what were your feelings as we lay side by side in the hay barn?"

She took a deep breath, then lowered her eyes from his compelling gaze. "There was a time when you kissed me and tried to make love to me that it took all my willpower to refuse you. I wanted you, Marcus. I admit it."

This time when he kissed her there was no staying the

188

power that drove him to subdue her. His mouth covered hers with an urgency that demanded satisfaction. He kissed her with a wild ferocity mingled with compassion, but it left no doubt in her mind who was the master.

She met his challenge with a fury of her own, intent on giving him value for value. Never had she met a man who could so completely stir her senses with a kiss. She felt herself sink into a cotton-wool world where nothing mattered but the bruising power of his mouth.

As he paused for breath his mouth sought the hollow place at the base of her throat, and with a groan he pulled her tightly against him.

CHAPTER FIFTEEN

The boat held obediently to its course, but Elizabeth found that her heart was less than eager to obey the commands of her head. She knew that she should keep a steady hand on her desires lest they run away with her, but she was prone to savor the warmth of his embrace.

Suddenly Marcus pushed her away, not ungently. She slowly opened her eyes.

"What it it, Marcus? Is something wrong?"

"Indeed." He gestured to a merchantman that was tacking to gain purchase on the slight wind. "A few minutes more and we would have risked going afoul of the shipping lane. See what you do to me, Elizabeth? Your very presence causes me to take leave of my senses. I'm beginning to suspect that Arthur is right. I have lost my ability to judge a situation accurately. My every thought is tied to you."

He smiled as he said it, but Elizabeth detected a serious note in his voice. She eased back against the cushion as he took control of the tiller. It disturbed her that she could not read the expression on his face. There was no doubt in her mind that he yearned to possess her, but did his feelings lie deeper than that, or was he seeking only the satisfaction of the moment? She rested her hand along the taut lines as she watched him. He was not unlike the boat. The urgency of his body was under tight control. If he ever allowed those feelings to run free—She shuddered. How desperately she longed to be the one to unleash them!

He returned her gaze with a look so warm and melting that for a moment she thought he might have read her mind. Reaching toward her, he took her hand and curled it within his as he pressed it against his chest.

It was nearly teatime when they returned to the castle. They had been close to each other in the carriage, thighs touching, fingers entwined, shy glances through eyes warmed by desire. Elizabeth felt a glow that was beyond description. Marcus, too, appeared in a mellow mood.

Since it was just the two of them, they took tea informally in the library. It was one of the few times Elizabeth felt perfectly relaxed since they had returned to the castle. Marcus leaned back in his chair and placed his cup on a table as he squinted his eyes at the dust motes that danced in the dying sunlight.

"This has been a fine day, Elizabeth, and I thank you for it."

She looked at him in surprise. "It is I who should thank you, Marcus. It is easy to see how a man can fall in love with the sea and make her his mistress."

He turned his head sideways and looked at her. "And is that what you think I have done? Given up marriage for love of a boat?"

"Hardly. But I knew a man once who did."

"Your betrothed?"

She opened her eyes wide. "You know about James?"

He nodded. "Your abigail mentioned something about your having lost a loved one to the sea. I confess to having questioned her rather thoroughly. Does that distress you?"

"I—no, of course not. I am flattered by your interest."

"Indeed. And if I may ask . . . are you still in love with the man?"

Elizabeth was startled by the intensity of his voice. She

191

studied his face carefully. "No, Your Grace. I am no longer in love with James. I know now that he was simply an infatuation." She smiled. "But I doubt that you can understand the feelings of a young girl."

The duke stirred uncomfortably and reached for his cup to drink deeply before he responded. "Has it occurred to you that young girls are not so different from young boys?"

She shook her head. "No. The young boys I knew were interested in horse racing, bear baiting, fisticuffs, and playing at soldiering until they returned home from boarding school and were full-grown men. Then, of course, it was another story."

He smiled. "Ah, yes. Boarding school has a way of sharpening the appreciation for the fair sex." He rose and went to a dark laquered chest with Oriental designs inlaid in ivory, and opened a drawer. When he returned to the chair, he was carrying a rectangular wooden instrument of sorts.

His hands stroked it lovingly. "I haven't played this since my mother died. She used to listen to me play by the hour."

"It's a wind harp, isn't it? Will you play something for me?"

"It's called an aeolian harp." His fingers rippled across the strings in a delicately sweet melody. After awhile he settled down to a simple tune and began to sing in a deep, gentle voice filled with the pathos of longing:

"I stole my love from the city,
where the wretched sigh and weep.

I wed my love on the headlands,
In the heather, wild and sweet.

In the heather, wild and sweet, oh,

192

In the heather, wild and sweet.

I wed my love on the headlands,
In the heather, wild and sweet.

There were several verses, which he sang with a hint of sadness in his voice, but during the refrain his eyes lighted with mischief and his mouth turned up at the corners.

When he finished, he grinned boyishly. "I should leave this nonsense to Arthur. He is much more accomplished than I am at playing the harp."

Elizabeth returned his smile. "You are too modest, Marcus. I can hardly imagine Arthur singing such a tender ballad. His style would be more appropriate to a bawdy house or a gaming room, I would suspect. Will you play another tune?"

He agreed, and for the rest of the evening, until it was time to dress for dinner, they sang simple folk tunes and talked about operas they had seen at Covent Garden in London. To their surprise they discovered they had both seen Richard Sheridan's two great comedies *Goldsmith* and *She Stoops to Conquer* at the Drury Lane Theatre after it had been rebuilt following the fire in 1809. The coincidence made Elizabeth feel closer to him.

Her feet hardly touched the floor as she dressed for dinner that night. It was as if she and Marcus had reached an understanding of their feelings for each other. He made no move to continue the passionate kiss they had begun that afternoon on the boat, and she was grateful. Indeed, if they had gone beyond the point where they had stopped, she would not now be so much at ease with her feelings. In truth, there were moments when she yearned desperately to pass over the barrier that separated maid from matron, but once over, there was no return. She was not sure she could in good conscience accept the dishonor that went with bed before marriage. Still, if it were a question of losing him . . .

She forced the thought from her mind. She was a product of her upbringing. With God's help she would keep her virtue until such time as she was spoken for. It was all she had to give a man. Little enough, by some standards, but there were those who set great store in maidenly purity.

Greta came in to brush Elizabeth's hair and fasten her into her wine-colored velvet gown, which boasted a sweeping décolletage. The abigail's eyes opened wide as she saw the abundant curve of bosom swell over the top of the gown.

"Aye. 'Tis out for the prize ye are tonight, your ladyship."

"I'm sure I don't know what you mean, Greta."

Greta raised an eyebrow but said nothing. Elizabeth was vexed, more with her own ill-concealed attempt to please Marcus than with her maid's recognition of the fact. She stared at herself in the long Empire mirror, which reflected a less than subtle picture of seduction.

"Is it *that* obvious, Greta?"

Greta's face softened. "'Hit don't matter what you'll be wearin' miss, 'tis written on your face. You've the beddin' fever sure and certain."

"Don't be ridiculous. I'm simply dressing for dinner, and I don't choose to overdress, but at the same time I want to look fetching."

"Yes, ma'am."

Greta came over to stand beside her, and although Elizabeth tried to hide it, it was obvious that Greta had seen the tears gather in Elizabeth's eyes, because she patted a fold of the skirt in place and spoke soothingly to Elizabeth.

"His Grace is a good man, your ladyship. 'E's not the kind to dance the jig then run away when 'e's tired o' the music. You've nought to fear wi' 'im as your protector."

Elizabeth looked closely at the girl who was so young,

yet old in so many ways. "I don't know if I could settle for having a protector. Could you, Greta. Could you really?"

Greta smiled slowly. "I could have once, my lady . . . but things have changed. The vicar has taught me the value of my own body." She grinned suddenly. "Not in the coin of the realm, mind you. I always knew I could turn a pretty price once I gave a man 'is way wi' me. But Chesley says as 'ow the most precious coin is what you 'ave inside. Speakin' for meself . . . I plans to keep it safe for a while." She shrugged, shifting with a sly grin from woman to child. "Besides, hit's nice knowin' hit's always there for a rainy day in case the right man comes along."

Elizabeth threw her head back and laughed. "You are truly intractable, Greta. There are times when I think you've completely reformed, then you turn right back into a little minx."

Greta grinned. "Chesley says I'm an angel in satan's clothes. But he says the angel is winning. And once I'm taken into the Church, Satan won't have a prayer o' gettin' 'is way."

"And do you truly believe that?"

"Not entirely, miss, but I'm workin' at it, and I'd trust the vicar wi' me very soul."

As Elizabeth walked down the stairs to dinner she considered the fact that except for her mother, she had never been so close to another woman as she was to Greta. The girls at school had shared their secrets with her, but she had always been the listener. No one had ever been able to see into her heart the way Greta could.

Reaching the foot of the stairs, she smiled at her reflection in the gilded mirror which hung between two ornate tapestries. A white shawl lay across her bosom, fastened at one side with a pink silk flower. The effect was more regal than seductive. She was pleased with the results

. . . but sighed for want of what might have been, had she left the shawl behind.

The footman told her that Marcus was waiting for her in the Assembly Room. She raised an eyebrow as she turned in that direction. Mrs. Patchen had said that the family used the Assembly Room for before-dinner drinks only on special occasions, more often preferring the comfort of the salon or library. Was he expecting guests? She waited while the footman opened the door and announced her.

Marcus rose and bowed in response to her curtsy. As the footman closed the door behind her Elizabeth noted with no little pleasure that she and Marcus were quite alone. He was wearing a soft-looking beige doeskin waistcoat and trousers. His high starcher was reddish-brown, ending in a cascade of ruffles that were secured with a diamond stickpin. Elegant indeed. It occurred to her that he too had taken the trouble to dress. He seated her in a chair and poured a glass of sherry, which he handed to her. As their fingers touched they looked at each other, and their gaze was an open admission of their feelings.

He stepped back and lifted his glass. "To what shall we drink?"

She smiled over the rim of her glass as she sniffed the fragrance. "There is always the King."

"Must we waste this moment on a madman?"

"You would prefer the Prince Regent?"

"What I would prefer is to drink to . . . life."

Elizabeth nodded to cover her disappointment as she touched her glass to her lips. She could have sworn he was going to say "to us." If so, why had he changed his mind? As he turned to pick up a book she caught a reflection of herself in the silver samovar. It was that infernal shawl. It made her look matronly. Should she have gone against her own judgment and left her bosom less concealed? He spoke, and she tried to erase the frown that creased her forehead but not soon enough.

"You look perturbed, Elizabeth. Is something wrong?"

"No, Marcus. I—" She put the glass down and spread her hands in a helpless gesture.

"Then let me propose another toast. To *your* life . . . and to *your* happiness. May you have everything that is good and beautiful."

"Thank you. That's very kind." As she studied his face she mused to herself that *he* was good . . . and beautiful. The thought brought the color to her cheeks, and she had to rise and walk away to keep him from seeing. Dinner was announced before she succeeded in making a fool of herself.

They were served in the refectory, another indication that the night was meant to be special. Between courses of fish Elizabeth gazed at the enormous Gothic fireplace, which dated back to the fifteenth century, and the ornate carvings and Flemish tapestries, which covered the walls on either side of the polished teak table, which could easily have seated two dozen guests. Massive glass and silver sanctuary lamps from Genoa were suspended from the wood and fresco ceiling.

Elizabeth sighed in wonder. "This surely must be one of the most beautiful rooms in the castle."

"I'm pleased that you like it. There is much of historical value in this room. The tapestries on the wall that faces you were created from designs by Peter Paul Rubens back in 1620." He pointed to a large water vessel that stood in the corner of the room. The wide mouth, cylindrical handles, and sturdy base were of black glaze, which highlighted the panel of figures banding the vase in the natural color of terra-cotta. "The Amphora is a fine example of some of our Grecian ware, which we know dates back at least to fifteen hundred."

"Does it not concern you that it might be broken?"

197

He shrugged. "If I put away everything of value, there would be nothing left with which to furnish the rooms. Treasures are meant to be used, otherwise what good are they?"

"I admire your point of view. The silverware alone is worth a king's ransom."

He laid down his fork in disgust. "Speaking of silverware, I hope yours is in better condition than mine. I must confer with Mrs. Patchen. It seems the kitchen help is not doing its work. I noticed also that there was dust on the sideboard this morning."

He rang the bell, and the butler appeared a bit more slowly than usual.

"Yes, Your Grace? May I serve you?"

"Indeed, Thomas, but this time with clean silver. I'd like a word with Mrs. Patchen. Would you send her to me, please?"

"The silver is my fault, Your Grace. As to Mrs. Patchen —" He shifted his weight from one foot to the other. "Begging your pardon, Your Grace, but Mrs. Patchen is feeling poorly and has taken to her bed."

"Indeed? Why wasn't I told?"

"She wouldn't permit it, Your Grace. It was her intention to rest for only a moment before she returned to her duties, but it's fair worn out she is, what with the fixings for Sir Arthur's party."

"Have you sent for the doctor?"

"Oh, no, Your Grace. Mrs. Patchen would never permit it."

"Well, I'm afraid that I insist. Please do so at once."

"Thank you, Your Grace. I regret not having told you before."

"Please inform Mrs. Patchen that I will be up to see her within the hour if she is well enough to receive me."

"Yes, Your Grace. At once."

When the butler had gone, Marcus leaned his elbows on

198

the table and rested his chin on his hand. "I fear we have a problem."

Elizabeth frowned. "Indeed? Do you think she is gravely ill?"

"She must be, or she never would have taken to bed. I am deeply troubled about her. She is alone in the world and has little to bring her joy. To add to her problem we have the party for Arthur, which is set for less than a week hence. It is too late to inform all of the guests that the party must be postponed."

Elizabeth sat up straight. "But why must it be postponed?"

"You jest. Do you have any idea how much remains to be done? There is food to be prepared for two hundred guests, and rooms to be readied for another twenty who will remain overnight."

"But the servants—"

"The servants work well, but only when they are supervised in everything they do. Suffice it to say that that is the reason Mrs. Patchen broke under the work. She is not young anymore. It was thoughtless of me to expect her to do the extra work."

"But I could do it in her place."

She saw the corners of his eyes wrinkle even though he managed to suppress his laughter. His lack of confidence in her ability irritated her.

"It may surprise you, Marcus, but I am not completely without womanly skills. For some time I saw to the management of the marquis's mansion in London."

"Be that as it may. I could not permit you to undertake such mundane labor."

"More than once I have said that I detest idleness. If I remember correctly, it was you, just moments ago, who said that you liked to make use of your treasures rather than store them away."

Elizabeth heard him draw in a sharp breath, then he fastened her with his gaze.

"Am I then to consider you one of my treasures?"

Her lashes fluttered, and she was unable to look at him as she carefully selected her words. "I would hardly consider myself a treasure, Your Grace. Suffice it to say that I am at your service, no matter what the task may be."

He rose from the table and came around to stand beside her chair. She dared not breathe as he bent down and put his hands on either side of her face, tilting it up to meet his.

"Never let it be said, Elizabeth, my sweet, that you are without womanly skills. You have the courage and determination of a hundred men, but your feminine appeal is enough to tempt the most hardy."

She slowly let out her breath as he pulled her up to face him. "Then you agree that the party will go on as planned?"

"If that is your wish."

"It is . . . one of them, Your Grace."

"Indeed? And the others?"

She was suddenly left without words. Her face flamed, and she heard him chuckle deep in his throat as he crushed her against his chest.

"As God is my witness, Elizabeth, I cannot face another night without you. Tell me that you want me, too."

But he gave her no chance to respond, because his mouth came down over hers in a kiss that ached with longing. It was only her fear that the servants would venture into the room to clear away their plates that kept Elizabeth from fully responding to his caresses. But the ardor she returned was apparently enough for him, because he seemed unaware that she was holding back.

His mouth traced the line of her eyebrows, and she felt the flick of his tongue as he smoothed them into softly curving arches, then moved on to her temple, where the warmth of his breath fluttered her hair.

Of their own volition her arms wound themselves around his neck. She squeezed her eyes tightly as if to ward off her need to excite him with her touch, to tangle her fingers in his hair, and hold his mouth firmly against hers.

Was it so insane to court danger without regard for the consequences? Surely it couldn't be wrong to yield to the hunger that cried out between them.

Greta's face swam before her closed eyelids, smiling, laughing over the game called love. If she yielded to her heart, she would lose in the end. She had to hold back.

But as it turned out the decision was made for her as the doors were flung open and Arthur strode into the room. He didn't appear to see them at first, and by the time his eyes adjusted to the light, Marcus and Elizabeth had separated from each other.

Arthur sprawled into a chair, his legs stretched out in front of him.

"God's blood, what a journey. 'Tis fortunate indeed that I took an extra mount, because I fair rode mine into the ground."

He finally managed to look at them. "I say . . . you don't look overjoyed to see me. Perhaps I should have bathed first, but I wanted to tell you the news. I succeeded in buying back the team, Marcus, and for less than half what I expected to pay."

"Fine. I shall, of course, reimburse you."

"That's hardly necessary." He sounded bewildered, and understandably so, Elizabeth thought. Marcus was less than gracious.

Marcus bowed. "I insist. But for now I suggest you repair the ravages of your ride. I will see that there is hot food on the table when you have finished."

Seeing Arthur's disappointment, Elizabeth spoke. "It's

good to have you back, Arthur, but you must be dreadfully weary to have made the journey in a day's time."

"Yes. More tired than I thought. Please excuse me."

After he had gone, Marcus turned to Elizabeth. His voice was controlled, but there was a coldness in his gaze that chilled her to the bone.

"Apparently, Elizabeth, you are overjoyed to have him back."

CHAPTER SIXTEEN

Elizabeth studied Marcus's face. "Indeed, I am pleased at Arthur's return. Can you not say the same?"

"Of course. But in truth, he has been gone but a few hours."

"It was not the time involved that concerned me, but rather the prospect of danger."

"Yes. It was not my intention to sound unfeeling. It was a question of his unfortunate timing. Arthur took me by surprise."

Elizabeth put her hand on his arm and smiled up into his eyes. "Perhaps his timing was less unfortunate than we are willing to admit. We must learn to keep our feelings in check, Your Grace, lest we become a scandal."

"As long as there are castles there will be scandals, Elizabeth, whether or not they are founded on fact."

"Granted, but I do not wish to be the one to provide that evidence, not only out of respect for your position, but for my own reputation as well. Now, if you will excuse me, I would like to begin setting my plans in order for the party."

He reached for her hands. "And if I choose not to bid you leave but order you to remain?"

"You would not do such a thing." There was a flash of spirit in her eyes, and she reached up to brush a kiss across his mouth. "But if you did, I would be forced to leave, even though I'd much prefer to stay. You do not own me, Marcus. I belong only to myself."

For a moment she thought he would reach out to grasp her, but she retreated in haste, dropping a curtsy as she turned at the door. He remained speechless, but she saw irritation mixed with grudging respect in his smile as he bowed low.

Before Elizabeth retired for the night she climbed the stairs to the servants' quarters to see Mrs. Patchen. The woman looked more fragile than ever, and her voice was barely above a whisper.

"I do beg your forgiveness, my lady. It is unlike me to be stricken to the point where I cannot perform my duties."

Once more Elizabeth was struck by the woman's obviously gentle breeding. "Please put it from your mind, Mrs. Patchen. I know His Grace is concerned only with your well-being."

"But the party for Sir Arthur. So much remains to be done. I fear it shall have to be postponed."

"It will go on as planned. What work is left to be completed will either be left unfinished or I will do it myself."

"Oh, Lady Elizabeth! Surely you can't—"

"But I can. Now, let's hear no more about it. I will ask Thomas for his help." Elizabeth reached for a small family portrait that was sitting on the bedside table. "What a lovely family. Were you in their employ, if I may ask?"

"No, my lady."

Elizabeth looked more closely. "Why, indeed! This is a picture of you, is it not? Is it possible that you are of noble birth?"

"Yes, Lady Elizabeth, although I had not intended it to be known. My parents have been gone for many years, and my sister and I were left penniless. We were separated by the church, which found positions for us. Unfortunately they considered her a bad influence on me and forbade our first employers to disclose our whereabouts. I haven't heard of her since that day."

"And is it your wish to see her?"

"Indeed, it is my most fervent wish to see her before I die."

Elizabeth was appalled. "Please, Mrs. Patchen. Speak not of dying! According to Thomas, the doctor has told His Grace that you suffer from exhaustion compounded by a congestion of the lungs. Plenty of rest and good food will see you feeling well within days."

The housekeeper smiled. "Dear lady, I am not afraid of dying, but I would much prefer to live, and I shall do my best to recover."

"Then you must begin by clearing your mind of thoughts about your housekeeping duties. I will do what I can to take over your work."

They talked for a while about their similar pasts. Mrs Patchen had chosen to go into servitude rather than accept the protection of a man who chose not to marry her. Elizabeth learned that the Patchen home, which had been in Dorset, now belonged to the widow of a wealthy importer of fine silks from China. Beyond that, the woman knew nothing.

Elizabeth liked and respected the elderly housekeeper, and along with the quantity of work to be done before the party, the woman's welfare was much on her mind. She spoke to the duke about it the next morning, telling him about the missing sister and how much Mrs. Patchen would like to see her. Although Marcus seemed mildly interested, his mind was obviously elsewhere.

"Yes, indeed. A great tragedy, I'm sure." He put his hand on Elizabeth's arm. "There's something I want to tell you."

She looked up, unable to conceal the apprehension in her eyes.

He smiled. "Do not look so distraught, Elizabeth. I only wanted you to know that I would be gone for a while on business."

"Oh. I see." She tried to keep the disappointment from her voice. "But surely you will return in time for Arthur's party."

"I will indeed. At most, I should be away for two days."

She slowly let out her breath. "Even two days can seem like a very long time, Marcus, but I feared it would be longer. Will you leave soon?"

"Yes. At once. Say you will miss me, Elizabeth."

"I doubt that it would be wise to let you know just how much." She feasted her eyes on his face, trying to read his thoughts, and what she saw there satisfied her. "I wish you a safe journey, Your Grace."

He pulled her into the crook of his arm and walked her into the grand entrance hall, where Thomas waited with a valise and Marcus's riding cloak.

He bowed. "The carriage is waiting, Your Grace. I bid you Godspeed."

Marcus thanked him, then turned to Elizabeth. Bending down, he brushed his lips against her forehead. "Watch over Emily for me, will you? I shall return as soon as possible."

Elizabeth knew her eyes were filled with tears, and she blinked rapidly. "Keep safe, Marcus."

He bowed, shrugged into the cloak, and took his leave. It occurred to Elizabeth that he had left rather abruptly. Was it to avoid showing his emotions? She had the feeling that he hated to leave almost as much as she regretted seeing him go.

Fortunately there was enough to do to keep her busy for the next two days. Most of her time was spent either in the

206

kitchen seeing to the advance preparation of food for the festivities or with Thomas, who marshaled his troops to turn out the rooms for the guests.

Emily came by on the afternoon of the first day and did her share to keep the servants from loitering. For the most part they were getting into the party spirit. It had been years since the halls of the castle had echoed with so much activity.

Emily found Elizabeth taking stock of the wines in the cellar and managed to persuade her to stop long enough for a cup of tea.

"Sweet saints, Elizabeth. You are beginning to act like a scullery maid, with all your hustle and bustle. Do sit back and relax."

Elizabeth's hands flew to her hair, which was tucked inside a plain white mobcap. "Oh, my. Do I look that disheveled?"

Emily grinned. "You could never look anything but beautiful. I only said you were acting like a scullery maid." She pushed her chair away from the table to allow additional room for her swollen abdomen. "Have you thought about putting up the banners in the refectory?"

"Banners? I don't know what you mean."

"The silk Palio festival banners from Siena. They used to be hung above the tapestries on either side of the dining tables that were set with the food." Her eyes sparkled with delight. "Any proper castle should have them displayed for a major celebration such as a son's twenty-first birthday. Besides, Marcus would be thrilled. He used to adore them when he was a child."

"Splendid. I will see to it that they are displayed, assuming someone knows where to find them."

"Finding them is one thing I can manage to do. As to hanging them, I'll ask one of the grounds keepers. Thomas would order me from the house if I added another task to his list." Emily added a dollop of cream to her tea and

207

sipped it slowly. "Speaking of my brother. When are you expecting Marcus to arrive home?"

"Tomorrow. He said he would be gone two days at the most."

"What kind of business could take him away at a time like this?"

"I really don't know, Emily, but it seemed rather urgent."

Emily shrugged. "If it were Arthur, I'd know it was a woman, but at least we need not concern ourselves on that score, not with you living in the castle."

"Don't assume too much, Emily."

"Do I have your permission to hope?"

Elizabeth gave her a look. "I think it is time we speak on another subject. Have you seen Arthur today?"

"I passed him in the lane. He said you had banished him from the house and he was going to seek solace from a more understanding lady."

"I can at least vouch for the first part. As for the second, I would be indeed surprised if it were not true."

"Indeed. I wonder if that was what the Royal Navy had in mind when they sent him home to recover from his wounds."

They laughed together over the foibles of men, then Elizabeth begged to be allowed to return to her duties. She stopped in several times during the day to check on Mrs. Patchen, who more often than not was sleeping. The doctor assured Elizabeth that sleep was the best medicine for the aging woman.

When nighttime came, Elizabeth retired to her room with a feeling of gratitude mixed with pride in her accomplishments. Tired as she was, her heart danced with the knowledge that Marcus would return on the morrow.

It was late afternoon when from an upstairs bedchamber she spied a carriage approaching up the hill. There was no doubt in her mind that it was Marcus. The carriage was new, and the Clendennon crest was emblazoned on its side.

She flew to her room and slipped into a fresh gown. While Greta saw to the fasteners Elizabeth pulled the mobcap from her hair and combed it into place. There was no need to pinch fresh color into her cheeks. The need to see him, to hold him, sent blood rushing through her veins.

She had just reached the top of the stairs when the row of footmen assembled in the grand entrance hall to receive the carriage, and Thomas opened the massive door. But it was not Marcus alone who entered. Preceding him through the doorway was an attractive woman dressed in a blue velvet traveling gown edged with quantities of elegant white fur.

Elizabeth shrank back against the wall. It wasn't so much seeing the woman that made her afraid. It was the expression on Marcus's face. She had never seen him so happy, so alive-looking. Emily's words came back to haunt her, but it wasn't Arthur who had been with a woman, this time it was Marcus.

She ran to her room and threw herself on the bed. Too numb to cry, she lay there with an ache as large as a tombstone lying against her heart.

Although it was less than a half hour later, it seemed like an eternity had passed when Greta entered to say that the duke had summoned her to the library. Greta looked at her with pity.

"Aye, so you've seen 'er. Gawd. The woman's old enough to be 'is mother, and brassy enough to be a doxy. Wot 'e sees in 'er is beyond me."

"Enough, Greta. She is a guest in the house. You would do well to mind your tongue." Then, with less irritation in her voice, "Have you learned her name?"

"Aye. A Mrs. Frettwell, so they say backstairs. She's a widow lady."

"Thank you. If you'll help me fix my hair, I had best go downstairs."

"You look white as the driven snow, my lady. Will you be all right?"

Elizabeth nodded. But she wasn't so sure later as she started down the stairs. Her knees felt weak, and she held onto the banister to make certain she didn't fall.

The door to the library was open as she approached, and she saw that Marcus was leaning attentively over the woman's chair as they discussed a paper she held on her lap. Marcus looked up when he heard Elizabeth enter, and she dropped a low curtsy. He bowed, and for a moment she could have sworn that the look she saw in his eyes was hunger.

His voice was casual when he spoke. "Do come in, Elizabeth. There is someone I would like you to meet."

She nodded, afraid to trust her voice as she walked toward them. The woman looked up, holding a lorgnette against her eyes to improve her vision.

Elizabeth was surprised. Indeed, the woman was truly *old*. Granted, she was well-preserved, but far too long in the tooth to present a logical threat where Marcus was concerned. Still . . .

Marcus stepped back. "Lady Elizabeth Cambridge, may I present another guest in our house, Mrs. Catherine Frettwell."

Mrs. Frettwell stood and dropped a token curtsy, but her voice was warm as she spoke. "Lady Elizabeth. What a pleasure. My sister tells me you have been taking splendid care of her during her illness."

Elizabeth was tongue-tied. "Y-your sister?"

"I should have told you, Elizabeth. Mrs. Frettwell is the long-lost sister to Mrs. Patchen. As it turned out, the widow lady whom Mrs. Patchen had heard bought the Patchen estate was none other than her own sister."

"How perfectly incredible," Elizabeth managed to say without letting her voice tremble.

"Even more unbelievable than you know, your ladyship. For the past twenty years I have believed my sister to be dead. It was only because of His Grace that I learned the truth. I shall be indebted to him for the rest of my life."

Fortunately the duke ushered Elizabeth into a chair, because she was incapable of standing another minute. Further conversation revealed that Mr. Frettwell had left their guest with enough money to permit her to live in style. Now it was her hope to take her sister home to share the wealth and try to compensate for the years they had been apart.

Elizabeth saw to it that Mrs. Frettwell was settled into one of the freshly cleaned guest rooms to rest before tea-time. When she returned to the library, Marcus was waiting for her, and he swept her into his arms.

"My dear Elizabeth, I was so frightened when I saw you. Your face was quite pale. Have you been working too hard?"

"No, Marcus. I have not been working too hard. It was—it was only that I missed you so dreadfully." She couldn't bring herself to admit the thoughts that had passed through her head. He would never let her forget it.

His mouth found hers, and he pulled her against him until she shared the urgency of his desire.

At that moment Thomas cleared his throat. "I do beg your pardon, Your Grace. There is a man who most urgently demands to see her ladyship."

Marcus released her, cursing softly at having been disturbed. "Yes, Thomas. And does this gentleman have a name?"

Thomas came into the room and handed the card over on a silver salver. Marcus picked it up and read it, then handed it to Elizabeth. "The Marquis of Farthingsham. Your esteemed brother-in-law, I presume."

211

Elizabeth nodded. "But what is he doing here?"

"There is only one way to find out, Elizabeth. Shall I see him for you?"

"No. I am not afraid to face him. Please. Ask him to come in."

Marcus nodded to Thomas, who again cleared his throat. "There is a lady with him; his wife, I believe."

Elizabeth sighed. "You might as well bid them both to enter, Thomas, if you please."

"Yes, your ladyship."

Marcus put his hand under her chin. "We knew this had to come about eventually, my dear. They must surely be concerned over your safety."

Elizabeth's voice was dry. "Do you think so? Well . . . we shall see."

In truth, Martha looked more worried than Elizabeth could ever remember. Elizabeth started to make introductions, but the duke reminded her that they had met, since he had once been betrothed to their daughter.

The marquis drew his fat little hands together in what Elizabeth knew to be a gesture of nervousness. "Yes, my dear sister. The duke and I are friends from years back. It was a scourge on my heart when I found it necessary to break the engagement between him and our Louella. It is only in the past month that I have been able to bring her to her senses."

Elizabeth felt her heart constrict in panic. "I—I don't understand. I thought Louella would have been wed by now. Her betrothal to the Earl of Pentland—"

Martha sat ramrod straight in the Queen Anne chair nearest the window. "Elizabeth, darling, we have finally persuaded dear Louella that she was wrong in breaking her engagement to Marcus. After all . . . he must have loved her dearly to have perpetrated an abduction to effect a reconciliation between them. Such a pity that you were the one he captured."

"Are you saying she is not married, or even engaged?"

"Alas." Martha clasped her hands together. "Isn't it a stroke of providence? Now she and the duke can be married as planned."

The duke moved into the circle of their conversation and bowed toward Martha. "I am indeed flattered by your generosity in offering your daughter's hand in marriage, Marchioness, but I fear I must decline. You see, I have already made other plans in that regard."

As Elizabeth released her breath Martha and the marquis gasped in astonishment. The marquis was the first to speak. "God's blood, man. Do you know what you are saying? Would you be cad enough to go back on your word?"

"My word is as good as any man's word, but I was relieved of my commitment by the Lady Louella when she accepted the offer of another man."

"It was but a childish whim," the marquis whined in his worst nasal twange. "Surely you are man enough to overlook it."

The duke folded his arms across his chest. "I regret to disappoint you, sir, but the subject is closed."

The marquis jumped to his feet. "The devil take you before I'm through with you. Either you marry my daughter, or I'll see you hung for kidnapping my sister-in-law."

Marcus threw his head back and laughed. To the marquis and his wife, this had to be the worst cut of all. They couldn't abide being to made look ridiculous.

Elizabeth stood and folded her hands in front of her as she faced her sister and the marquis. "Look at me. Is there any court in the land who would believe I am here under duress? I have never been happier in my entire life. I really think it would be best if you left, now."

After a few unkind words about the ingratitude of destitute relatives, they went outside to their carriage. While

Elizabeth and Marcus watched, the marquis threw a trunk to the ground.

"Keep the whore and be damned," he shouted as the carriage sped away.

One of the footmen hurried down the steps to retrieve the jumble of clothing that had spilled from the trunk.

"'Tis nothin' but a bunch o' worn clothing, Your Grace. Wot would you 'ave done with it?"

Elizabeth interrupted. "They belong to me, Jimmy. Please send them up to my chambers."

He was deeply shamed, but her smile helped to ease his embarrassment.

Marcus put his arm around Elizabeth as they returned to the library. He poured a glass of brandy and handed it to her. "Here, drink this. It will steady your nerves."

She sipped a drop or two, but she was still shaking inside, not so much from her encounter with what remained of her family. They had no power to hurt her directly, nor, she suspected, could they touch the duke. It was the sudden realization that she was alone in the world, with no place to turn for help. She had nothing, nothing . . . save the clothes on her back, and even they, in truth, belonged to Emily. It wasn't like her to resort to tears, but they came, unbidden, and she was ashamed of her weakness.

The duke put his arms around her and held her as he would a child, stroking her hair and whispering soothing things against her temple.

When she was finally able to control the convulsive sobs, Marcus offered her his handkerchief, and she dabbed at her face.

"I am t-truly sorry, Your Grace. It was childish of me to carry on so. Please forgive me."

"Stop apologizing for being human, Elizabeth. I thought you behaved admirably. I'll wager we've seen the

214

last of that lot, and we're better off for it. Do you not agree?"

She nodded.

"Good. Will you be all right if I leave you alone for a moment?"

She moistened her lips and lifted her chin. "Please. Don't concern yourself over me. I'll be fine."

"I must fetch something that I brought back for you."

CHAPTER SEVENTEEN

Elizabeth was still numb with shock when he left the room, not only because of the unexpected visit from Martha and the marquis, but from her own complete loss of control. It had been some time since she had indulged in the luxury of tears. Marcus must think her quite immature. She dabbed at her eyes and patted her hair into place just as he came into the library.

He was carrying a small package, a gift she assumed, even though it was not wrapped nor tied with a ribbon.

As he handed it to her, he watched her face with serious intensity, a fact that made her rather uneasy.

"A gift for me, Marcus? You are more generous than I deserve."

"Would that it were true. In truth, it is not a gift but something that was rightfully yours from the outset."

"Indeed? But what could it possibly be?" His words had mystified her, and she opened the box with a vague reluctance, as if unwilling to submit her emotions to yet another devastation. Lifting the thick layer of tissue, Elizabeth looked up in astonishment. "I can't believe it! My mother's necklace. How did you ever manage to come by this?"

"It was not as difficult as I had expected. The blacksmith to whom you traded it for the horses and wagon sold it to a goldsmith in the next village. The goldsmith was more than eager to sell it to me."

"Oh, Marcus. If you only knew how much this means to me. I know you must have spent a great deal of money to reclaim it. How can I ever repay you?"

"By wearing it to the party." He smiled and twirled a lock of her hair around his finger. "Buying it back for you was one of the least things I could do to make up for all you have done for me. I shall ever be in your debt, Elizabeth."

"Then let us hear no more talk of debts. You can be assured I will wear it to Arthur's party."

"Am I to assume that the arrangements are coming along as we planned?"

"Everything is in order. Of course, there will be a multitude of last-minute things to do, but we have some girls coming in to help with those preparations. You have not changed your mind about tomorrow?"

He looked blank. "Tomorrow? Have we an engagement?"

She studied his face. "Tomorrow is the Sabbath. Have you forgotten that you promised to attend services at the church?"

He rubbed his hand across his chin. "In truth, I had. But do not despair, Elizabeth. My word stands."

She smiled and touched his arm. "I'm so pleased. May I invite Greta to ride with us in the carriage? She would be so honored. I know that she is feeling a bit fainthearted now that she has taken the step of joining Reverend Fleetwood's flock. It could only give her courage if we were at her side to bolster her confidence."

"Indeed she may. You are a good person, Elizabeth. So considerate of others."

"It is you, Your Grace, who deserves that credit. Who else would undertake such a journey to bring two long-lost sisters together?" She smiled up at him. "I suppose you know you may well lose your housekeeper. Mrs. Frettwell

217

is talking about taking Mrs. Patchen to Dorset to live at the family estate."

"Mrs. Patchen deserves to spend the rest of her life in luxury. Hers was not an easy lot. But then you of all people must be aware of her hardships."

"Her suffering far exceeded mine. I always had family to turn to—that is until now."

He took her hands in his. "Never fear, Elizabeth. You will always have family. As long as you live I hope you will consider Heatherwood your home."

She waited for him to go on but apparently that was all he had to say. She inclined her head and in a quiet voice expressed her appreciation for his generosity. After that she excused herself on the pretext that she had tasks that remained to be finished before teatime.

Alone in her room, Elizabeth lay on her bed and stared at the wooden chest that contained the clothing the marquis had thrown on the ground as his carriage departed. In offering her a place to live for the rest of her life, the duke had been more than generous . . . but she felt letdown nevertheless. They had been close, very close in the past few weeks. Indeed, had circumstances not intervened, there was more than once when she would have yielded herself to him. It had been in the back of her mind that he might offer for her. Tonight would have been the opportune moment, but he let it pass without voicing his intentions. Perhaps she was living in a dreamworld . . . the way Greta had dreamed about marrying a rich man. Tears began at the back of her eyes, and she would have given in to them had she not heard Greta come in through the sitting room door.

"Oh, are you up here so early, your ladyship? 'Tis not yet time to dress for tea, is it?"

"No, Greta. I've simply been resting. It has been a long day."

"Aye. But not as long as tomorrow."

218

"You are still concerned about joining the church? Is it your faith that wavers?"

"No, indeed, your ladyship. 'Tis only that I fear I might disappoint the reverend. Chesley is a foine man, finer even than I thought at the start. 'Tis not often you see a man of such beauty who also 'as a goodness of the 'eart."

"Trust my judgement, Greta. You will not disappoint him. Have you planned what to wear tomorrow?"

She shrugged. "Me brown muslin, I suspects."

Elizabeth got up from the bed and went to her trunk. Searching through the jumble of clothing, she came to a carefully wrapped package. When opened, it revealed a gown of fine white lace, slightly yellowed now from the years but still in wearable condition.

"It was my coming-out dress, Greta. If you like it and it fits well enough, I'd like you to have it. I think you will find the style simple enough that it will be appropriate for church."

"You can't mean that, your ladyship. It's far too splendid for the likes of me."

Elizabeth handed it to her. "It's yours to keep. I hope it brings you happiness."

"Lawd! Can you imagine me standin' in front o' the pews, dressed like an angel?" Her eyes pleaded with Elizabeth. "Would it be askin' too much if I were to try it on right now?"

"Please do. I can't wait to see how you look." When Greta hesitated, Elizabeth motioned to the next room. "Why don't you go in there and undress." Greta sighed in obvious relief, and Elizabeth realized that she had guessed right when she thought the girl might be ashamed of her undergarments.

When Greta came into the room a short time later, Elizabeth was amazed by the metamorphosis. Save for a slight straining of the bodice from an overripe bosom, the dress fit very well.

Elizabeth smiled broadly. "You do look like an angel, Greta. Come, look at yourself in the mirror. Take off the mobcap and let your hair fall down."

When she saw herself, Greta looked astounded, and for a moment her old impishness came back. "Lawd almighty. Will you look a' that. I would 'ave settled for just a knight, but with a body like this I could 'ave got me a duke."

Elizabeth laughed. "You haven't changed your mind, have you, about joining the church?"

"No, my lady. I'd never do that. It would break Chesley's 'eart." She hastened to add that it was not just for Chesley but for the sake of her own immortal soul. The two women looked at each other with an even deeper understanding than they had known, and at the same moment reached out to hug each other in a gesture of affection.

Greta was thrilled to ride in the State carriage with the rest of the family. It seemed everyone from the small community had turned out once they heard the duke and his household would be in attendance. The church was packed to the doorway. It was a simple but touching ceremony followed by a rousing sermon based on discipleship.

The duke, with Elizabeth at his side and Arthur and Emily on the other side, sat as regal as a king among his subjects. Elizabeth with pleased by the respect shown him. This probably had a great deal to do with the fact that she too was treated with respect. Apparently the vicar was true to his word that he would do his best to stamp out the idle gossip concerning her unexpected arrival in the village.

Arthur had obviously experienced some difficulty keeping his gaze off Greta, but once she sat down his head turned toward an attractive red-haired woman seated on the far side of the church. She was with an elderly man whom Elizabeth guessed to be her husband. Was this perhaps the infamous Mrs. Walpole whom Emily accused Arthur of seeing on the sly? Apparently she too had a roving eyes, because Elizabeth caught her giving the duke a close inspection.

Much of the talk after the services centered around the party, which was to be held in two days. Since everyone was invited to the castle, it was not necessary to choose one's words in regard to the subject. Arthur appeared as excited about it as a little boy, and Marcus seemed the doting older brother. For once there was no sign of dissension between the two men. Elizabeth prayed that it would stay that way for as long as Arthur remained home on leave from the Royal Navy.

Emily accompanied them back to the castle after services. She looked happier than Elizabeth had ever seen her. The rest of the day passed in doing simple things in preparation for the party. Most of the heavy work was already completed.

Finally the day was upon them. Nearly all of the house guests arrived just before lunch, with stragglers trickling in just before tea. Arthur or Marcus made it a point to be with Elizabeth to greet them as they arrived, since they were strangers to Elizabeth. Once they were settled into their rooms she invited them downstairs to the morning room, where a buffet was kept supplied with a collation of cold meats and fresh fruit. She made a special effort to connect names from the guest list, which she had memorized, with the various faces of the people as they arrived.

There was the Marquis Wellesley, who had been the British Governor General of India until 1805, then became Foreign Secretary until, for lack of support of the Peninsula Campaign in 1812, he had been replaced by Lord Castlereagh. Elizabeth was a little in awe of him, but his friendly manner soon put her at ease. Other guests included Aaron Murray, an editor of the *Morning Post,* and his wife Maybelle. She was a twittery little woman with a constant twinkle in her eyes. A direct contrast to her was the hatchet-faced Duchess of Grenwald. Elizabeth had resolved to be on her guard with this woman, but she proved to be the most friendly of all.

A number of other couples had made the trip from Weymouth, where it was rumored the King had recently spent a few days during one of his saner periods. At least one of the couples declared the rumor an outright fabrication.

The main festivities began after teatime, when the local people were invited to attend. The musicians brought in from London were to stay overnight in a suite in the servants' wing. They were already in their places and had begun to tune their instruments for the dancing, which would take place in the Petite Ballroom after the feast, which had just taken place in the refectory.

Emily, looking rotund and robust in a dark-blue chiffon gown that did little to hide her condition, came over to speak to Elizabeth, who for the first time that evening was alone.

"Did you ever find time to really enjoy this fabulous food, Elizabeth?"

"In truth, I have been too excited to eat. I drank a small glass of claret early on and managed a few slivers of partridge pie, but that was just to keep from being muzzy-headed. What do you think, Emily? Has everything gone aright so far?"

Emily laughed. "Look around you, dear. Can you question what your eyes see? Everyone has eaten of jellied salmon, reindeer tongue, pigeon pie, glacéed fruit, and of course the delightful iced apricot tarts, until they can scarcely breathe. I wonder how they shall ever summon the energy to dance?"

222

"Oh, but they must! How would it look to have an empty dance floor?"

"Silly goose. I was simply teasing. Of course they will dance. The young people can hardly wait for the opportunity. Look at my brother. He can hardly keep his hands off that young Whittier girl who works in the chandlery. I'll wager Mrs. Walpole is seething."

Elizabeth laughed. "You are irrepressible, Emily." She looked around. "Have you seen Marcus since he left the table?"

She patted Elizabeth on the arm. "Don't fret now. He is in the library, talking to the marquess about the possibility of starting some new investigations into the legality of the Corn Law Act. Since your adventure with the riot, the subject is close to his heart. I'm sure you know that he agrees the laws are unfair to the small farmers."

"Indeed, but I feared that our experience might leave him embittered. I'm grateful that he is able to see their side of the matter."

"Here he comes now. He doesn't appear to have accomplished very much."

"No. Apparently not."

Emily looked at her in amusement. "Go on, go to him. I can see that you are about to perish from want of it. Besides, in that Persian ivory brocade dress you will do more for him than a special act of Parliament."

Elizabeth's face colored. "Don't say such things." She laughed. "But will you be all right if I do?"

"Indeed. Go along with you."

Marcus's face lit up when she came toward him. "Elizabeth, have I told you how beautiful you look tonight?"

"More than once, Marcus, but it is food for my soul. Are you happy with the way the party is going?"

"It's perfect, my dear, but I'm sure you must know that by now."

"It was kind of you to have Mrs. Patchen carried down

on the chair so that she could share in the festivities. Her sister is very protective of her."

"Indeed. They seem to be making up for all the years they were separated." He looked at a clock that hung at one end of the hall between the colorful rows of banners. "I think perhaps I will ask Thomas to announce the dancing to begin in the ballroom. Will you excuse me?"

She nodded but continued to watch as he walked away. He was elegantly attired in a pale-blue long-tailed coat with tight-fitting trousers of a perfect cut. His snow-white ruffled cravat was embroidered in fine blue thread to complement his formal evening shirt. The older men wore the traditional satin knee britches and black stockings, but Elizabeth was pleased that both Arthur and Marcus would have been completely at home among the beau monde at Watier's or any of the fine clubs in London.

A half dozen of the diners remained on to refill their plates, but nearly all of the two hundred guests filed on down to the ballroom. It was resplendent with garlands of leaves and flowers strung across the ceiling. The room smelled of roses and lavender, a combination that rested well on the faint breeze that filtered in through the open windows.

Arthur and Emily started off the dance with a grand march down the center of the room, slow-paced, Elizabeth was sure, out of regard for Emily's condition. Marcus bowed, and they too joined the line of marchers. When it was over, the musicians played a lively reel that the younger people in particular enjoyed.

Arthur, as if born to the role, made certain to give each lady, whether young or old, a few moments of his time. When it came Elizabeth's turn, he swept her onto the floor in time for a gay mazurka.

Elizabeth smiled up at him. "Are you having a good time, or are you simply putting on a brave show since you are the guest of honor?"

He grinned. "In truth, I am having the best day of my life, and I owe it all to you, Elizabeth. What a pity I waited so long to abduct you."

"Hush. Someone is sure to hear you."

"They would forgive me any indiscretion tonight. In regard to that . . . why not dance a jig of our own in the privacy of my quarters as soon as the others have gone?"

She gave him a look. "'Tis fortunate for you, Sir Arthur, that I know you well enough to know you are jesting, otherwise I might take offense."

"Have you not heard that there is always a measure of truth in every jest?"

"I have heard, but for your sake let this be the exception that proves the rule."

"You would make a memorable birthday gift, Elizabeth."

Marcus chose that moment to cut in. "If I may, Arthur, you have spent more than your share of time with Elizabeth."

Arthur inclined his head. "I bow to age, Your Grace, but with reluctance, I assure you."

Marcus took her into his arms as the music drifted into a waltz. "What was this talk about a birthday present?"

Elizabeth colored. "Nothing of great importance. You know Arthur's penchant for casual conversation."

"Indeed. Only too well."

They were silent as he whirled her around the room. He was an accomplished dancer, less inclined to hold her close, as was Arthur's wont, but his nearness had its effect on her nevertheless. His hand where it held hers was warm. As he bent his head to look into her face, his fingers curled over the top of hers in a secret gesture of affection. Had she been slow-witted enough to miss the meaning, there was no doubting the message in his eyes.

"The party is well under way, Elizabeth. It can do without us."

Elizabeth looked up questioningly. "You are tired, Your Grace?"

He laughed. "Tired? Hardly. Unless it be of the constant clack and gabble of our guests. They are enjoying the festivities, but all I want is to be alone with you."

Her heart caught in her throat, and she was unable to speak. His hand tightened around her waist. "Come. Will you walk with me on the headlands?"

"If that is your wish."

"But what is *your* wish, Elizabeth?"

"To walk with you on the headlands . . . 'in the heather, wild and sweet.'" She sang the last part as she remembered the song he had sung while playing the wind harp.

He smiled, and his heart was in his eyes as they feasted on her face. "Then come, we'll slip out through the French doors, and no one will be the wiser."

Someone will be, Elizabeth thought. Emily was watching them as they left, and when she smiled, her eyes were filled with love.

It was the time of the full moon. From the water just beyond the rocks and some distance below, the soft murmurings of the waves beat in accompaniment to the flutter of Elizabeth's heart. They were alone. His arm across her shoulders gave warmth to her body, but her soul was warmed by the mere fact of his presence. How she loved this man.

They followed a narrow path that skirted the boulders along the cliff where the heather bloomed like tiny stars against its dark, coarse foliage.

Marcus stopped and pulled her around to face him. His finger traced the top of her gown where the slightest curve of her trim bosom shone white as snow in the moonlight.

"Oh, Elizabeth. It stirs my blood to touch you like this, to have you so near . . . yet *not* to have you. Do you know

226

the sleepless nights I have spent since you came into my life?"

There was nothing for her to say. She simply looked at him, and her hand went out to touch the fine hair that curled against his wrist.

And then she was in his arms. All the aching need that she had denied came into being. When he kissed her, his mouth demanded satisfaction, and she gave it without holding back. Their bodies melded together, striving for a closeness that wasn't quite possible, yet greedy with a hunger that knew no bounds.

His hands circled her waist, then slid downward, cupping her body against him. Strong! She gloried in his strength and tried to match it with her own.

"Elizabeth," he groaned. "You are the blood of my veins, the very nourishment of my life. How can I face the rest of my life without you?"

She pulled back to study his face. Had something happened she did not see? His words were ragged with longing, yet they seemed to speak of endings, as if their love for each other could never be.

She measured her words carefully. "I love you, Marcus. But you must know that I have nothing to offer you, save myself. What little money my parents left me is gone. Where I go, I go empty-handed."

"Do you think that matters one whit?"

"What, then, Marcus?"

He looked at her for one long moment, then turned and strode toward the lights of the castle.

CHAPTER EIGHTEEN

Elizabeth felt as if she had turned to stone. Her feet were granite-heavy as she retraced her footsteps to the castle. For the love of Heaven, why had she failed to return to London when she had had the chance? Her common sense had warned her that nothing good could come from remaining here. It was over. The fragile dream that Marcus might someday fall in love with her and offer for her hand in marriage had vanished like the mists over the moors.

Far above her a night bird's plaintive call echoed the loneliness in her heart, contrasting sharply with the laughter that bubbled from the open windows of the Petite Ballroom.

It would be difficult to face them all, but she must. She had willed herself not to cry, but Emily would know. Perhaps that hurt most of all. She resisted the temptation to enter through the inner court and go directly to the stairway. She had to see this through. When the last guest was gone and the house was put back in its normal state, she would leave. To go where? Anywhere! Anywhere she could lose herself and not have to spend each waking moment thinking of Marcus.

Marcus. The mere thought of his name brought the ache to the surface like pushing on a sprained ankle. One was hard put to know whether to cry out from the pain or to rub it with a soothing balm. But there was no balm to soothe this particular agony.

As she slowly entered through the French doors, the music and merriment smote her ears. The young people from the village were performing an intricate folk dance called "The Needle and Thread." Standing nearest her were Greta and Chesley Fleetwood, clapping in time to the music but hardly aware of anyone but themselves. Elizabeth smiled at the joy with which they seemed to overflow. They were in love. That was plain to see. She wondered if anything could ever come of it.

Skirting the dancers, she started to move on to the refectory to see if the work there was proceeding as it should, when Emily intercepted her and took her by the arm.

"Come with me, Elizabeth. I must talk to to you."

Emily was the last person she wanted to see now; Emily, with her plotting and planning to bring the duke and Elizabeth together.

"Please, not now, Emily. I must attend to something."

"Nonsense. Come with me. We can talk in the study."

There was no getting out of it without making a scene, so Elizabeth dutifully accompanied her. "Has something happened? Is one of the guests ill? It seemed to me that everyone was having a good time."

"Everyone save you and Marcus. I saw him come in just moments ago. He looked like he had just been sentenced to the gallows." She closed the door behind her and stood with her hands on her hips. "If you tell me you turned down his offer of marriage, Elizabeth, I shall never forgive you. Marcus needs you. Surely you must know that. Do I have to remind you how much he loves you?"

Elizabeth shook her head. "No. I know that he loves me."

Emily flopped down into a chair. "Then what? Do speak up, Elizabeth. Ladies in the family way should not be subjected to such tension."

Elizabeth pressed her hands together in front of her and

walked toward the window. It would hurt to say the words; it would make it so final. But she must . . . for Emily's sake.

"Marcus did not ask me to marry him. For some reason I cannot comprehend, he let the opportunity slip by." She pressed her lips together and fought back the tears. It was moments before she could continue. "I—I thought perhaps it was the lack of a suitable dowry, but he said it didn't matter."

"Of that I can assure you. Although Marcus would naturally seek someone of noble birth to insure a pure line of succession, it would not enter his head to refuse you simply for lack of a dowry. Your father was the Baron of Wendenn. Your bloodline is as pure as anyone could desire." She rose and quickly paced the floor despite her bulk.

Elizabeth feared for Emily's health should she continue to be distraught. "Please, Emily, you must not concern yourself. The baby is all you should be thinking of for the present." She forced a smile. "I fear it would take some of the attention away from Arthur if you were to go into labor during his birthday party."

But Emily was beyond seeing the humor in it. Suddenly she smote her forehead with her hand. "That utter fool. Could he have been so obtuse as to have believed him?"

"Whatever are you talking about, Emily?"

"Your brother-in-law. When he took his departure, he called you an unkind name. One of the servants told me about it."

"But surely Marcus must have realized the man spoke out of vindictiveness when he called me a—a prostitute."

Emily's voice was dry. "A man in love is apt to believe anything. I must go to him and set things aright."

"No, Emily. Please, I beg of you, don't speak to Marcus of this. It would be too humiliating."

Emily's voice was soft but unrelenting. "Be honest with

yourself, Elizabeth. Would it not be better to have it out now than to worry over it for weeks to come? For all your strength you are too tender when it comes to seeking your own happiness. Left to you, the misunderstanding might never be resolved."

Elizabeth started to protest, but Emily held up her hand. "Hear me out. I know Marcus better than anyone. He has a moral code that he refuses to violate. Where Arthur is free and easy with his favors, Marcus is more selective. That is not to say that he has as yet to experience the delights of the bedroom. What it does say is that he expects the woman he marries to be untouched. I think perhaps he might be inclined to forgive a single affair, but he would never consider taking an adventuress as a wife. Do I make myself clear?"

Elizabeth nodded as Emily continued.

"No. I doubt that I have. To understand Marcus you have to know the entire story. When Marcus was barely seventeen, he fell madly in love with a beautiful young girl. She was the daughter of a count, but she lived with a chaperon in her own suite of rooms at a posting inn in London. On the surface all the requirements of Polite Society were obeyed, and Marcus spread the word that he intended to marry her. When the truth came out, she was revealed to be under the protection of the King's chancellor, who had discovered her working in a French brothel."

Emily spread her hands. "So you see . . . although Marcus might appear to be overly concerned about reputations, one can hardly fault him. Do you not agree?"

Elizabeth nodded.

"All right, then, Elizabeth. Let me speak to Marcus."

"No. I cannot permit—"

At that moment a tap sounded on the door, and when it opened, Marcus was standing there. "Thomas told me I'd find you here. I'd like to speak to you alone, Elizabeth."

Emily put her hand on Marcus's arm. "Before you do, Marcus, there is something I must say to you, since Elizabeth refuses."

Elizabeth walked toward them. "No! Please excuse us, Emily. I am sure we will not be long. Perhaps you would be good enough to see to the needs of the guests."

It was not a question but a command. Emily accepted it as such, curtsied awkwardly to Marcus, and left the room. When the door closed behind her, Marcus linked his hands behind his back and strode over to the window.

"There is much I have to say to you, Elizabeth, and I find it difficult to know where to begin. Although you have been here but a few short weeks, circumstances have brought us so close together that it seems as if I have always known you."

She saw the rigid set of his shoulders, but his face was turned away, and she could not fathom his mood as he continued.

"You have defied me, you have angered me, and you have delighted in making me look the fool. You have irritated me with your independence, but"—his voice softened—"you have made me come to admire that very source of my irritation. Finally you have set fire to my blood until I find that I no longer choose to live without you. I love you, Elizabeth. Will you do me the honor of becoming my wife?"

She was stupefied. "I—you're asking me to marry you?"

At last he turned to face her. "I am. I want to marry you. Were it possible, I would plead my case before a senior member of your family, but circumstances being what they are, I must offer directly to you. Will you consent to become the Duchess of Heatherford?"

Suddenly all the dreams she had ever dreamed appeared to be coming true. She curtsied low, and when she arose, her eyes were shining with the love she felt in her heart.

The faint quaver in her voice gave evidence to the depth of her emotions.

"I . . . am deeply honored, Your Grace. My answer is yes."

As if released from some terrible tension, the duke reached her in two quick strides and whirled her into his arms.

"Great Heaven! I was so afraid you would refuse me."

She nuzzled her face against his chest. "Surely you know how much I love you, Marcus?"

His hands pulled her against him so tightly that it seemed as if their bodies were one. "No, Elizabeth, I don't know how much you love me. Will you not show me?" He teased.

She felt her face turn pink. "I—I don't know—"

"It was a kiss I had in mind. Once before you kissed me of your own volition. Could we not again share this experience?"

She suddenly felt like a shy schoolgirl. After a pause she pulled his head down to her level and kissed him chastely on the mouth.

He let out a guffaw. "In truth, you have a great deal to learn about making love."

She lifted veiled eyes. "I trust that you will teach me the finer points . . . once our vows have been said."

He cupped her face in his hands and bent so close that she could see the tiny vertical line in the generous curve of his lips.

"Indeed, although I confess it will not be easy to wait that long. Will you be an eager pupil, Elizabeth?"

"If I told you how much I long to begin the lessons, you would think me a shameless wanton. Suffice it to say that I do not look with disfavor upon the bedding rights."

His voice was husky. "You are everything a man could desire, Elizabeth. How proud my father would have been to know the woman I have chosen to father my sons."

"I will do my best to bring honor to the House of Clendennon. How soon do you wish the ceremony to take place?"

"As soon as possible. Four days?"

"Marcus! Surely you jest? A wedding takes time. There will be gowns to make, announcements to be made. You surely will want to invite the people of Heatherford."

"Only if we must. In truth, I suppose we owe it to them to make this a festive occasion. It has been years since the marriage of a duke has taken place at Heatherwood Castle. I will leave it to you to set the date."

"I think it could be done three weeks hence."

"As you wish."

"But there are two things, Marcus. For propriety's sake I must move out of the castle before our betrothal is announced."

He made a face, but it was plain that he agreed. "And what else?"

"I would like to tell Emily. She feels responsible for having brought about an understanding between us, and the news will make her very happy."

He laughed. "My dearest, there is no possible way of keeping the news from Emily even if we choose to. Tell her tonight if you wish . . . and Arthur, too."

There was a knock on the door. As Marcus went to open it he said, "That will be Emily now, or I miss my guess."

But it was Thomas. "Beggin' your pardon, Your Grace, but I have a message for Mr. Walpole. Would you know where I might find him?"

Elizabeth spoke up. "The last I saw him, Thomas, he was in the library speaking with Mr. Crenshaw. I think you might still find him there."

"Thank you, your ladyship."

When he left, she turned to Marcus. "We have been

away from our guests overlong. We must join them before they come looking for us."

"Regrettably. But first—" He pulled her into his arms and kissed her with a tenderness that went beyond passion. Her hand stroked the back of his head, and he groaned with pleasure. "Oh, Elizabeth, my sweet. Let me give you lesson number one. One must never begin something so exquisite when there is no time to finish."

She brushed a kiss on his cheek and darted away before he could lay a hand on her.

The music had slowed to a more sedate pace, reflecting the weariness of the musicians, Elizabeth guessed. More and more of the revelers had begun to fill the chairs on either side of the dance floor. At the far end near the door a table had been set with crystal and silver punch bowls. At a signal from Marcus the footmen began filling fragile footed glasses with arrack punch or creamy syllabub laced with wine. It was time for the toast. When all the glasses were filled, Marcus nodded to the trumpeter, who blew a lilting fanfare that effectively silenced all conversations as the people waited to join in the proceedings.

Carrying his glass, Marcus walked over to where Arthur, looking even more handsome than usual in his uniform of a lieutenant of the Royal Navy, stood among a group of admiring young people. The crimson neckband on which hung the Star of the Order of Bath, which he was awarded at the same time he was knighted for meritorious service to the Crown, gave him a certain dignity that usually eluded him.

The cheers went up until they resounded throughout the high, vaulted room. When the toasts were over, Arthur made a pretty little speech about his joy at being among friends on his twenty-first birthday. After it was over, the musicians again took their places, and a few hardy souls returned to the dance floor.

Elizabeth happened to see Mrs. Walpole and asked if Thomas had found her husband.

"Oh, yes, rather, your ladyship. My mister went off in the gig to see a merchant from London on some business matter."

"Indeed. How unfortunate that he had to leave early. Be assured, Mrs. Walpole, that I will have Thomas see that you are sent home in our carriage whenever you choose to leave."

"Oh, that won't be necessary, Lady Elizabeth. I've a'ready been promised a ride home, though I am much obliged for your kind consideration." She dropped a curtsy, all the time looking up with wide-eyed innocence.

Elizabeth inclined her head, then excused herself. The nerve of that hussy! Beyond doubt it was Arthur whom she had prevailed upon to see her home. She had the look of a spider about her, but alas, Arthur was a grown man. He had to learn not to lift each and every skirt that pleased his fancy.

For fear of taking some of the glory away from Arthur, Elizabeth had planned to wait until the guests had gone home to break the news to Emily, but it was a vain hope, because Emily was not to be put off. When Elizabeth told her of the betrothal, Emily nearly wept with happiness.

"My dearest Elizabeth," she said. "I have always wanted a sister of my very own. But more than that I want Marcus to be happy, and I want an heir for Heatherwood. Much as I pretend to laugh at Marcus's love for the castle and all the tradition that goes with it, I love it, too, as does Arthur, and I want it to go on forever."

They embraced, and Emily looked up at her in merriment. "You see! Did I not tell you the Persian ivory brocade dress would conjure miracles?" They giggled together over their little joke, much to the amusement of the bystanders.

Finally the last guest was gone save for Mrs. Walpole,

who was waiting for Arthur to take her home. Emily offered the use of her carriage, but Arthur demurred, saying that he needed the fresh air. Both carriages left at the same time, so that Arthur could first make certain Emily arrived home without mishap.

The overnight guests had retired to their rooms, and the servants were given permission to leave most of the cleaning up for the morrow. Mrs. Patchen had long since been carried up to her room. Elizabeth was grateful that the brightness of the woman's eyes came from her pleasure and excitement, not the fever, which had broken four days ago.

When just the two of them remained in the refectory, Marcus put his arm around Elizabeth and held her close. "This was one of the loveliest parties we ever had at Heatherwood, and we owe most of the credit to you. You will make a splendid duchess, Elizabeth. Shall we go to the study for a glass of wine?"

"I think not, Marcus. In truth, I am more weary than I had imagined I could be. If you will forgive me, I would like to retire. There will be much to do in the morning to see that our guests are fed and packed off to their various homes."

"You are right, of course. But before I bid you good night, I must tell you that you have made me a very happy man tonight."

"With God's help this will be the first of thousands of happy nights. I love you, Marcus."

"And I you, Elizabeth."

He kissed her lightly on the mouth and walked her up the stairs to her bedchamber, where he left her at the door.

Greta was still waiting up to help Elizabeth disrobe. The girl looked as fresh as she had that morning.

"I didn't see you socializing with the people from the village, Greta. Were you not having a good time?"

"Aye, that's a good one, your ladyship. In truth, I'll wager I 'ad the best time o' me life."

"But whenever I noticed you, you were sitting and talking to the vicar. That couldn't have been very entertaining."

"Oh, couldn't it now? Well, I didn't see you dancin' much, your ladyship, but one would be 'ard put to find a jewel that could outshine the sparkle in your eyes."

"Touché. Can you keep a secret, Greta?"

"Aye, if need be, though should Chesley ask, I'd be bound to tell him."

"Indeed, why? We have no confessional in our church."

"I've learned one thing, your ladyship. There are some people you just can't lie to. Chesley is one o' them."

"Well, I shall have to trust you. I tell you only because we have become such good friends. The duke has offered for my hand, and I have accepted."

Greta's face beamed. "I can't be more happy, my lady. You, a duchess. I'll wager there's none o' us who will be surprised. Not since the day you brought 'im home safe from the riots. 'E was a doomed man, so to speak, but I knew 'e was taken wi' you even before." There was a silence, then Greta again spoke, and her voice was tight in her throat.

"What would you think, Lady Elizabeth, if I told you the vicar has asked me to marry him?"

"Greta! Is it true?"

"Aye. But I 'aven't said I would. 'Tis a big undertaking for one such as me, and I don't know if I could do 'im proud."

"Do you love him?"

"More than I ever 'oped to love any man."

"A vicar's life is not an easy one, Greta. You must know that there will never be much money for one of his calling."

Greta smiled broadly. "A jolly good joke, wouldn' you

238

say, for one who set great store in selling 'er virtue to the 'ighest bidder? Me, a vicar's wife!" Her face sobered at the thought. "Could I learn, do you think, Lady Elizabeth?"

"I think you can do anything you really want to."

"Then I'll tell Chesley 'e can go ahead and talk to 'Is Grace. Hit seemed fittin', since my folks is gone."

"I wish you all the happiness in the world, Greta."

"And I wish the same for you, Lady Elizabeth."

They hugged each other briefly and then said their good nights.

Elizabeth lay in bed for what seemed like hours before she drifted off to sleep. Her body ached with weariness, but her mind was filled with incredible thoughts. It was all too good to be true. Would she waken in the morning only to find that it had all been an impossible dream? Elizabeth Cambridge Clendennon, the Duchess of Heatherford, mistress of Heatherwood Castle. If only her parents could have been alive to share the joy in her heart. She closed her eyes, and finally sleep became a reality.

It was just after four in the morning when a knock sounded on her door, and she struggled up out of the fuzziness of a dream. "Who is it?" she called. There was no answer. Pulling on a dressing gown, she went to the door of her sitting room and opened it a crack. The hallway was dark outside. "Marcus, is that you?" Her voice was unbelieving.

"It's Arthur. Let me in, Elizabeth."

She felt his foot press against the door. "Arthur, have you been drinking? Behave yourself and go to your own room." She tried to force the door shut, but his weight prevented it from closing.

"Help me, Elizabeth." He sagged against the door.

"Dear Lord. You're bleeding." She grasped his arm. His other hand was pressed against his chest. She was shaking now, but she fought to control her voice. "Come inside and sit on the bed. What happened, Arthur? Have you been shot?"

He grinned lopsidedly. "Nothing so dramatic as that. Suffice it to say that I ran into an irate husband who used to be a boxer. The bloke let me have one on the chest, and I think it reopened my wound."

"Here. Let me unbutton your shirt. Oh, dear. It is bleeding rather badly. We really should call the physician."

"And have it all over the village? I'd as leave bleed to death. I brought a pocketful of lint and bandages from the kitchen. If you have some scissors, that's all we need to tie it up proper."

She reached into the sewing basket and brought out the scissors, then snipped away the stained bandage. "You may be right. It seems to have stopped bleeding. If I bind it tightly, it should hold the edges of the wound together."

"You're a treasure, Elizabeth. My brother's a fool to let you get away from him."

"Not such a fool as you think, Arthur. He has asked me to marry him . . . and needless to say, I have accepted."

Arthur let out a whoop. "Great lack-a-day! What a birthday this has been. My only regret is that I am not the lucky man."

Elizabeth snugged the bandage tightly across his chest and tied it in place. "You would never be content without the sea under your feet, Arthur, as you well know. There, now. That should do it. I suppose you will have to ask for an extension of your leave to give this wound a chance to heal."

He grinned. "I considered it, but ruled it out. As you say, the sea is in my blood, and it's about time I got back to it. Were I to remain here, I would doubtless encounter another jealous husband."

They were still laughing as he walked toward the sitting room, buttoning his shirt on the way.

As Elizabeth opened the door to the corridor she gasped in surprise. Marcus was standing there.

CHAPTER NINETEEN

At the sight of Marcus both Elizabeth and Arthur stopped dead. His face was ashen, his mouth a dark gash against the gray of his skin, and when he spoke, his voice was leaden.

"I trust the two of you have had an enjoyable time." Before either of them could speak, he bowed and, turning abruptly, strode toward the stairway.

Elizabeth ran after him. "Wait, Marcus. You don't understand. Arthur—we—"

But before she could finish, he had reached the entrance and gone out the door. It seemed like only moments later that she heard hoofbeats pounding through the outer court. Then crossing the gravel, they disappeared into the night.

She sank down on the top stair and buried her face in her hands. She was too numb to cry. Arthur sat down beside her and put his arm across her shoulder.

"I seem to have a penchant for being around at the wrong time. God's blood, Elizabeth, I do hope you can forgive me. As soon as I right this wrong, I shall take leave of this place and return to my ship." He wiped his hand across his eyes. "I have meant nothing but trouble to you since the moment we met."

She folded her arms in front of her, gripping them to keep from trembling. "Stop talking like that. Had it not been for you, I would never have met him. Perhaps it was a backward favor, but it was a favor, nonetheless. I will always be grateful to you, Arthur, whatever happens."

"Don't start thinking it's all over. As soon as he gets his temper under control, I shall talk to him and set things aright."

"Where do you think he might have gone?"

He shrugged. "Only Heaven knows, but I'll wager his mount will have a run he won't soon forget. You might as well try to sleep, Elizabeth. He won't return for hours. You can be assured of that."

She nodded. "Good night, then."

"Good night, Elizabeth. Try not to worry."

She chose the chair near the window, where she could see him if he returned. There was no good courting sleep, the ache in her heart was too new to be stilled for long. Even the walls of the castle seemed to sigh in sympathy with her grief. A trick of the wind, she thought. A breeze had freshened after midnight, bringing with it the rattle of branches against stone walls and the crisp tang of drying seaweed. She had grown to love the smell. How hard it would be to return to London, with its open sewers running dank and putrid in the afternoon sun.

Would she be able to make Marcus understand what had happened? It was no wonder that he had thought the worst, with Arthur buttoning his shirt and she clad only in her nightdress and robe. Added to that, they had been laughing like two giddy children delighting in their latest prank.

Dear Lord, she thought. If I can make him see the truth of what happened tonight, I will spend the rest of my life proving to him that he is the only one I desire. She played with the thought of confronting him after his ride, but good sense prevailed. He needed time to consider his hurt and place it in proper perspective.

Given time, he would surely realize he had acted out of

hand. Had he waited but a moment longer he would have saved everyone a sleepless night. But even amidst her pain, her honesty prevailed. Suffice it to say, she thought, had their situation been reversed, she doubted that she would have acted less stupidly.

The dawning came like a slow awakening as the sun crept over the fringe of trees. It boded fair, despite the thick tendrils of fog that clung to the low patches of land like newly shorn lamb's wool to fustian breeches. Sleep had eluded her.

Elizabeth mussed her bed, then dressed quickly lest Greta wake and discover that she had not slept. Marcus still had not returned by the time she went down to the morning room.

The staff was already at work clearing away the remnants of last night's party and setting things to right for the guests who would be down for breakfast in less than an hour. They would meet in the morning room for coffee or hot chocolate, then retire to the refectory, where the sideboard would again be heaped with food.

The mere thought of food caused Elizabeth's stomach to churn. There had been too many times when things seemed to be going well between her and Marcus, only to become upset by his wrongheadedness. This time their differences must be resolved, one way or the other. He would doubtless return before the guests were due to take their departure. Marcus was too much the lord of the castle to allow his ill humor to override his good manners.

She had dressed with care, knowing that their next time together could be a turning point in their lives. The dark smudges beneath her eyes bore evidence to her sleepless night, but the gentian-blue organdy gown bordered with pink silk flowers made her skin look translucent rather than pale. She had brushed her hair until it shone with the

244

luster of warm honey, then tied it back with a pink satin ribbon.

From outward appearances Elizabeth was as busy as the least of the servants, but inside, she waited. For all intent time had ceased to exist. All that mattered was Marcus and her need to see him.

Breakfast was served to the overnight guests, who were requested to help themselves from the sideboard at the appointed hour. Emily had been invited to return to the castle to share their repast. She arrived in a veritable tent of yellow chiffon with an overskirt of dusty sage-green, intended to minimize her expectant condition. She threw her arms around Elizabeth.

"In truth, Elizabeth, I can scarce believe our good fortune. Have you told the others about your betrothal to Marcus?"

"No, Emily. And I beg of you to be silent in that regard."

She gave Elizabeth a look. "Indeed?"

"I—Marcus left suddenly during the night. The guests, of course, wondered why he was not here to receive them. I advised them that he was called away quite unexpectedly."

Emily swore expertly over the follies of men, and Elizabeth looked up in surprise.

"Please. You must not say such things. In truth, Marcus is not entirely to blame."

"Indeed? Am I to understand that there was some truth in his suspicions?"

"Hardly. It seems that we have had a misunderstanding. He saw Arthur leaving my room early this morning. What he did not know was that Arthur's wound had reopened during a bout of fisticuffs, and he had come to me to refresh the bandage." Elizabeth spread her hands. "It is but the latest in a series of misunderstandings. In

245

truth, I am beginning to wonder if your brother is capable of trusting me."

"Remember that he is a man once burned. Knowing Marcus, I would say that he is already regretting his abrupt departure."

"Would that I could believe it!" Elizabeth sighed.

Hours passed and still she waited. The last guest had departed, and the servants relaxed visibly as they returned to their daily chores. And still Marcus had not returned. Arthur, Emily, and Elizabeth were sitting in the library, all three of them at a loss for words. Marcus's abrupt departure had left a void too deep to fill with mere conversation.

Finally Elizabeth stood up. "I've come to a decision. The time has come for me to leave. In truth, I doubt that I could stay another hour under the cloud that hangs over Heatherwood Castle." She turned to Emily. "Would it be asking too much if I were to beg shelter from you for a few days until I can make other arrangements?"

Emily shook her head. "I—I don't know, Elizabeth—I don't think it would be advisable."

Elizabeth was shocked by her refusal, and she tried unsuccessfully to hide the pain in her eyes. Emily quickly put her arm around her.

"Silly goose. I didn't mean you weren't welcome. I only meant that the move might be poor strategy."

Elizabeth felt her temper rise. "Please. Don't speak to me of plotting and planning. In truth, if I have but one more setback, I fear I shall lose my mind." She moistened her lips before she could continue. "I thought that falling in love would be a wondrous thing, but the pain is beyond belief."

Arthur put his arm around her. "I'm going to find him and set him straight. He has no right to do this to you without so much as a chance for us to explain."

246

Elizabeth gently moved away. "He has every right, Arthur. You know what thoughts must have gone through his mind. Can't you imagine how much he was hurting?"

Arthur nodded.

"Then, please, leave this matter to the two of us. We will work it out in our own way."

Emily nodded. "Very well. Then if you still wish to return with me to my house, consider yourself welcome for as long as you wish to stay."

"Thank you. I think that would be the best thing for the present. Perhaps Marcus will return home if he knows he will not have to face me."

They were silenced by what her words implied. Finally Arthur spoke. "I will never believe it is all over for the two of you. That is a condition I cannot accept."

Nevertheless it was Arthur who helped carry her things downstairs to the waiting coach, and it was Arthur who waved at the departing coach as the women disappeared down the lane toward Emily's house.

Greta had been almost as upset as Arthur about Elizabeth leaving the castle. Elizabeth had decided to make some excuse for her sudden move to Emily's house, but Greta admitted that she had been listening to what had taken place in Elizabeth's bedroom the night before.

"Men!" She stomped her foot as her eyes blazed. "Hit matters not one whit that they alley-cat from bed to bed, but should the woman want a little o' the same, they sings another tune. My Chesley would never have run off without first askin' was I guilty. A pox on the nobs, for all their fancy ways. Present company excepted, your ladyship."

Elizabeth had finally managed to soothe the girl's feelings and assured Greta that she would see her before she left the village for good.

She was hardly aware of settling into the suite of rooms on the second floor of Emily's country estate. The bed-

247

chamber, sitting room, and dressing room were comfortably appointed, but not ostentatious. Burgundy rugs nearly covered the shining wood floors, blending nicely with burgundy draperies edged with gold braid. The walls were covered with a soft gray silk moiré fabric that caught the fading afternoon sun in a myriad of patterns.

And still she waited. Would he come to her? He had to if they were ever to resolve their differences. One thing she knew for certain, she would not go to him. She had her pride to consider.

She laid aside the coverlet and stretched out on the bed in an effort to rest. Emily was resting in her own rooms, more for the sake of the baby than herself. Elizabeth knew that Emily too was far too distraught to truly rest.

She had been lying down for less than an hour when she heard a gig drive into the approach in front of the house. Running to the window, Elizabeth caught a glimpse of the black geldings that belonged to the castle stables. There was no mistaking that fine pair of blooded horses.

She pressed her hands together so tightly that the pain spread up to her elbows. The waiting was over. Marcus had come to claim her. Oh, God, let it be true, she thought as she hurriedly tore the ribbon from her hair and let it fall down over her shoulders. There was no time to wind it into a twist. Instead, she brushed it until it shone like sunlight on a wheatfield in September.

At the top of the stairs she paused just long enough to catch her breath and assume a small degree of composure before the emotional confrontation that was sure to follow.

She heard voices in the library. Apparently Emily too had heard Marcus arrive. Elizabeth felt a moment of regret. She would like to have seen him alone. They had a great deal of sorting out to do. But there was no turning back. Lifting her chin, she went downstairs and stopped at the open door of the library.

They turned as she entered; first Emily and then Arthur. For it *was* Arthur and not Marcus as she had hoped. Emily spoke.

"Elizabeth, my dear, have you heard?"

"Heard what?"

"Marcus has been found."

Elizabeth felt her heart rise up in her throat. "Been found? I don't understand. Has he—"

Arthur cut in quickly. "God's blood, Em, you make it sound as if he were hurt or something. He is perfectly well, Elizabeth, at least physically. Where his mental faculties are concerned there is considerable doubt, at least in my mind."

Elizabeth reached to a table for support. "Then he did wait until I had quit the castle to make his appearance?"

Arthur looked a bit uneasy, but he brushed her aside. "In truth, he never really left. He has been riding over the hills and headlands of the duchy for the past several hours."

She nodded. "I see. It was good of you to let me know that he is safe. For that I thank you, Arthur. Now, if you will excuse me, I would like to retire to my rooms." It was all she could do to keep her tears in check.

But Emily would have none of that. "Your rooms! But don't be absurd, Elizabeth. You must go to him. He needs you desperately. On that I would stake my life and that of my child."

Elizabeth was horrified. "Don't say such things, Emily. I cannot go to him. It is up to him to come to me. It was not I who rode off into the night with my heart full of anger and hate."

Arthur put his arm around her. "But it *is* you, Elizabeth, who must forgive. Marcus knows the truth of what happened, but he is so deeply shamed, he cannot face you." He paused as if to consider his words. "True, in time he will come to you, of that I am convinced, but would it not be wiser to forgo the hours of pain that lie ahead for both of you? All you have to do is go to him and tell him that you understand."

"You told him that our meeting in my rooms was innocent of wrongdoing?"

"That was my intention, but he already knew."

"Indeed? But how?"

"It was Greta who searched him out and told him the truth of what happened. At first he refused to listen, thinking that she was but a pawn in your employ. But you know Greta." Arthur grinned as if visualizing the scene. "She was quite firm with him, or so Marcus led me to believe. She quite royally took him to task for his wrongheadedness." He turned Elizabeth to face him. "Surely, now that you know the whole story, you will go to Marcus. He awaits on the headlands."

Elizabeth shook her head. "I cannot. I just cannot."

Emily swore roundly. "But you must, Elizabeth. This may be your last chance."

Arthur gripped Elizabeth's shoulders. "Heaven deliver me from an obstinate woman! You must do as I tell you, Elizabeth. Go to Marcus while there is still light enough to see." There was a slight pause before he continued. "If need be, I will abduct you and take you to him. I still have an extra pad of lint with the potion to make you sleep."

Elizabeth smiled despite herself. "I am tempted to say that you wouldn't dare, Arthur, but I know you too well for that." She pressed her hands together to keep them from trembling. "Very well. If you must . . . take me to him."

Both Emily and Arthur hugged her at the same time, and Elizabeth was amazed to see that there were tears in their eyes, as there were in hers.

Arthur would not give her time to put on a fresh gown. "You look lovely, Elizabeth. Once I said I'd give my right arm to see your hair falling down around your shoulders in a golden cascade. Now, seeing you like this, I vow it would have been worth it."

Elizabeth brushed a kiss across his cheek. "I know you speak in jest, Arthur, but your words give me the last ounce of courage I need to see this through." She took a deep breath. "Shall we go?"

Arthur left her at the end of the lane nearest the path to the headlands. It was unlike him not to offer to accompany her, but he doubtless knew that she would want to see Marcus alone. He had kissed her on the forehead before he drove away, and as the gig disappeared she stood there watching, afraid to go on, yet unable to turn back. Finally she pulled her shawl tightly around her shoulders and turned toward the sea.

The setting sun slanted pale-gold rays across the narrow pathway, tinting it with shades of mauve and lilac that darkened into misty purple in the shadows of the rocks. Far below, the hypnotic susurration of the tide at ebb echoed the loneliness in her heart.

She had expected him to meet her as soon as they were alone, but he was nowhere in sight. Had he changed his mind about waiting? She felt something curl up inside of her. Could she face yet another disappointment? There had been so many, so many.

Her fingers reached up to touch the ruby and pearl necklace. Somehow it comforted her as if her mother, on some far-off heavenly plane, were watching over her. She took courage and continued on down the path. It was better to have done with it, whatever the outcome would be.

As she rounded an outcropping of boulders where the path dipped low into the heather, a shadow separated itself from the rocks and stood waiting. It was Marcus. There was no doubting those broad shoulders and the tall frame that looked muscular even in the fading light. He spoke, and his voice was ragged with fatigue.

"Elizabeth. I feared that you would refuse to see me."

She walked toward him, slowly, as if in a dream. His voice continued, so heartbreakingly near, yet beyond her power to reach out to.

"Can you ever forgive the wrong I have done to you? It breaks my heart to know how badly I mistreated you." His voice caught in his throat. "If—if you can find it in your heart to forgive me, Elizabeth, I promise I will never mistrust you as long as I live."

And still she waited. The sun, low now against the horizon, deepened the lines in his face where the pain of those last hours was written clearly for her to see. His eyes were dark hollows with no light to mirror the need in hers. She waited, afraid to speak for fear her voice would betray her.

His hands fell useless to his side. "Marry me, Elizabeth. Be the wife I have always dreamed of, for in truth, if you deny me now, I fear I shall never love again. I am consumed with my need for you, and I shall love you until the day I die."

Suddenly the waiting was over. His final words had released her, and she opened her arms to him. He stood for an instant as if spellbound, then with an anguished cry swept her into his arms.

She was dimly aware of the seabirds' cries as they winged their way home for the night. It occurred to her that she too had come home, and her heart was near bursting with the joy of it. Marcus loved her. She belonged to him, and he belonged to her. Beyond that, nothing mattered.

When he finally released her, he bent to pick up a circlet of flowers he had woven from the pink heather that grew beside the pathway. First touching it to his lips, he placed it on her head, then held her at arm's length.

252

"This must suffice for now, my dearest, but in a few weeks I will place upon your head the duchess coronet of diamonds and rubies. It is a treasure of great price, but it pales in comparison to the love I hold for you."

He kissed her then, and she no longer heard the seabirds or the whisperings of the tide. She had surrendered her spirit to him, and he was all that existed.

Love—the way you want it!

Candlelight Romances